A King Production presents…

So Hood
So Rich

A Novel

Joy Deja King
Peter Mack

Cover concept by Joy Deja King

Library of Congress Cataloging-in-Publication Data;
Mack, Peter
So Hood So Rich: by Peter Mack

For complete Library of Congress Copyright info visit;
www.joydejaking.com

A King Production
P.O. Box 912, Collierville, TN 38027

A King Production and the above portrayal log are trademarks of A King Production LLC

Acknowledgements:

Greetings beautiful people. Thank you for your sharing this novel with me. It was truly a joy to write. I'm thankful to Joy Deja King for choosing me to represent her with my flow and Monica Jones for being such a great communicator and enthusiast for creative fiction. I've been writing for many years and there are so many who have shared in my journey. To all my friends and family, I thank you for your continued support and encouragement. And as always, LIVE RICH DIE READY.

A KING PRODUCTION

So Hood So Rich

A NOVEL

Joy Deja King
Peter Mack

Chapter One

The tension in the air would hold a feather still in its thickness. The staid but venerable oak desks, occupied by sharply dressed professionals gleamed a tradition of defeat and misery under the glaring florescent lights.

No motion. Expectation pushed through the rich fabric of the dapper professionals. The lawyers occupying both desks on either side of the sterile expanse of courtroom watched with measured patience. Those pale long fingers of the judge sitting on high shuffled through the latest dismissal motion of the defendant. His skin stood in stark contrast; pale against the dark robe of final judgment. His thin neck reached out of the rich folds terrified at the vulnerability of being uncovered. Exposed. The steel gray eyes and shiny mop of silver hair were what conveyed his power and authority, even more so than his robe or the high copper base relief of the scales of justice hanging from the wall above his high backed chair.

BoDeen watched him intently. He noticed the low involuntary movement of his thin lips. White people intrigued him. The ones who had the power all looked the same to him. The spirit of authority pressed against their form giving them the same shape. Like an image illuminated when lightning strikes. The same sense of authority and surety. His college football coach. Pale. Slight. Sure. The detective that put him on death row. The silver shiny hair. The Warden at San Quentin. Those penetrating steel gray eyes. But this time he had one of them fighting for him. Not making him tackle. Not arresting him. Not locking him up. This time he was meeting them on their own turf with one of their own—though paid for handsomely enough—fighting for his freedom.

BoDeen watched the heavy gold Ivy League class ring move on the thin pale finger next to his thick, dark, scarred hand. He leaned closer. "Rubin, what's he doing?"

They both looked up at the judge, who was mumbling to himself, squinting at the notepad. His hawk eyes scanned the room above their heads. BoDeen knew without turning what Judge Steinberg was surveying. The courtroom was full of shiny suits and pretty women. Hoodlums in stingy brim hats and gangsters in Khaki suits occupied a respectable number of rows.

Coffee-, toffee-, vanilla-, and pecan-hued women with diamonds weighted in their ears and finely tailored clothes sheathing delicate limbs, sat pertly, protected by the ghetto security of the men they'd chosen to be their husbands, boyfriends, and baby daddies. All had a stake on the decision the Judge was about to make with BoDeen's life. Some privately wished he wouldn't be allowed to interrupt their hustle; others hoped he'd return them to former glory.

BoDeen could feel the heat from Missy's eyes burning across the distance. She held their son close. He'd grown since the last time BoDeen had seen him. Where Missy was vanilla-colored, their son, Dimp, was a deep mocha; his nine-year-old body was already forming into the sturdy sure shape of an athlete.

Dimp watched him from behind. His strong thick neck escaped the white shirt collar and his broad shoulders stretched the dark suit jacket. The light bounced off his bald shiny head. Dimp ran his own small fingers through his thick curls and wondered if his mom would let him cut his hair off like his father. When BoDeen turned suddenly to catch him looking, Dimp's eyes never wavered, but communicated a strength that made BoDeen smile, proudly.

The Judge cleared his throat for attention or annoyance. He looked from one table to the other. His penetrating gaze finally settled on BoDeen's lawyer, Mr. Rubin.

"I've considered the defense motion for dismissal

at great length," Judge Steinberg began. "It seems the district attorney will agree that since the key witness in this case has expired—mysterious circumstances to be sure—this court can't go investigating every murder in this God-forsaken city." He looked at Mr. Rubin with an unspoken communication then continued. "There lacks here the key testimony to hold the defendant."

At this, BoDeen's ears were plugged up with the alternate shouts, cries, audible gasps, and rustling of jewelry and footsteps of the people behind him. He vaguely felt Mr. Rubin shake his hand and hug him around his big shoulders. The gravel in the pale hand on high moved to pound in slow motion: case dismissed.

After nine years on death row, the infamous Bo-Deen was free; the ex-Arizona state, all-star linebacker who blew his knee out at the NFL Combine. The man who came home and turned his popularity and charisma into a million dollar drug business. Cop killer. Free.

Chapter Two

It was cool inside the garage. Billy Bob rolled the powder blue dice across the thin mat. "Get'em girls, daddy need new shoes," he whispered in his trademark
drawl that sounded country scratched from yelling at
an extra-inning baseball game. He'd developed this
voice four years ago just before turning 16 years old.
It was right after that late night killing—the one that
earned him his rep. A lot changed after that. No one
talked about it. Not even the red-faced detective who
came around now and then. He had started the investigation into the shooting, but the lady who said she'd
seen a boy on a bike shoot the man firing at Milo, had
recanted her story. Since then, the red-faced detective,
Big Red, kept his eyes on Billy Bob. It paid off.

"Point made, Bru," Billy Bob drawled in a fashion his mother had grown accustomed to, though she

knew not where he picked it up. They'd never been down south.

Bunchy didn't have to hear him to know the point was made by the way Billy Bob snatched up the five ten dollar bills that lay next to his big faced fifty. "Shoot!" Bunchy responded, throwing another fifty down. Green eyes stared intensely out of a pale face. Red braids cornrowed back in tight twists, hung down his neck over a bright multi-colored Tommy Hilfiger dress shirt. A diamond bezel Rolex peeked under open cuffs. A thick gold rope hung loose, heavy, and long over his neck, anchored by a large gold "HR" plaque crusted with diamonds. Baggy jeans. Old school Timberland boots. Bunchy was the mirror image and closest confidante to Billy Bob.

They'd met in Juvenile Hall. Big Red had been coming around more often after the murder on the block. Milo quit the dope game and opened a sports bar in the Marina, leaving a void in the hood. With a murder under his belt, Billy Bob began testing his legs in the game. Every time Big Red saw Billy Bob, he pulled up on him for a search.

It was the gun Big Red found on him that landed Billy Bob in Juvenile Hall; with an admonishment from Big Red that Billy Bob should use the time to think about what his next move should be. The direction he wanted his life to take. He didn't understand at first, but remembered how Milo's father, Haitian Jack, never went to jail and made millions. Milo quit the game because he didn't want to get in bed with Big Red when he got up on him. Milo really didn't have to mainly because he pushed weight out of state. But things were different now. Lefty was dead and the nigga Billy Bob gunned down for Milo was a minor incident. The hood was wide open.

A few weeks in Billy Bob noticed a green-eyed red hair kid named Bunchy. Bunchy had sliced some hater who pushed up on him in the mall. He was famous for his skills with a switchblade. The hater thought that since Bunchy was light-skinned with long hair and pretty, that he was a pussy. Bunchy had sliced him so quick and smooth, the sucka thought the warm feeling across his face was water until he had felt the sting when the air hit the raw meat under his skin. His fingers had slid over the area coming back across his eyes magenta red and glossy. Bunchy had been holding the switchblade away from his body, watching his victim's eyes grow wide with disbelief and surprise.

They had become like brothers. Kindred spirits. Billy Bob and Bunchy roamed Juvenile Hall making plans for the future. Building on their reputation as killers. Young and handsome, they were two peas in a pod; same weight, height, and gleaming eyes. One dark. One light. Both wrong.

The garage door was pulled up. The street beyond was visible around Billy Bob's squatted powder blue Escalade on 26" rims. Behind it, closer to the street, was his mother's new Maxima; an update from her almost always broken-down older model. Bunchy's powder blue Navigator on 24" rims was parked at the curb.

Stutterbox, 6'2" and weighing 230lbs, lounged lazily on the couch in front of the big screen TV watching a porno; the dice game going on to the side of him. When Billy Bob's mom appeared at the front of the garage with a tray of fried chicken, he jumped to attention. Not his body, but his otherwise cold, lifeless eyes. They dully traced her shapely figure.

Elaine favored stretch pants. Pink. Accentuating her flared hips and heart-shaped gap lodged between her legs, allowing daylight to highlight her sex appeal. Her ass hung heavy inside the ribbed stretched cotton. She had the same dusty complexion as her son, with hazel eyes to match. Elaine was ghetto fine. One to make you pay utility bills just to hear her say thank you. Gold chains draped her long neck and diamond topped gold rings dangled richly on her tapered fingers. She'd grown used to Stutterbox's dull glare and crooked smile.

"Set the dice down and eat something. Y'all ain't gon' do nothing but spend it on each other anyway," Elaine said into the garage, inwardly proud that Bunchy and Billy Bob were so close. In the background, Fabolous rapped through tall speakers about shiny trinkets and fine hoes. Her son was engrossed with the rhythm of his roll, trying to hit his point. Elaine put the plate of chicken on a nearby table, then turned towards the house, ass rocking and rolling like two guerrillas fighting in a pillowcase.

"Back up off moms nigga..." Billy Bob rasped, not looking up at Stutterbox, who lazily looked away from Elaine's rocking ass back to the big screen.

Stutterbox changed the channel to BET's noon Rap Party. He took notice, as he always did, when Billy Bob addressed him. He wasn't "Bru" like Bunchy or Milo. He didn't share the easy relationship Billy Bob had with Bunchy. Stutterbox was developing a simmering jealousy sparked by the fact that he was older than both of them by three years. He was 23 years old, yet he lacked their status as reputables in the hood. He was fresh out of prison from a two-year bid for assault with a deadly weapon. He was the muscle, though they didn't need it. As much as he tried to be as valuable to Billy Bob as Bunchy was, there was always something he did wrong to annoy Billy Bob. No matter how many clowns he beat down or choked out, he couldn't be a "Bru" to him. He wanted more. Maybe it had something to do with being on Dollar Bill's team before he got murked by the South Siders. He didn't come up with Billy Bob, but since he covered his back on a developing intricate plot, Billy Bob gave him a pass. Still, his envy simmered.

Haitian Jack's was filled with a professionally dressed lunchtime crowd. Open four years now, Haitian Jack's was the place to be any time, day or night.

Milo was having an intense conversation with his famous dreadlocked bartender. They stood shoulder to shoulder with success discussing a new mix drink suggested by a dark skinned, longhaired cutie at the bar. They'd both laughed when they heard the name 'dirty white motherfucker'. When the drink was mixed and offered to a few hot ladies, it became a fast favorite of the popular crowd. They enjoyed saying it almost as much as the smooth fruity taste.

Sherrie's long rust-colored hair moved around her beige freckled face as she came trotting on high heels through the office door next to the kitchen holding a cordless phone. "Milo," she huffed, extending the phone across the bar in his direction. "Missy's at the court-house. They dismissed the charges against BoDeen."

Milo reacted with wide eyes to her gray eyes flashing newness and surprise. He quickly grabbed the phone, waiting to hear Missy's voice. "Is that right, sis?" he asked.

"He's coming home," Missy replied, the reality of it settling her earlier excitement. Something prayed for yet unprepared for. Neither could be sure what to expect from BoDeen. So much had changed since last he was home.

The light was escaping the day heading for the cover of night. The big screen TV was the only light Billy Bob had to work with, so he squatted in front of a triple beam as he finished the last of measuring out one ounce portions of powder cocaine and placing them into plastic baggies. On a smaller table beside him, a stack of larger bags were filled with dime size chunks of rocked up cocaine.

"You ready, Bru?" Bunchy asked, coming from the room above the garage. He was descending the wooden stairs looking at his pager. "Ruff tryin' to holla. He waitin' on us."

"Fuck that nigga. We get there when we get there," Billy Bob responded, his fingers sliding across a powdery Ziplock bag, securing the ridge tight. His head bobbed. "Niggas clock us, next they wanna rob us. Can't touch us, wanna be us," he rhymed in his raspy voice. His thin frame moved under a baggy Sean Jean dress shirt. His dust colored dreads swung over his shoulders with each head bob. "Can't see us. HoodRich be the elite nigga kiss the feet. My money come in lumps, my pocket got the mumps."

"Aw, Bru! You bitin' now. Don't bite," Bunchy interrupted, grabbing the bags of dope, and dumping them into a duffel bag. He was thinking privately to himself that it was almost time to do something with the money they made. Billy Bob could rap and his uncle Chubb had given him a little game on the music business. He knew they could be larger than G-Unit.

"That nigga 50 ain't no joke tho.'" Billy Bob was smiling at his main man, guilty he added a verse to his rhyme that wasn't his own. His eyes grew steely. "Look at the nigga." He nodded towards Stutterbox, who lay reclined in front of the big screen asleep. "Wake that nigga up."

"Yo, Box. Yo, Box!" Bunchy yelled.

Billy Bob became annoyed. He walked over to where Stutterbox reclined and shoved his heavy boots off the wooden table, sparking a quick movement from Stutterbox. "Let's roll," Billy Bob announced, ignoring the glare in Stutterbox's eyes.

"We was just comin' to see y'all," Towana said from the driver's seat of her Honda Accord. "Where y'all goin'?"

Billy Bob, Bunchy, and Stutterbox were walking from the backyard to Stutterbox's Suburban. Stutterbox looked to see who was in the back seat of her car as he opened the door of his car. Towana was talking to Billy Bob, who was carrying the duffel bag full of powder and rock cocaine.

Towana and Tomika were girls. They stuck together like sweaty butt cheeks. Where Towana was thick in all the right places, Tomika was thin with meat. They both had the same butter complexion and long sandy hair; a plus in any hood.

"Hey Bunchy, that's how you're goin' to treat me, huh? Not say nothing? Tomika got something to say to you," Towana said looking past Billy Bob to Bunchy who was about to get in the back of the Suburban. She'd waited long enough for him to be polite.

"Yeah, yellow nigga. I got somethin' to say to you!" Tomika yelled from the passenger seat, leaning over Towana's lap.

Bunchy came strolling around the back of the Suburban into the middle of the street. "Check this out, bitch!" He strolled lazily to the passenger side of the car. "Don't be yelling at a nigga, bitch," he said, reaching into the car. He grabbed a fist full of her ponytail and yanked on it, forcing her head back.

"Ouch!" Tomika screamed. "Stop it, Bunchy!" She winced, trying to keep the roots of her hair in place and stay in the car at the same time.

Towana looked over to Billy Bob. "Tell him to stop, Billy," she pleaded.

Billy Bob watched for two more beats. Crazy bitches. *They know Bunchy damn near crazier than me,* he thought to himself, a crooked grin on his face. "Yo, Bru. Chills," he said calmly in Bunchy's direction. The 'Bru' did it.

Bunchy released her back into the seat. Tomika held her composure, flipping down the visor mirror to check herself. "Damn, Bunchy. You fucked up my hair. Now I got to get it done again." Tomika pouted, avoiding his steel green eyes for the moment. Waiting for his reply.

"Get at me right, you don't have to trip like that," he answered, leaning in to console her. Tomika kept her attention in the mirror as he kissed her hot cheeks. A smile spread across her face despite the tears in her eyes.

Towana rolled her eyes. *Both them niggas crazy*, she thought to herself. She turned to Billy Bob, whose attention was down the street, preoccupied. "So what's up for tonight?" *This nigga better come correct*, she thought privately looking at his thin frame and sexy hazel eyes staring off into the distance. *Damn you sexy.* He aroused her just by the way he stood. He always seemed to be half somewhere else. She couldn't understand why this made her so mad and turned her on at the same time. She'd long ago learned to be patient and not repeat herself because that annoyed him and when he was annoyed, he was out of reach. Sometimes she wished he would blow up like Bunchy, but knew that whenever his temper erupted someone got seriously hurt. Not just hair pulling. He was

14

only 20 years old and had grown ass men in this hood shook.

He turned to face her after resolving whatever was on his mind. "Check me out later at Haitian Jack's." His face had erased his previous thoughts. He was unreadable no matter how she tried. He looked over at Bunchy, who was leaning into the passenger window kissing Tomika. "Let's roll, Bru."

With that, they hopped into the Suburban. Stutterbox lifted his hand slightly at the dark skinned girl in the back who'd scooted next to the window for a better view and to be seen. She smiled in response as Stutterbox drove past.

The stock gray Suburban with 35% tint hit the corner in a smooth menacing motion. The windows vibrated with Gorilla Black's fat voice rapping over a deep bass. When the Accord was out of sight, Stutterbox hit the mute button, leaving an echo thumping through the cabin.

"Yo, Billy Bob, why you gettin' twisted with Towana when you know your girl is on her way back from college? And you know how she is," Stutterbox said, but what he really wanted to know was, who was in the back of the Accord.

"'Cuz her pussy long as a thirty dollar roll of nickels," interjected Bunchy with hard laughter.

"Pussy so fat it hang down like a pair of boxing gloves," Billy Bob added, twisting in his seat to give his man dap.

Stutterbox grinned, knowing better than to think he'd get a straight answer. He hit the mute button again, bringing the bass pounding. Their heads bobbed in unison as they rolled through traffic behind tinted windows. Dope in a duffel bag.

Lonnie Ray was the first to see the familiar gray Suburban hit the corner. The music signaled its approach, the bass reaching his ears before he could see the trademark stock Chevy with tinted windows. He sat in his wheelchair on the porch, watching the Suburban appear. "Ruff, peep game," he yelled through the black iron screen door. The inside of the house was alive with the smell of cronic smoke and fried chicken. The aromas fought for space through the wrought iron screen door.

The front yard was hard dirt surrounded by a low gate. On the opposite side of the driveway, a red-nosed pit bull with an oversized head tugged at a chain anchored to a steel spike planted in the middle of the yard. The pit bull trampled over a chewed up plastic bowl as he tested the limits of the chain.

The driveway was lined with two brightly painted '79 Regals—one electric blue, the other forest green. Triple gold Dayton rims and Vogue tires provided the feet. Dubb's small black shaved head bobbed in the driver's seat of the parked green Regal closest to the street. Drak's peanut butter skull was reclined in the passenger seat. He was pulling on a fat blunt, smoke crawling over the interior of the car. They both made easy movements to get out of the car when they saw the Suburban pull to the curb in front of the barking pit bull. Thick gold chains dangled from their necks, anchored by the same diamond crusted plaque with the "HR" emblem Billy Bob and Bunchy wore.

Lonnie Ray raised a manacled three-fingered hand at Billy Bob as he opened the half-hinged gate, creating a new outburst from Kujo, the pit bull. Kujo snapped the thick chain with each lunge at the feet of Billy Bob, Bunchy, and Stutterbox as they walked the stone path to the rickety wooden stairs. The duffel bag was slung over Billy Bob's shoulder.

"Down, Kujo!" Ruff commanded from the doorway in his heavy bass voice. He stood taller than Stutterbox and weighed close to 500lbs. His neck was crushed between a massive torso and huge head that squished beady eyes between fat cheeks and thick eyebrows.

Kujo yelped one last time, giving a sorrowful glance up at Ruff, who was smiling at Billy Bob. He wondered if Billy Bob knew.

"You gettin' too big to holla back?" Ruff asked, covering his large oil stained fist over Billy Bob's. He watched his face, the place where he usually got most of his information because Billy Bob rarely said what he thought. He acted on it instead. Billy Bob didn't know, Ruff saw.

"You hear BoDeen out?" Lonnie Ray eagerly asked from his wheelchair.

Mixed emotions danced inside Billy Bob as he watched the gnarled, twisted grin on Lonnie Ray's two-tone face. His face was made joker like by the battery acid he drank by mistake from a beer can.

Billy Bob was putting the pieces of a puzzle together. First, source of the information: Lonnie Ray. Older than BoDeen by ten years. Shermhead, but respected in the hood as a G. He was BoDeen's boy before he got locked up. Since then it's been all bad for Lonnie Ray. He fried his throat by drinking battery acid high on sherm. Now he sounded like a toy doll. He was paralyzed by a drive-by shooting. He only survived because he was high on jet fuel. Non-factor. Loved drama. Wanted to see other people as miserable as he felt.

Now, Ruff. BoDeen's age, but not one of his crew. Ruff built low-riders and sold double up and ounces of cocaine to a few local thugs who entrusted him with their rides. Occasionally, Ruff would get a request for half a bird of powder or rocks. This was happening more frequently, giving Billy Bob yet another high cash flow spout. Ruff did his own thing and wouldn't be swayed one way or another by BoDeen's release.

Billy Bob knew they were watching him. He knew what they thought. Milo's boy. A killer. Milo got his respect off his father's reputation. Haitian Jack was a legend. BoDeen was Haitian Jack's boy. They were waiting to see how Billy Bob would react to the new equation. And if he could handle it, 'cuz shit was definitely about to pop.

Billy Bob decided not to answer Lonnie Ray. It was good to know BoDeen had won his appeal. He'd heard stories about how BoDeen had the hood on lock and had a baby by Milo's sister, Missy. He was like family, but had been locked up since Billy Bob was eleven years old. He'd see Milo later on. He looked forward to it. Billy Bob was secure in the fact that no matter what was about to happen, Milo had his back.

"What that Hood Rich like?" Dubb said, climbing the few steps to stand beside Billy Bob. Fresh as baby milk and not much older. Dubb and Drak were the younger set to Billy Bob and Bunchy. They were joined at the hip. All were interchangeable in their understanding of the game and ability to walk through the valley of death.

"Filthy," Bunchy answered for Billy Bob. The four all gave each other dap and hard air punches to the chest. The camaraderie was evident.

As the scene played out, Ruff noticed the envious expression on Stutterbox's face. Just when it became clear to him, Stutterbox looked up and caught Ruff's gaze over the heads of the youngsters. Stutterbox tried to wipe the expression off his face, but it was too late. His only assurance was the fact he knew Ruff was not the type to speak on business that wasn't his.

"Let's go inside. See what you got for me," Ruff said, opening the screen behind him and leading the way inside the dark house.

Missy was happy, anxious, nervous, and perplexed. Mixed emotions fought for space in her stomach. So much had changed since BoDeen had been locked up. Dimp had been barely a year old. He'd been all she had for nine years. Now her man was back. Her mind was caught up as she moved the pan of baked fish from the oven. *How did he expect it to be? What should I expect?* She knew one thing for sure, she wasn't going to be thrust into the old life again; the one that put Bo-Deen on death row. The one that got her brother shot down in the street. So much had changed. Mom and Dad had passed away. Milo almost died. Thank God he survived and had enough sense to quit the game and open Haitian Jack's. Missy smiled at the way God had blessed her family despite the hardship. Her beauty salon, Missy's Magic, was very successful. Her brother's sports bar was also doing very well. And BoDeen was not about to fuck that up, she admonished herself firmly.

"What's on your mind?" BoDeen asked, coming into the kitchen. Prison had preserved him. Made him stronger. More menacing, if that was possible.

Missy looked at him with the awe and memory of seeing him all those years ago standing beside her father. "Oh, just thinking how happy I am," she answered vaguely, forcing a smile. So much was on her mind. *What are his plans?* "Dimp show you all his trophies? He swears he'll be the next Randy Moss." A proud smile flashed across her face.

"Yeah." BoDeen sighed. "He's so big," he said, shaking his head, sad that he'd missed out on so much.

"Daddy... daddy..." Dimp stepped into the kitchen. "Come play 'Fight 4 New York' with me." His soft palm touched his father's hand.

BoDeen looked up at Missy, confused. "It's a wrestling game on the Xbox," Missy said against his bewildered look. She turned her attention to Dimp. "It's time for dinner baby, go wash your hands. We'll all play after dinner.

"Okay Mommie," he said with a wide grin, turning and scampering down the hallway. A new kind of happiness wrapped in his bounce.

BoDeen was watching her pile dirty rice, broccoli, and fish onto fine plates. He was proud of her. The way she succeeded at business and holding the house together. Mostly at the way she handled Dimp. And she was just as fine now as when he first laid eyes on her. He'd never seen her hair cut this short. It stood in dark loose curls over her head, barely covering her ears. The rich curls contrasted darkly against her pale complexion. She was still slender, but with more meat in the best places. Her gap-toothed smile still had the same effect on him. She was familiar still yet strange. Far removed from the woman he'd known. All those years. Lost. *I've got to get back*, he thought to himself.

"Now it's my turn to ask, what's on your mind?" Missy interrupted his thoughts, catching him staring at a spot beyond her. It was if they were tiptoeing around each other. Like holding a large chunk of crushed ice; not wanting to move too fast for fear it would crumble. Better to let it melt at normal motion and room temperature.

BoDeen's eyes came into focus on the two plates of hot food she held. He followed her into the dining room where Dimp was having a seat at the table. He was smiling with a pleasure only a son could have for a father returning home after a long journey. Dimp watched his every move: the way he held his fork, the dark rings around his knuckles, the shape of his mouth when he chewed, and the timbre of his voice. He was enraptured by the presence of his father seated next to him. Drinking in his aroma. Watching his mother's reaction to him. There was a certain feeling of wholeness that his father brought to his life. Dimp was happy... expectant... excited... calmed... made whole.

It had been a while since he'd been able to stretch fully in his own bed. The bed he bought for Missy when he bought the house. As he lay on his back atop the thick cream-colored comforter, it was too real to be a dream. Even though his son was in the bed with him, he didn't want to go to sleep. Dimp kept opening his eyes, fighting against slumber to see if his father was still there watching him. Finally, he couldn't fight anymore. When BoDeen gently stroked the shiny cinnamon complexioned high cheekbone, then rubbed across Dimp's thick curly hair—there was no movement—he was satisfied his son was sleep.

He thought he could handle all this so smoothly. Being alone with Missy for the first time. When alone he stole glances in a mirror. In the restroom. The small one in the hallway. The long one on the back of the bedroom door. Missy was getting out of the shower. One last glance. The thousand push-ups a day preserved his powerful physique; the body of a linebacker. Briefly, he wondered if he was in shape—good enough to play pro ball. Briefly. He hopped back into the bed in time to watch Missy stroll under dim light from the bathroom—a fresh scent of steam and fragrance on her. The pink negligee cascaded over her slim body, teasing the bottom of her knees.

Missy walked slowly over the thick carpet, watching him watch her. She hid her nervousness well. She saw him rising beneath cocaine white boxer briefs. "You still look good," she whispered.

"What?" he said, breaking into the distance between them.

"You still look good." Missy smiled, lifting the comforter for her entrance.

BoDeen rolled under to join her. His large hands found her under the covers, treading the curves of her soft, warm body. She melted into him, feeling the hardness of him wrap around her. His longing and attraction finding its way trapped between her thighs. Pulsing. Waiting. Probing.

Missy sighed into him, letting his fingers work her panties down her legs. Almost laughing out loud at his clumsiness, feeling him toss at the effort to remove his own underwear.

He was free. He stood hard under the covers, barely able to contain himself with the knowledge of a hot body ready to receive him laying near.

Missy gently pulled him on top of her. Placing one firm petite breast into his mouth, then the other. She opened her legs to him. Her warmth breathed onto him, guiding his hardness to its source.

The soft hair tickled him as he moved past to her wetness. She was tight. Warm. Yet opening more with each gentle circular probe. Smoothly he went into her, halfway at first, then coming back out. The air on the retreating wetness motivating his return to her warmth. Fully this time, making his back arch with the pleasure.

Missy tightened around him, opening to receive him wholly. She felt him grow inside her. Hot. One stroke. *Don't do it, BoDeen.* Two strokes. *Damn, it feels good.* Three strokes. *Hold on. Not yet.* Four strokes. *Don't move like that baby, you're going to make me...* a half stroke. *Cum! Damn!* Plunging into her. *Aww shit!!*

Missy breathed against the side of his collapsed head. She squeezed what juices he had left in him. Satisfied he was empty, she whispered, "Get up. They're waiting for you at Milo's."

Chapter Three

Haitian Jack's Sports Bar & Lounge was rocking an old Parliament beat. The atmosphere was electric. Beautiful people milled around the large bar that dominated the center of the floor. Heads bobbed, holding bright-colored drinks delicately. To the left over the row of dimly lit pool tables, people danced behind a glass wall suspended from the ceiling. The DJ was mixing on the turntables. BoDeen was immediately infected with the success Milo had accomplished. Above the bar, eight small television monitors showed muted videos of the hottest rap and R&B artists' videos. BoDeen was flanked by two of his homeboys from his days when his name rang bells and he commanded the hood. This crowd was nine years removed for his heyday. He was surprised when he heard his name interrupting the music, announcing his arrival. Droop and

Maniac looked at him with renewed respect. Many heads in the foyer turned his way.

"Y'all heard me right. Milo's brother-in-law, Bo-Deen, is back. For those that don't know, it's better that you don't. For those that know, check yourself," the DJ warned.

BoDeen looked up behind the DJ booth and recognized the smiling face of Pooh, who used to DJ at Club Flex in West Hollywood every Tuesday night. BoDeen gave him a respectful head nod. Pooh cranked the music back up with LL Cool J's 'Headsprung'.

"I told you folks, Milo did the damn thang. But it's true, he ain't in the game. Believe me, I would know. But the crew is still tight. Look, there go Rolando right there." Droop another member of the crew nodded over to where Rolando's beefy frame did damage to a chair at the corner of the bar. Rolando was looking their way, holding eye contact with BoDeen.

Rolando, BoDeen murmured to himself with a smile, remembering when Haitian Jack had first moved his mother and sisters over from the island. Rolando reminded him of Biggie Smalls then. A young hungry kid with a keen eye for the street. He'd heard that Rolando was security for Missy's Magic and rumors that he and Missy had hooked up for a minute. His smile faded when this thought occurred to him.

"What's up, Bru. Long time no see," a familiar voice said behind BoDeen as he walked towards Rolando.

He turned around, arms wide. "Man! Milo, what's up!" BoDeen answered excitedly, grabbing him in a warm hug. "Bru-n-law, back up. Let me get a look at you." They both smiled with the appraisal.

Milo was in his customary dark, tailored, wool, single-breasted suit with magenta pocket square matching the ribbon around a royal blue Fedora. His high open collar shirt was of the finest cream linen. BoDeen was slightly self-conscious of his Sean John denim outfit. He was accustomed to being the sharp-est in the group, now Milo was all grown up. He was the picture of success and good living, smiling a co-caine white prosperity.

Droop looked on with calculating envy. Maniac was casting his sharp eyes on the crowd searching for anyone who might owe him money or an enemy who he'd robbed, shot, or been shot at by.

"Follow me," Milo said. "Kilroy is upstairs waiting for you in the V.I.P. room." Turning to Droop and Ma-niac, Milo said, "Round of drinks on me." Nodding to-wards the bar. He got Dreads attention and motioned towards the two, holding up one finger. A nod of agree-ment.

"Man! How's Kilroy doing?" BoDeen asked, ig-noring the disappointed looks of Droop and Maniac. They'd never been invited to the V.I.P section and were silently hoping this would be the day. BoDeen really wanted to know if the pimp had really settled down with Silk's people, Lola May from Chicago.

"Kilroy's cool, Bru," Milo assured him as they passed Rolando, who gave BoDeen's back a hard slap. Welcome home.

From the loft of the V.I.P section, BoDeen was impressed with the view from above. Seated comfortably in an overstuffed leather recliner, he was treated to a private pole dance by Heather, a personal friend of Kilroy's. She bounced large, tanned breasts to a deep bass and shimmied down the silver pole, casting pale blue eyes at BoDeen.

Kilroy emerged from a discreet door behind the wet bar next to the narrow stage where Heather gyrated. He was as graceful as BoDeen remembered. Dressed in a tailored silk leisure suit that was as rust red as his shoulder length hair.

"Look what the wind blew in," Kilroy drawled in his smooth trademark delivery honed by years of pimping.

"Hey, old timer," BoDeen responded with a genuine smile, moving in for a familiar embrace.

"Good to have you home, Bru," Kilroy said, having a seat across from BoDeen.

Everything was different. These niggas had they shit tight. No more grinding in the street. No more pigs sniffing up your ass. Milo had done all this, and brought his crew—the family—with him. I'm BoDeen. This used to be me. The nigga everyone look up to. "Yo Milo," BoDeen began, breaking from his private thoughts. "So, you strictly legit huh?" A nod and wide smile.

Kilroy looked on suspiciously.

"That's cool," BoDeen assured, taking the shot of Hennessy Milo offered when a commotion on the floor of the foyer caught his attention.

Billy Bob, Bunchy, and Stutterbox had entered through the front door in a grand display of bravado trailed by the equally excited duo of Dubb and Drak. Chants of "HoodRich! HoodRich!" reverberated through the lobby competing with the music. "HoodRich! HoodRich!" They were heading towards the bar.

Rolando stepped in to remind Dread that the only one old enough to drink was Stutterbox. Just then, Towana, Tomika, and three of their fly ass friends tumbled through the doors followed by a rugged crew of thugs upset that the girls claimed they had boyfriends already.

Billy Bob and Bunchy stepped to Towana and her girls in the middle of the foyer when Rolando placed his frame between the two groups of young riders.

"As every one can see, HoodRich is in the house," DJ Pooh said comically, trying to diffuse the tension.

Droop and Maniac stood at the pool tables eyeing the scene, hoping BoDeen saw how Billy Bob had grown since he'd been gone.

The young Khaki-suited Crips grew wide-eyed at the exclamation of "HoodRich" shouted by Dubb and Drak. "Fuck HoodRich! This Dirt Gang Crip!" shouted Midnight, the beady eyed one at the center of the seven deep crew. His hands were balled into fists at his stomach.

Milo moved towards the door leading to the spiral staircase that would take him downstairs. BoDeen followed close behind.

Towana and Tomika moved behind Billy Bob and Bunchy as Stutterbox sized up who he'd take out first. The fly ass friends dissolved into the periphery as the tension mounted with violent expectation.

"We won't have that in here," warned Rolando, his 360lb frame heaving with the challenge, eyeing Midnight.

"Fuck HoodRich!" Midnight grumbled.

"Fuck smut gang crabs nigga!" Billy Bob hurled the worst insult, moving past Rolando quickly, followed by Bunchy, whose silver blade flipped out of its hiding space.

The music died, replaced by the dull clap of a 9mm Glock, followed by chairs squealing with scared movement and high-pitched screams. Clap. Clap. Clap.

Fighting through the commotion at the back of the bar Milo couldn't believe that blood spurted from the beefy arm of Rolando as he tumbled towards Midnight and his gang, taking shots as if to save everyone else.

"Stay down!" BoDeen warned as Milo attempted to rise, calling out to Rolando.

"Fall nigga!" Midnight shouted as he emptied his clip into Rolando. His words were muted by the chaos of people screaming and scattering as Billy Bob began shooting towards Midnight, hitting two of his home-boys as they began moving toward the front door.

Dubb and Drak hopped over Rolando's fallen body busting their pistols, dropping two more of Midnight's homeboys.

Midnight was the first to escape, jumping over prone bodies and pushing his way through the screaming crowd.

Bunchy kneeled over one of the enemies as blood leaked from his chest. "Fuck smut gang," he whispered, bringing his knife next to his temple and slicing it across his throat. "HoodRich nigga," he whispered as he let his head drop back to the floor. Bunchy looked up quickly, searching for Billy Bob, who was deftly putting bullets into a bleeding thug that was trying to crawl out the door. Cool as a fan.

The screams and bullets subsided. The empty clicking of Billy Bob's pistol echoed in the silence.

"Bru." The familiar voice broke Billy Bob's spell. He looked up to see Milo, cautiously advancing his way, stepping over a frightened Towana. In his glance, people rose cautiously from behind pool tables to his left; dining tables overturned to his right. Stutterbox rose next to Rolando's fallen body, bleeding from his cheek and arm, stumbling towards him in a daze.

"Bru. Let's go." Bunchy was pulling at Billy Bob, grabbing hold of his jacket, propelling him over dead bodies towards the door.

As BoDeen cast his eyes across the carnage, he was met by the "I told you so" stares of Droop and Maniac, who rose above the edge of a pool table.

Milo looked around calmly as people checked themselves for blood. Sirens wailed in the distance. Rolando was at his feet. He kneeled to hold the big man's head in his hands. Rolando was gasping for air. "Hold on. Help is on the way. Hold on, Bru," Milo whispered, staring into Rolando's eyes, pleading.

Chapter Four

Jody attempted a smile as Milo grasped her hand in his. Assurance. Surely, he felt her the sun was blazing 'high noon' overhead. The shiny green grass breathed in its brilliance, drinking in its rays throughout the straw of its blade. Granite headstones glistened under the brightness. The trees made no sound. They too seemed entranced by the somber baritone of Reverend Lovejoy as he sang the praises of yet another fallen man in the youth of his life. Jody quietly glanced around Milo, where Mrs. Sempier held her beloved friend, Mrs. Kern. She felt sad for the distinguished shiny black-skinned woman who had to watch her son get buried.

Anxiety at what would happen in the next few days. Although she privately hoped he didn't, but after five years together this was unlikely. She put on a brave face.

Hutch was customarily dapper, filling out his dark pinstriped suit. He and Gwen had gotten married by the same Reverend Lovejoy who had wed Milo and Jody. Gwen was swollen with pregnancy. Jody had only just begun to show. Jody rubbed the tender mound with life growing inside, thinking how ironic that life was being born as one was being laid to rest.

"Don't be sad for Rolando. No. No. Don't be sad. He's finally home. Yes, indeed, he's finally home," Reverend Lovejoy finished, shaking his beefy salt and pepper head.

The money-green casket with gold trimming reflected the sunlight as one by one his family placed flowers over it. His mom, helped by Mrs. Sempier, followed by Milo, Hutch, and Kilroy.

Rolando's body was lowered into the ground covered by the dark of night, long after his loved ones had left footprints on the breathing dew covered grass.

The time of peace and ease was at its end. There would be more bloodshed.

Milo was caught up in his own thoughts as he drove the quiet streets of the early afternoon on his way to Billy Bob's house. Jody protested when he announced he had to go to the city. She was shedding her black pantsuit she'd worn to Rolando's funeral. He assured her he'd be right back, but didn't tell her the reason he was leaving, though she knew. Billy Bob.

Fallen leaves decorated the streets casting an innocence against the tall school gate. Inside the steel wiring, mocha-, almond- and chocolate-colored children mingled with vanilla and toffee hued laughing, running playmates. Milo smiled inwardly at their innocence, protected against a grown up world of responsibilities and loss. Rolando. Milo heard Rolando's laughter in his head. The grief on Mrs. Kern's face as she watched her son's casket resting on the cemetery lawn was enough to make him wince. H slammed his hand hard against the wood grain space on the steering wheel. His other hand gripped the thick leather padding. He thought he might snap the steering wheel. Hutch was motionless until now in the passenger seat. His small eyes darted over to his long-time friend, peering beneath the thick folds of his face. He again looked straight ahead without saying a word. No music. No sounds. In their reflections of a sad occasion and preparation for what the killing meant, neither had made a move to push play on the CD console.

Bunchy was the first to see Milo's sleek black on black Lexus GS turn into the driveway, parking behind his Navigator. He'd expected to see Stutterbox come through, but strangely he was in traffic somewhere. *Probably tricking*, Bunchy thought.

"Yo, Billy! Yo, Billy!" Bunchy shouted over the voice of Lil Jon screaming through tall speakers. He hit the mute button. "Hey, Bru. Milo and Hutch here!" he said, watching the sturdy stride of Milo as he approached. Hutch's wide frame offered a silhouette behind him. They looked as gangster as the first time he'd met them. Only this time their expressions were pensive. Somber. The black suits did little to lighten the mood.

Milo took a seat beside Bunchy. "Where my boy at?" he asked Bunchy, offering his dark fist for dap. Hutch grabbed up the remote and filled the leather loveseat in front of the big screen TV, happy to be seated comfortably.

"Right there." Bunchy motioned his head towards Billy Bob who was coming down the stairs from the second level of the garage.

"'Sup, Bru!" Billy Bob said as he reached the landing. "Figured you come through. Sorry I didn't come to the funeral. Me and the cemetery don't get along."

"Imagine that," Milo answered, tapping Billy Bob's fist with his own. He watched the growing boy who seemed to not be affected by what made Milo step out of the game.

Billy Bob slid easily into the leather recliner between Milo and Hutch. Glancing around the player's den of comfortable appointments, he turned back to Billy Bob. "Where's Stutterbox?"

"That nigga bin flakin' lately. I'ma have to cut that nigga loose," Billy Bob said with a seriousness Milo knew well. "Shit about to crack and this nigga MIA," Billy Bob offered as an afterthought.

"Ain't to be trusted," Hutch said almost under his breath. A keen observation Milo had learned to trust a long time ago. But that would have to wait. Milo looked to Billy Bob. "Let Hutch know what you need."

"Now we talkin'," Billy Bob exclaimed, rubbing his hands together. He turned to the beefy faced man he regarded as a trusted friend and brother. "Bru, cop me a couple of those .45 Grizzly semi's with extra 15 round clips, some grenades and a few of those new lightweight bullet proof vests."

Hutch exchanged a knowing glance with Milo. Kid knows what he wants.

"And get me a pair of binoculars, the kind they used in Iraq." He looked at Hutch hopefully, waiting for the nod of agreement. "I'm straight on everything else. You still got that plug at the car lot? I need a van I can dump."

Hutch gave him the nod again, privately excited at the drama about to unfold, yet mature enough to be satisfied that his hands wouldn't get dirty.

The business complete, Milo made his way to the sleek black coach parked in the driveway. Billy Bob followed.

"Damn, Bru, this joint is like a space ship," he said, sticking his head in the door, admiring the interior.

Milo's attention was on the dark blue Chevy Malibu that crept to a halt at the curb. Big Red smiled grandly from the driver's seat. He exited the car. He was a lumbering man with a low center of gravity and a broad frame. His shoulders seemed weighed down with corruption.

"Seems like an ironic parody," he began, pleased with his choice of words, "that I'd find you here," he finished, casting a smart smile at Milo and Hutch. Two beats of silence. "I 'spect there's going to be some bloodshed. You're not going to let Rolando go down like that right?" He looked at Billy Bob. "And those kids that died, Midnight ain't gon' like that." He was having fun now, knowing he'd stumbled up on the beginning of a war. He bounced his fat hand against his protruding belly. "Billy, how 'bout I check back with you in a few days. Make sure you don't get in any trouble," he said with a wink and turned back towards the Malibu with a wave.

Milo watched him drive off. "You can swim with the sharks only so long before they get hungry," Milo said to Billy Bob.

"I feel you, Bru. He gon' come in handy right now though." Billy Bob was calculating his next move.

"Ooh shit!!" cried Coretta as Stutterbox pounded into her petite frame. He gripped her ankles wide as he longstroked her, his feet planted firmly on the floor, her ass at the edge of the bed. He watched his dick slide in and out, shiny with her wetness.

"Take that, bitch!" Stutterbox growled, turned on by her screw face and shouts of pain. "Make a nigga wait all this time for the pussy," he panted, still pounding, watching her eyes shut tightly and her mouth twist shut.

BOOM!! The motel room door busted open, letting in the brightness from outside silhouetting bodies moving through the door quickly. "What that Dirt Gang like nigga?"

Stutterbox immediately recognized Midnight's voice. His dick slid out of Coretta as she scooted up towards the headboard. He looked wide-eyed from Coretta to Midnight. "Bitch, you set me up?" His answer was a slap across the head with Midnight's pistol. Stutterbox fell to the floor naked, holding the spout where blood leaked from his head.

"You set yo' self up nigga," Midnight said, pointing the large tre57 at his head. Stutterbox instinctively put his hands up and closed his eyes. "I ain't gon kill yo' bitch ass." He watched Stutterbox look around confused, relaxing his hands. For a few seconds he became conscious of how he must have looked naked on the floor.

Watching Midnight sit on the bed he just fell from, he rose tentatively to reach for his clothes strewn on a corner chair.

"Y'all niggas think y'all run this shit huh?!" screamed Midnight, reaching for Coretta who'd managed to slip her panties and bra on. He moved her next to him on the bed. "You was Dollar Bill's boy, now you running with them HoodBitch niggas. What's up with that?"

Stutterbox was still figuring who he'd kill first. Coretta for playing him or Midnight for humiliating him. He still didn't answer.

"You can't talk nigga?!" Midnight hissed, jerking the large pistol in Stutterbox's direction.

Stutterbox knew he was out of pocket. If he could get his clothes on he would feel better. He got his jeans on before he began to relax. He sat up in the chair, his broad chest heaving with uncertainty. "So you ain't gon' shoot me, what's up with the 21 questions?"

This brought a smile to Midnight's dark face. Coretta smiled in echo, secretly proud of Stutterbox. "Dollar Bill was my boy. He put me down. When I got out the pen and heard you was with them niggas, I couldn't understand it. You grimy like me and Dollar Bill was. Them niggas is pretty," Midnight said this with a screw face. He wanted to spit. He gripped the pistol tight. "I

41

can't see you with them niggas!"

"I don't give a fuck about them niggas," Stutterbox said plainly in a way not to be confused with being scared into saying it.

Midnight tilted his head and squinted his eyes in an effort to see the truth of what Stutterbox just said. "What you fuckin' wit them niggas for?"

"'Cuz Billy Bob looked out when I hit the bricks. I didn't have shit."

"You ain't got shit now!" Midnight countered. "What you got? A truck?"

Stutterbox wasn't mad anymore. He knew what time it was. He did want to fuck the shit out of Coretta though. He wanted to hurt her bad. A slow smirk turned up the corners of his mouth.

"So what's up, nigga?" Midnight nodded. "Don't trip. You stay close to them niggas." His eyes communicated a newfound agreement and loyalty. He relaxed, pulling Coretta's head into his lap. She tried to resist at first, but the sharp yank of her hair convinced her to do what he intended for her.

As Coretta worked to free his dick through the zipper, Midnight waved Stutterbox over with his pistol. Coretta began sucking Midnight's dick as Stutterbox pulled her panties down and slowly pushed his dick into her tight ass. She winced with the intrusion but knew better than to stop what was about to happen. She could just as easily get beat up. She was tossed up like a salad by two angry men who were close to death.

When they were done with her, all she could do was curl up in a fetal position as they left the motel room.

BoDeen sat quietly in the overstuffed leather chair as Droop gave him the details of Billy Bob's distribution network. "Yeah, we gotta holla at Ruff if we wanna get plugged. He fuck with everybody. S.A. niggas going out of town and local niggas. Get him to cop from you and you got one foot in the hood."

They were in Droop's living room. BoDeen dropped Missy off at home after leaving Chatsworth. Milo mysteriously disappeared after returning from Rolando's funeral. Maniac was listening to Droop try to convince BoDeen to interrupt Billy Bob's connect with Ruff. Maniac was a robber and jacker, not a dope seller and could care less. He was waiting to hear the part about how they should run up in Ruff's spot and jack him for everything. He saw it unfold in his mind. Running up in they spot. Killing the dog and everything else moving. So caught up in his own dream, he didn't hear Droop calling his name.

"Damn Yac! Where you at? Ey, where Billy Bob cop from?" Droop asked. "South Siders."

"Yeah." Now Droop remembered. "Billy Bob had beef with Dollar Bill and somehow got in bed with the

S.A.'s. They got his back."

"You sure Milo ain't pushing weight?" BoDeen asked.

"That's your folks. You don't know?" Droop tested, only to be answered with a hard stare.

"That nigga out the game, but who knows how it gon' crack wit his boy Rolando gettin' merked in his spot," Maniac offered.

"Yeah, that's another thing," Droop said excitedly. "It's about to be some shit I know. Milo ain't gon' let that shit rest."

"He ain't gettin' his hands dirty either," BoDeen interjected.

"Billy Bob," Maniac whispered, his mind working to figure how he could fit into the coming feud and come out with some bread, dope, or both.

BoDeen's mind flashed back to the night Rolando was gunned down. These youngsters quick to pull their pistols out. With all that he'd heard about Billy Bob, he was sure Rolando's death was only the beginning of more, especially since he killed some of Midnight's crew. Suddenly he was weary. He rose to leave. "I'll catch y'all later. We'll holla at Ruff in a minute."

"Later." Droop said, watching BoDeen walk into the bright sun.

"Dat nigga gon' to get some pussy," Maniac said with a sinister laugh.

"I ain't mad at him. I wouldn't mind hittin' Missy myself," Droop whispered to make sure his wife, who was in the kitchen, didn't hear.

"Where have you been?" Missy asked calmly, though secretly angry. She didn't want to appear like she was putting pressure on him.

"Handling some business," BoDeen answered vaguely as he walked past her into the den where Dimp was playing NARC on his Playstation II with a cell phone to his ear. A slow smile crept across his face as he sat next to his son on the leather sofa. He caught snatches of the one-way conversation Dimp was having with a girl. A young player already, BoDeen thought to himself.

"So that's it, huh?" Missy followed him into the den. She was standing at the edge of the couch over Dimp. "Handling some business? What kind of business?" Her voice was a threatening low timber. Menacing. Independent.

BoDeen seemed captured by Dimp's play of the video game. A drug dealer was shooting it out with the police. Not wanting to argue in front of Dimp, Missy shot BoDeen one last look—a dagger—and turned away towards the kitchen. BoDeen never looked up as she walked away.

BoDeen occupied himself with Dimp for as long

as he could before his son announced that he was tired. Ironically, it was about the same time he figured his mom would be announcing his bedtime.

Missy disappeared into the bedroom after having cleaned up the kitchen and putting a plate in the microwave for BoDeen. The day had been depressing. One filled with fear and anxiety. The deep knowledge that a testing time was near that would threaten her family moved within her. She knew Milo would not let Rolando's death go unanswered. Surely as she knew this, she was still unsure as to BoDeen's plans. A sinking feeling told her he'd been enamored by the success of Milo and felt he had to play catch up. Though she hoped her misgivings weren't true, she had doubts. Privately, she hoped that Milo would handle his vengeance quietly and quickly and that Billy Bob would be OK when it was over. She was no match for the insanity that pulled the men in her life to a world of revenge and violence.

When BoDeen slid into bed, Missy's body was warm. He felt a certain brief appreciation for the softness of the mattress and thickness of the comforter. So far from the steel bunk and wool blanket of the cold impersonal cell. He grimaced with the memory as he moved to erase it from his mind, placing his hand on the soft hip of the warm body next to him. Marvin Gaye sang 'Distant Lover' on the radio. BoDeen moved spoonlike up against Missy.

"I'm sorry, baby," he whispered. "Everything's going to be alright," he continued against her bare back. Kissing her softly.

"I can't do more time with you," she responded hoarsely, not moving from her warm position.

"Neither can I, baby." And he believed this now more than at any other time as he rubbed his fingers over the lace of her panties. He felt her softening to him. Everything was happening so fast and it seemed he was being pulled right into the motion that came natural to him. "I ain't going nowhere, baby." He tried to assure her. BoDeen sensed that much was on her mind, but she didn't want to argue.

She wanted to trust him. She'd been through this with Milo.

"It's going to be okay," BoDeen whispered, sliding her panties down over her raised knees. Missy worked her legs to move the panties free. He was hard behind her as he entered her gently. He stroked her softly, slowly, and tenderly with the love he'd been intending for her all those lost years. Imagining what it would be like to make love to her while alone in his cell, he called up those feelings now. He moved to the tune of Marvin Gaye's 'Keep You Satisfied'. He couldn't see the tears that rolled slowly across Missy's face, wetting the pillow.

"I just want you to be careful, that's all," Towana said. The rising morning sun was just barely making its way into the upstairs garage window. She was under the covers naked, watching Billy Bob stand at the window looking down into the driveway where Stutterbox was pulling his Suburban to the curb. Billy Bob's eyes glazed over with mistrust at seeing, up until now, the absent Stutterbox. Billy Bob remembered him wanting to know who the girl was rolling with Towana and Tomika.

He turned back to Towana. "Who was that girl y'all had rolling with y'all that day?"

"What day?" Towana asked, stifling a yawn.

"What day you think?" Billy Bob said impatiently. "How many bitches you have wit you?!"

"Don't be yelling at me, Billy Bob! You need to show me some respect." She exercised a temporary grace period after giving him phenomenal brain. She knew she couldn't talk this way in a few more hours. So she was surprised when he called her a bitch and told her to drop that other bitch's name. "Coretta," she huffed, throwing the cover off and walking nude to the bathroom.

When Billy Bob walked downstairs, Bunchy was grilling Stutterbox. "Nigga, you act like we ain't bin hollerin'. You MIA when you ain't 'spose to be."

"You was with Coretta?" Billy Bob asked quickly, hoping it was some new pussy that had him foreign.

"Na-na-naw," Stutterbox stammered, his eyes widening more than they should have.

"Damn nigga! What had you missing then?" Billy Bob asked, disappointed at what his instincts told him.

"I was with this other shorty."

Tomika knew he was lying because Coretta had told her she was going to be with Stutterbox the day before. She couldn't wait to talk to her to find out what the deal was. When she saw Towana coming down the steps, she rose from the couch next to Bunchy. "You ready to go girl?"

Towana rolled her eyes. "Yeah, let's roll."

Chapter Five

When Maniac came bobbing through the wrought iron gate of the low level fourplex in Hawthorne, all he could think of was the pussy he just got off and the cronic sack he had waiting in the car. He'd left it in the glove compartment the night before because he didn't want to share with the hoodrat he just finished fucking. She had two bad ass kids he knew he would have to wait for to fall asleep. So last night it was a bottle of Hennessy and light blowjob until he was sure they were asleep.

He didn't see the black van with the tinted windows parked across the street from his electric blue '76 Cutlass on gold Dayton. He was thinking about the cronic and hooking up with Droop and hopefully hearing from BoDeen. He needed some money. He was broke as hell. Maniac didn't finish his thought.

The van made a quick U-turn in the street and the side door opened behind him as he stuck his key in the car door. He was snatched off his feet onto the hard metal floor of the van. The door slammed shut and a smelly canvas sack was pulled tightly over his head. No one said a word. He was scared to death. He tried to guess how many people were in the van with him. He scooted tentatively and was met by a sharp blow to the head. He involuntarily pissed in his pants. Now he was ashamed. They'd know he was scared. He hoped his dark baggy jeans would cover the wetness. But they'd smell his piss.

"Pissy ass nigga," Dubb said with a laugh.

Maniac didn't recognize the voice, but knew he was about the same age as him.

"Nigga gon' shit 'fore it's over," Drak said in his menacing pitch.

Maniac didn't recognize this voice either. Young like him too. He wondered what they wanted.

Stutterbox didn't know where the van was headed. It was weird that Billy Bob wanted to ride with him in the Suburban and follow the van. He knew he should've been driving the van. And Billy Bob's pager kept going off. Towana had called, but Billy Bob had told her to call back. He wondered if Towana had talked to Coretta. It was a comfort to him that his .44 was pressed coldly against his stomach.

"Bunchy. G-Rob say come 'round back, Bru. He got the gate open," Billy said into the phone.

G-Rob. Stutterbox's mind worked fast. They taking Maniac to one of Billy Bob's dope houses. If he wasn't mistaken, G-Rob's spot had a basement and there was little traffic because he served halves and wholes of hard and soft.

"Catch this green light, Bru," Bunchy said into the two-way as he sped through the last intersection before busting a quick right onto a quiet residential street.

The smelly oil stained canvas sack was snatched off roughly. His eyes blinked rapidly trying to adjust to the bright overhead light bulb. He was strapped to a chair. His hands were tied behind him and his legs to the legs of the chair. Slowly four figures dressed in black khaki suits came into focus before him. He recognized Bunchy and Billy Bob immediately, then knew that the other two had to be Dubb and Drak. He didn't see Stutterbox at first. He stood off to the side dressed in baggy jeans and a white t-shirt. It was like he wasn't a part of them, but he was worried just the same.

"Where Midnight spot at?" Billy Bob asked into the silence.

"Who?" Maniac asked back, squinting like he didn't understand the words coming out of Billy Bob's mouth.

"You know who he talkin' 'bout nigga! You fuck wit dat nigga. Where dat nigga be at?" Bunchy said, moving across the floor to stand in front of Maniac.

"It's cool, Bru. He wanna play." Billy Bob looked over at Stutterbox. "Make him tell us where he at Box."

Stutterbox knew it would come to this. If Billy Bob knew what time it was, this was a test. If he didn't, it was still a test. He stepped quickly to Maniac without hesitation and hit him square in the nose. He felt the bone break under his fist. Blood squirted away from his face as if released from a high-pressure valve.

Maniac fell backwards in the chair, his head banging against the floor. He couldn't hold his nose, so his face screwed up in a desperate attempt to staunch the pain and flow of blood. "I don't know where he stay!" he yelled like a stuck pig.

Stutterbox stood him back up in the chair. He grabbed Maniac's nose roughly and moved the broken bone around with his fingers. "You know, nigga," he hissed against the screaming and spitting of Maniac.

He was pissing on himself again and his asshole was warm and mushy. He didn't think this could happen to him. Then Stutterbox reached for Maniac's lap. When he figured what Stutterbox was trying to do, he squirmed in his chair trying to prevent him from pulling his dick out through the unfastened belt and open pant. Stutterbox gently placed his dick between a pair of pliers and began squeezing slowly. Maniac screamed loudly, barely able to breathe. He took two deep gulps of air as the pain increased. "Oh God! Please! Please! Eighty-third! Midnight on Eighty-third!" Maniac hissed through clenched teeth, tears rolling down his screw-up face.

Droop was hanging up the phone in disgust when Bo-Deen knocked on the front door. He'd been trying to reach Maniac for over three hours.

"What's up, Bo," he said, opening the front door.

"What's crackin'? You got them new plugs?" Bo-Deen asked, hoping he did. Nothing was the same for BoDeen. Most of his contacts were either legit or in jail. His most difficult obstacle had been the death of Haitian Jack. He was his main connect nine years ago. Even the same spots they had on lock were gone or controlled by Billy Bob. That would change soon.

"I'm waitin' on Maniac so we can go meet them cats, but that lil' nigga ain't nowhere to be found."

"We got to shake. Holla at him later. Get at the connect and cop that. I'm going to holla at Ruff," said BoDeen, pushing matters.

Droop didn't want to meet the Jamaicans alone. That's why he was waiting on Maniac. And nothing was happening if BoDeen didn't have the loot to cop with. "Roll with me, then we'll holla at Ruff. You sure you wanna cop before we holla?" Droop asked, pretty sure that Ruff was a loyal dude and wouldn't be easy to turn away from Billy Bob.

The Jamaicans were his best option to cop quality dope at a cool price. After Rolando's funeral, BoDeen had a brief chat with Milo. He'd wanted to thank him for all his help all those years. BoDeen was in his debt for no less than a hundred grand easy. Even though they were family, he felt he had to square his end up. He thought for sure Milo would help him get back into the game, but that was not the case. BoDeen was smart enough to know that Milo really wanted him to be cool and be home for his family.

I got to catch up, BoDeen kept telling himself. He didn't take Milo's decision not to help him with his plan to get back in the game personally. He just had to find another way. And Missy just didn't understand, he'd said to himself over and over again after enduring yet another argument about what he planned to do and how he should consider Dimp, his son. How he needed a father.

"I am his father," he'd shouted. "I am here!" Missy just looked at him then. She didn't understand; he stared back. Frustrated, he shouted, "What I know? What I'ma do?! Work in the salon?!" He thought he'd made a good point until she challenged him to stay out of jail. Told him that he must like jail. That he didn't appreciate how her family fought for him.

BoDeen couldn't deny her point and he was flustered for a minute. Still, she didn't understand what it was like looking at everyone around him have everything and he had nothing but his reputation. And that was worth nothing but a fake greeting and niggas watching you. He could easily be a major factor again. This was something he knew how to do. The only thing he knew. Sell dope. He'd learned his lesson. This time he'd make it right. He needed to do it his way until he could get enough money to do something better. He needed to meet the Jamaicans for himself anyway, he thought as he came out of his thoughts, seeing Missy's incomprehension in his mind.

Arguing in the back room broke him from his thoughts. Droop had left him at the front door to get something.

"I need more than this! How am I supposed to go shopping with $200?!" Droop's wife was demanding as she followed Droop towards the front door waving the money in the air. "Give me some more money, Anthony!" Patricia demanded.

Droop sighed, bowing under the pressure. He flung a few bills at her and turned to BoDeen. "Let's get outta here."

Patricia was cursing from the door as Droop got into the passenger seat of BoDeen's Durango. "She killing me, Bo," Droop complained once they drove off, leaving Patricia, long limbed and red amber from rage, standing on the porch.

Chapter Six

Billy Bob left Maniac tied up in the spot with instructions for G-Rob to keep an eye on him. Bunchy wanted to put him in a steel drum and dump it in the ocean like Scott Peterson did Laci. Billy Bob thought it best to hold onto him. He might come in handy.

It was barely getting dark by the time they got back to Billy Bob's house. Before Stutterbox could follow them to the back, Billy Bob told him to take the van they used to kidnap Maniac to his buddy Juedo who ran a chop shop downtown.

Billy Bob's mom was at the backdoor when he got to the garage. Dubb and Drak stopped in their tracks to get a good view of Elaine in a neck to toe body suit. She was nothing but tits, hips and ass.

"Y'all take a flic, it'll last longer,' Bunchy said before motioning them into the garage.

"Billy, come in here boy." Elaine said, moving back into the house.

"What's up, Mom?" Billy Bob asked as he came in through the back door.

Elaine had her back up against the kitchen sink. She looked serious. "You forgot huh?"

Billy Bob looked confused as he searched his mind for what it was he could've forgotten. So much was on his mind that he had no clue what his mother was talking about.

"Florence," she said, raising her thin eyebrows.

"Snap! Momma, I forgot!" He checked his pager. He knew Towana had been trying to reach him, but doubted she accounted for the extra 14 messages he saw on his pager. He reached into his pocket for his phone.

"It's off," Elaine said shortly. "We've been trying to call you. Where have you been boy?"

"In traffic. Where Florence at?" he asked eagerly.

"In your room." She watched a genuine smile, something she rarely saw, spread across his face as he walked out of the kitchen.

He'd totally forgotten that Florence was flying in from Virginia where she was attending college. She was taking a semester off before transferring to UCLA. She was his jewel; sanity in an insane world. They'd met at L.A. High his senior year before he went to camp for that gun charge. She was a junior and completely opposite to the girls who usually were attracted to him. They had been in the same Spanish class. She was plain, but beautiful. Wide mouth and long naturally wavy hair that she wore in a ponytail religiously. The way she'd looked at him then had him open. She saw past his bravado and the deadness in his eyes that scared most people. Something in her he found attractive besides the fact she didn't wear tight or revealing clothing. She wore no make-up. Her gold-rimmed glasses gave her a seductive sex appeal no matter if she wore long print dresses. Florence was smart, homely, and had been a virgin. He had been her first. They were inseparable before she went off to college.

When he went to his room Florence was asleep on his bed. Her hair was fanned out over the pillow. He'd never seen it straightened. Its dark strands contrasted against her almond complexion. He watched her breathe before kneeling down to give her a soft peck on the cheek. She opened her long lashed eyes slowly. Smiling.

"Hi, Billy," she whispered sweetly. "I missed you."

"I missed you too, baby," he responded, his loins stirring.

She raised up on the bed, her nose crinkling. "Why are you dressed in all black?"

"Don't trip on that," he answered, unbuttoning his shirt and unbuckling his belt.

He moved onto the bed beside her, rubbing his hand over the soft material of her cotton summer dress. "Sorry I forgot you were coming," he whispered between kisses on her neck.

"As long as you weren't with another girl. What have you been up to while I've been gone?" She was almost afraid to ask, hoping not for the truth but a little reassurance. She didn't mind that he smelled like gasoline and gunpowder. She was happy to see him. To be in the room where she lost her virginity.

"Nothing like that. Just missing you." He was now taking off his boxers.

She saw his excitement. "Good answer," her voice was husky with anticipation as he lay on top of her, covering her wide mouth while expertly pulling her panties down.

Everything was going according to plan. BoDeen got respect from the Jamaicans and a cool deal to cop as much powder and cronic as he needed once he had a steady stream of demand. He copped a half bird of powder straight up to put a one on and distribute to the few people he'd locked in.

It was eerily quiet when he turned onto Ruff's block. He'd anticipated a few people out front, but even the dog was absent from the front yard. He wondered where Dubb and Drak were. And where was Lonnie Ray?

"This spot is dead. That nigga Lonnie Ray don't go nowhere though," Droop said as they got out of the Durango and pushed through the gate.

Before they could get to the porch, the graveled voice of Ruff came through the black metal screen door. "You niggas got a lot of heart."

BoDeen couldn't see through the screen door and Ruff made no move to open it. He knew the big man was standing just behind it watching them.

"Ey Ruff, you know BoDeen, Milo's folks."

"I know Milo," Ruff interrupted Droop cryptically.

Droop was shook. "He just wanna holla at you."

"Now ain't a good time."

Bo spoke up, "I used to run this hood."

"Don't know nothin' 'bout that," Ruff stopped him.

Droop was getting nervous. He guessed that he might be out of pocket for showing up unannounced with BoDeen. He didn't take into consideration the funk that was in the streets. He knew better than to provoke Ruff. Droop was a coward when it came to the actual business of conflict.

BoDeen was at a disadvantage. He couldn't see who he was talking to. He didn't expect not to be welcome to a conversation.

"State your business and be out," Ruff barked.

"My man Droop say you cop powder. I got my hand on some cool flake. Whatever you get yours for, I got it better," BoDeen offered. In his day this offer would be followed by violence if it wasn't accepted. He realized it was a polite intimidation and was not surprised, given Ruff's demeanor, at what he said next.

"Get off my porch," Ruff commanded.

Droop could feel the big man behind the black grill looking at them.

BoDeen understood perfectly what his mistake was. First, he overestimated what it meant to have Droop as a go-between. Obviously he wasn't respected. Second, he disrespected the game by not meeting Ruff on his own terms.

Chapter Seven

By the time Billy Bob got up off the cock, he was ready to go put in work. When he got to the garage Bunchy was telling a story to Dubb and Drak, passing a blunt between them. Smoke rose like angelic halos above their heads. "I switched up on that nigga like I was a south paw. You got to be careful 'cuz in real life your friends really be your enemies and your enemies really be snitches." Bunchy reached for the blunt.

"Where that nigga Stutterbox?" Billy Bob asked as he came through the side door. The sliding garage door was pulled down.

Everybody looked at each other like they hadn't noticed he was gone. It'd been at least three hours since he was sent to dump the van at the chop shop.

"Sumptin' up wit dat dumb nigga. I'ma slice that nigga," Bunchy warned, pulling on the blunt again before passing it to Billy Bob.

"Not if I see 'im first." Drak raised his pistol, pointing it at a spot on the wall. "Blow! Blow! Rest in hell!" he slurred, releasing blunt smoke into the air.

"You got the bucket?" Billy Bob asked Dubb.

"Out front."

"Let's roll."

Bulletproof vests were secured and guns of choice were being examined. Bunchy was admiring the chunk and heft of the .45 Grizzly that Hutch had gotten for him. "This muthafucka fat!" he exclaimed. "Can't wait to Knock-Knock-Knock," he said, jerking it in his outstretched hand.

While Billy Bob was spending time with Florence, Drak had taken Dubb to pick up the bucket, an often painted over old school Caprice Classic with a 454 engine. It was used for dope runs and other dastardly activities.

As the crew made their way to the bucket, Towana pulled up with a serious screw face. "Billy, why you don't answer your phone? Where have you been?" she asked in succession as she hopped out of the car. Tomika was in the passenger seat and the dark girl he'd seen before was in the back seat. "I need to talk to you. It's serious, Billy!" She pushed up on him.

"I got something to do right now." He tried to brush past her.

She jumped between him and the passenger door of the Caprice, putting her hand on his chest feeling the vest. "Where Stutterbox at?"

"You sure are asking a lot of questions. Move out the way." He tried to get in the car.

"He fucked my friend!" she shouted, getting Billy Bob's attention. She was pointing at Coretta in the back seat of her Honda Accord.

"So," he said, raising his shoulders.

"And Midnight was there." She dropped the info that was sure to get his attention.

"What?"

"Yeah. He was fucking her and Midnight broke in on them. And he said he didn't give a fuck about y'all."

Billy Bob's mind was working fast as Bunchy was making his way over to Towana's car.

Tomika jumped out of the car. "Bunchy, don't!"

"She knew that nigga! Set up our nigga too!" Bunchy screamed, opening the door and reaching for Coretta. "Come here bitch! Snake bitch!"

"Stop, Bunchy!" Tomika yelled, running around the car to stop him.

It was all clear to Billy Bob now. He was thinking of where Stutterbox might be as he watched Bunchy grab Coretta by her hair and pull her out of the car. She was on the ground crying as Bunchy started to kick her with Tomika grabbing at his arms.

Towana was screaming, "That's my friend, Billy! Tell Bunchy to stop!"

Billy Bob was looking at Towana with disgust. "Where you meet her at?'

Her mind worked quick. "That don't matter. I didn't have nothing to do with it."

"That bitch trying to get me killed. She your friend?"

Coretta's screams were dying as Bunchy continued to kick her in the head and stomach. Tomika was crying, trying to protect her from the blows.

"Bunchy! Get off that girl!" Billy Bob's mom shouted as she stormed through the front door and out to the street. Florence looked confused as she followed to the mayhem. "Have you lost your mind?" Elaine was asking as she pulled on Bunchy.

Towana's attention was now focused on the pretty girl in the long summer dress who'd stopped at the curb looking at Billy Bob. She had his attention too. "Who's that?" Towana asked loudly, pulling on Billy Bob's arm to get him to look at her. She looked from him to Florence, hands on hips, forgetting about the whimpering Coretta who was struggling to get to her feet with Tomika's aid.

Elaine turned to her son. "Billy, what the hell is going on? Don't be having this shit in front of my house."

"Who is that bitch?" Towana shouted, locking eyes with Florence.

"Bitch, who are you?" Florence answered in defense thinking back to the girls in high school she had to beat up because she loved Billy Bob.

Elaine moved in Florence's direction looking at Towana. "Don't start no shit over here little girl," she warned.

Tomika was fuming. "What the fuck wrong with you crazy ass nigga!" she screamed, throwing her arms against Bunchy as he backstepped her advance.

As Elaine tried to stop Bunchy from hitting Tomika, Towana dashed to the curb to confront Florence. "You here for Billy Bob bitch?!"

"I ain't your bitch, bitch. You better get out my face," Florence said, balling up her fist.

Towana hit her two times in the face before Florence grabbed her by the hair and slung her to the ground.

Elaine was screaming at Billy Bob as she tried to keep Tomika from jumping in to help Towana. "Get them!"

Dubb and Drak were already trying to pull Florence off Towana with half-hearted effort. They tussled on the ground swinging and pulling each other's hair.

A police siren chirped loudly, getting everyone's attention. Big Red jumped out his Chevy Malibu followed by his young partner. "Don't make me take you girls to jail," he warned as he moved across Dubb to coax the girls apart. He turned to Elaine. "Take this girl in the house." Then he shoved Towana towards her car. "You get out of here before I take you to jail." He saw Coretta leaning against the car. He didn't want to know what happened to her. If it was serious she could make a police report. That wouldn't be his problem. He'd come to handle more important business. Getting his cut to keep Billy Bob out of jail and talk about what's turning into some sort of turf war.

For once Billy Bob was glad to see the pig. Shit was crazy. He watched Towana drive off cursing at him and everyone else who caught her sight. Her hair was sticking out at all angles. Coretta was laid out in the back seat. His mom had Florence under her arm, taking her into the house. He wanted to go speak with her and try to make shit right but he had so much on his mind. With Florence being as pissed as he was he knew talking to her right now would only makes things worse. He hoped his mom could keep her calm. Bunchy was grinning, happy with the drama. Dubb and Drak were giving each other dap. Billy Bob was looking at Big Red with a mixture of appreciation and disgust as he watched him crack a yellow-toothed grin.

"Got yourself a real love rodeo here, huh?" Big Red remarked. He was looking around at the new calm, then at all the fellas dressed in black with bullet-proof vests on. He could see the bulge of a fat Glock in Billy Bob's waist.

Billy Bob knew what he wanted and really didn't have time to talk to him. Other things were on his mind. Namely, Midnight and finding Stutterbox. He went to his Escalade and disappeared inside. He came back with a small envelope, handing it to Big Red. "For your trouble. Holla later," he said as he got in the Ca-price. Although he didn't trust Big Red since he was responsible for sending him to juvee, Billy Bob wanted to keep him in his pocket for certain business dealings that would be beneficial to him.

Big Red was tapping the heavy envelope as the four deep crew sped off down the street. He wondered where they were going. Hopefully out of his jurisdiction.

G-Rob had just come up from the basement. He was getting tired of hearing Maniac beg him to untie the ropes around his hands and ankles; pleading with him to let him go. "Nigga straight punk," G-rob said out loud.

"That nigga still crying?" asked Teardrop. He was playing dominoes with Crazy-O. They were both half-breeds with light skin and long silky black braids that hung to their shoulders. Teardrop used to be a golden gloves middleweight champion until he started smoking sherm sticks. Now he was just a menace. Crazy-O was his younger brother who was known for his quick left hook at the slightest provocation. They often came through G-Rob's spot to chill and try to stay out of trouble and maybe make a few dollars off the baseheads.

"Hell yeah," G-Rob answered with a disgusted laugh. "Smell like piss and shit down there." He walked to the front door to look out the window. A familiar looking van had just passed slowly.

G-Rob had only left the window by a few steps when the front door came crashing down with a loud bang. He was startled as a fat black man came tumbling into the living room followed by a slim man who was the color of midnight. Dark purple he was so black. G-Rob could hardly react before Midnight shot him in the leg then ran up on him to unload two more bullets into his falling body. Fatboy was shooting from pistols in both hands towards Teardrop and Crazy-O. The flimsy card table was quickly chewed up and dominos scattered through the air. Teardrop made it as far as the kitchen door before a bullet found the back of his head. Crazy-O was slumped over the fallen table.

When Midnight opened the basement door, he was assaulted by the powerful stench of shit, piss, and fear. He almost vomited when he got down the stairs and got a good look at the beaten, bloody, swollen face of Maniac. He was looking at Midnight through puffy eyes. Fright. Surprise. Embarrassment. Submission. His face showed all these emotions as Midnight walked towards him with the hot Glock gripped in his hand.

Maniac said that Midnight's spot was the blue house on the corner of 83rd and VanNess. Bunchy parked the

Caprice on the opposite corner. There were no street-lights on this corner so they were covered by the night as they ran towards the blue house. Someone was looking at a TV in the living room. Bunchy had eased up to the front window and peeked through a crack in the curtain. Stutterbox was sitting in a leather reclin-er in the corner. A light-skinned girl had just come in from a back room and sat on the couch next to some buff dude with no shirt on. Bunchy whispered over his shoulder to Billy Bob what he saw.

Billy Bob told Dubb and Drak to go around back and gun down anybody coming out. He lit a malatov cocktail and threw it through the front window. He and Bunchy stood on the front lawn and fired into the house. Flames erupted inside the house. People moved around frantically trying to escape, screaming as bul-lets flew through the front window and door.

Dubb caught two dudes running fast out the back door. They were caught by surprise as the bullets flew into them. The buff dude stumbled through the door right after them. Drak shot him three times before he fell to the ground.

There was a lot of commotion in the house as gunshots rang out from the back yard. Stutterbox jumped out a side window. Billy Bob saw him crash to the ground on the side of the house as he stood at the edge of the lawn in the front yard. He ran towards him as he was getting up, brushing glass off his arms. He was bleeding from his forehead. His eyes bulged when he saw Billy Bob standing in front of him pointing a Glock at his head. "Bitch ass nigga!" Billy Bob shouted over the gunshots and the fire. "Where Midnight at?"

Stutterbox was speechless. Before he thought it was better to say something, Billy Bob shot him in the chest and when he fell, strode over to him and shot him two more times in the head. It exploded onto the sidewalk.

As all four trotted across the street, leaving Stutterbox dead on the sidewalk, a woman could be heard screaming from inside the burning house. She was too scared to run outside.

Chapter Eight

Elaine spent much of the night comforting Florence. She genuinely liked her and preferred her over that "rowdy bitch" Towana, as she'd confided to Florence. "Honey, my son don't even like that girl. All he talk about is you," she'd said, only to be stumped by Florence's reply.

"Then why he forget I was coming?" she asked while standing in the bathroom mirror dabbing alcohol on a scratch across her cheek. Her lip was puffy and her eye was red. Elaine was looking at her through the mirror, not knowing what else to say except that Billy Bob had a lot on his mind at the moment. *That's the least of it*, Florence thought to herself. She'd talk to Billy when he got home, she assured herself.

Florence was in Billy Bob's bed when she heard footsteps run past the window and into the backyard.

She saw the upstairs garage light come on through the bedroom window. She knew Billy Bob's walk. He'd run upstairs, then run back down. A few more minutes passed before she heard a lesser amount of footsteps pass by going out towards the front yard. Then the motors of no less than two cars came to life—one with loud music made louder at one in the morning. She was relieved when she heard the back door close. She waited. The bathroom door closed and the shower came on. Her mind traveled fast as to what all the sounds meant. Where had he been? What smell was he washing off? She couldn't imagine what he was doing in the streets this late at night.

He smelled like Caress soap. She felt the violence in him when he slid into the bed beside her. A tenderness began to take over as she tried to read a story across the ridges of his rib cage and the rises across the muscles of his stomach. She wanted to know where he'd been, but dared not to ask. The answer might be better left unsaid.

"I'm sorry about what happened today. Sorry. I forgot you were coming," Billy Bob whispered for the second time that day, against the top of her head as she lay across his chest.

She wanted to be mean. Say something smart. She wanted him to say that that girl meant nothing to him. She wanted him to say how much he loved her. She wanted to be able to love him wholly; with abandon. He called what she felt for him 'thug passion'. She knew it was true. Even with her face scratched and her lips dipped in Vaseline, she felt exhilarated. She was proud of herself. She relived the fight over and over in her mind. The two hits she suffered were nothing compared to the way she grabbed that bitch's hair and slung her to the ground. She smiled with the memory of how Towana cried out when she pulled it, feeling the roots snatch.

"What's so funny?" Billy Bob asked, feeling her cheek move against his chest.

"She tried to serve me, huh?" she asked in the dark, smiling.

He smiled with her. "Bitch couldn't see you."

"Is that what men like? To see two women fight? It feels like high school all over again." Her hand traveled over the ridges of his stomach.

"Not you, baby. I don't like to see you fight. Never did."

She chuckled. "Coulda fooled me the way I always had to fight for you." She looked up at him then. "Still, I do handle myself don't I?"

"You represent, baby." He didn't want to dwell on it. She didn't seem like she was tripping too much. Not like he thought she would. She was moving her fingers through his pubic hairs. His dick stirred, making him take a deep breath. "You and me like peanut butter and jelly. You ever try to pull apart that shit? It tear up the bread."

She giggled at this. He always knew how to make

her laugh. She moved her head towards the spot where her fingers stopped at the base of his pubic hairs. She hoped the swelling would go down on her lips by morning. It only hurt a little, but not enough to stop doing what she really wanted to do. She pulled his hardening dick through his boxers and filled her mouth with the swollen meat. She was hungry for him. Her appetite was heightened by the day's activities and his absence. She was so aggressive on the dick she took Billy Bob by surprise, making him jump. She sucked so hard and strong, he gasped at the intensity of the suction. She heard him. Felt him. Secretly proud of herself for making him lose control. She was on her way to giving him phenomenal brain. *The best he'd ever had and he'd love me for it*, she thought as she hungrily deep throated the whole of him with a quick move of her neck.

When Midnight turned the corner off 82nd, his chest thumped at the site of the fire trucks and police cars. His spot was burned to the ground, leaving a shell of three walls. Firemen walked through the rubble looking for bodies. Yellow tape surrounded the house. He rolled past staring at the scene. Yellow plastic blankets covered a body in the front yard. Another covered a body on the side of the house. Two bodies were covered in the back yard surrounded by burned debris.

"Aw shit!" Maniac gasped, involuntarily looking over at Midnight, then at Fatboy.

"What you tell them niggas?" Midnight demanded as he turned on to a quiet street away from the chaos and bright lights.

"I didn't tell 'em nothing man!" Maniac pleaded.

"That's why you piss and shit on yo'self! Cuz you didn't say nothin'!" Midnight shouted.

"Man... man..." Maniac cried, holding his head in his hands.

Fatboy looked over at Midnight with a knowing glance. Midnight was hurt deeply and mad as hell as he turned towards the marina. He had something to show Maniac.

Chapter Nine

Billy Bob heard the banging on the door. He thought he was dreaming and the banging was actually the sounds the large pit bull was making in his dream as it chased him down the street. But the banging slowly woke him. Florence was still asleep, snuggled close to him. He looked over at the bedside clock. It read 8:45 a.m. He knew his mom had to be gone. She went to work fifteen minutes ago for the drive to the valley. The banging on the front door continued. *Bet not be that bitch Towana*, he mumbled to himself as he moved through the living room barefoot in his boxers.

"Who the fuck at my door..." he began as he opened the door. He'd expected to see whoever it was through the screen door. It was open, propped by the wide body of Big Red. Billy Bob was confused. Big Red looked mad. *What he pointing a gun at me for?*

"Come the fuck out the house! Turn around and put your hands on your head!" Big Red yelled. His young partner behind him with his gun down.

Big Red handcuffed Billy Bob and grabbed him by the arm. He ran with him to the Chevy Malibu and shoved him into the open door of the back seat. He moved so fast Billy Bob was on his toes for most of the way. He felt like he was being kidnapped. No other police were around. He was shoved into the car head-first. The door slammed and Big Red sped off, leaving Florence at the front door scared and confused.

Big Red didn't take him to the police station like Billy Bob thought he would. They pulled into an abandoned warehouse downtown. The area was a deserted rail-way station. Brisk early morning air filled the vacant space escorting a rising sun. Old, broken machinery was pushed to one side of the warehouse leaving the other side partly kept. The cleaner side had a desk and file cabinet against the wall. At the far back wall, under broken windows and dusty steel beams stood a lone wooden stool.

Big Red parked in the middle of the concrete floor and snatched Billy Bob out of the back seat. Clad only in his boxers and barefoot, the cold cement sent a jolt through his body.

Anger screwed his face up. "What the fuck is up with this shit? Take these iron bracelets off!" Billy Bob shouted into the sparse room.

Big Red hesitated before moving to take the handcuffs off.

Released, Billy Bob rubbed his wrists and hopped onto the warm hood of the car. "You kidnap a nigga in his draws!" He had to chuckle at the absurdity of it all.

"Shit ain't funny. You think you pay me so you can kill at will? The Feds are in my fucking precinct! This little war you got going on has reached all the way to the Governor Terminator. I got to answer to this shit! And I ain't gonna lose my job and pension for no piece of shit like you!"

"I ain't killed nobody!" Billy Bob said calmly.

"You ain't!"

"I ain't," Billy Bob said, returning the incredulous stare.

Big Red stood a few feet in front of Billy Bob with his legs spread apart and his arms folded. His fat fingers started popping away from his palm as he ticked off the murders. "Three dead on 29th street and a basement that smells like shit. Looks like somebody was tortured down there. On 83rd, I got four people dead." He popped two more fingers off his other hand. "And a burned body in a burned down house." One more finger. "Oh... and if that ain't enough. A body was found on the beach with a bullet to the back of the head.

Wouldn't mean nothing except that it looks like he may be the guy that was tortured on 29th street." He grandly held his hands up with eight extended fingers. "All in a day. Now, you see my dilemna?"

Billy Bob was putting it all together in his mind. G-Rob must be dead. They got Maniac and figured he snitched and domed him at the beach.

Big Red looked at him quizzically. "You think I'm stupid huh? No. You just think you're smarter than me in your undeveloped mind. I'm the police!" he screamed as if newly upset, moving closer. "You and Midnight got beef!" he said this with a flourish and stepped back to let that sink in. Then he smiled. "I've been doing this since before you were born. You think your game tight. You're too late in the game. Back in the day you could carry a pistol, bag of weed, and shoot somebody and get probation. Now you carry a pistol or have a bag of weed you go to jail for a long time. If you shoot somebody, heck, just shoot at somebody and you go to jail for life. You're late, Billy. This ain't the time to be a thug." Big Red got a wistful expression on his face, remembering a better time. "Know who was game tight? Milo's father, Haitian Jack. Even Milo couldn't follow in his footsteps. It was a different time. Luckily Milo found the right time for his game. Now, you think you got the recipe?

"You kill Midnight's boys. He kill your boys. And what for? Crumbs. The game is sour." He moved to-wards Billy Bob with a sad look on his face, suddenly tired. "I take your money because I can. You'll be dead soon because you think you can do wrong the right way." He was up on Billy Bob again, closer than he'd ever been. Like his father should've been if he were around. "Get off my car. Next time you get in it, I'll be taking you to jail."

Billy Bob hopped off the warm hood onto the warming concrete. He watched the two pigs get in the car and begin backing out of the warehouse. "Hey! Y'all just going to leave me here?" he screamed.

Suddenly Big Red sped back into the warehouse and stopped next to Billy Bob. He had a weird smile on his face. "And no one get away with killing a cop. Watch BoDeen closely. Maybe it'll be a lesson for you. Think of that on your way home." He winked, then backed up out of the warehouse, leaving Billy Bob standing there barefoot in his boxers.

When Florence saw the powder blue Escalade creep to a slow turn into the driveway and park behind Billy Bob's Navigator, she rushed out the front door. "Bunchy! The police took Billy!" She was frightened.

"What?!" Bunchy asked, getting out the truck. He didn't understand what she was talking about. He briefly wondered if it had anything to do with him beating down Coretta in the street. The fat .45 Grizzly was weighted comfortably in his waistband. His demeanor betrayed the murderous activities of the night before. He was shocked to hear about Billy Bob.

"What's going on, Bunchy?" Florence asked, looking into the deep green-gray of his eyes. Hidden in the crystals was a rage subdued by a slightly lesser violence. She felt him calculating his answer.

"Ain't shit," he responded, moving towards the garage where he'd feel more comfortable. "How long ago he left?" he asked, moving through the side door followed by Florence. He turned on the widescreen and sat down in the leather recliner.

"About 10 minutes ago." She watched him all the while he made himself comfortable. He put the gun on the table in front of him. Checked his pager and phone before laying them beside the gun. "Did he take his phone with him?"

"All he had on was his boxers. He didn't even have on any shoes," Florence said seriously. Eyes wide.

Bunchy couldn't help but to smile at this. Florence wasn't surprised. She was quickly learning he was the type to find humor in such madness. "Bru got snatched up in his draws!" he was saying to himself with a low chuckle. "He'll call. Don't worry," he said, reassuring Florence as he picked up the remote and flipped to BET RapCity.

Florence felt like she wasn't even in the room. She was conscious of the fact they were alone and a weird sort of bond held together by an affinity for violence. She imagined he got the same type of rush she did after her fight. Yet, he didn't mention anything. He acted like yesterday never happened. She was intrigued that he seemed not to want to talk to her too much. Maybe it was out of respect for Billy Bob. She drew plenty of dudes who had girlfriends or knew she had a boyfriend, but would still try to get at her or ask stupid questions to disguise their interest. Obviously Bunchy was different. So was Billy Bob. This brought about a certain comfort. She relaxed against the leather couch to watch a Lil Jon video.

"Bunchy," she began after a few minutes of rapping and ass shaking. "Where do you see yourself in three years?"

Is she serious? he thought to himself as he rotated his gaze on her. She was serious. Something deep inside him tugged. It was so easy to get caught up in what was going on. Her question reminded him of what he really wanted to do. That was to be bigger than G-Unit. "Why you ask?" he finally asked harshly to see if she would be intimidated. She acted like she wanted to care, he'd reasoned.

"I just wanna know."

"Who are you to know?" His stare was even.

She didn't flinch. "You scared to tell me," she said with a slight smile. He wasn't so tough.

"I ain't scared of nothin'. Why you askin' so many questions?"

"I asked you one question, so don't even try it."

"How many gon' follow that?" He didn't need to be so tough.

"Haven't planned that. Let's start with that one." She saw him relax. Trusting.

Bunchy took a shallow breath and turned his attention back to the widescreen. The Game was on a block in Compton. This both inspired him and upset him. He knew he and Billy Bob could do that shit. Billy had flow. They had loot and rep. He pointed to the video. "That's where I wanna be in three years. We could be there next year if..." He was going to say if they wanted to, but that would start more questions he wasn't prepared to answer.

Florence watched him retreat into his thoughts. She knew Billy Bob liked to rap and she'd jokingly urged him to make a record. He'd never taken the initiative to pursue his skills. He was caught up. So was Bunchy. Yet, she knew that they had more intelligence and promise than the guys at college. It's just that they were in two different places. She wondered what it would be like to have people like Billy Bob and Bunchy, Dubb and Drak, on college campuses everywhere. Natural thugs and hustlers going to school. That would be incredible. "You ever thought about going to college?" she asked, watching his eyes register her question.

"Naw. Not really," he answered vaguely. Bunchy knew she'd have more questions. He hated being questioned. *Why won't she just chill? Shit, why she out here anyway?* Now he was getting aggravated and began to worry about Billy Bob. "Who got Billy? Was it a big fat pig?"

"Yep."

"Was he by his self?"

"No. There was another guy with him."

"Naw. Was any more cars? Just one car?" he asked hopefully.

That seemed odd. "Yeah. It was only one car."

Bunchy nodded his head. Suddenly Tupac's ring-tone voice came from his phone laying on the table: 'Me Against The World'. Bunchy picked up the phone. "Yeah. What's up, Bru... I heard... Where you at? I'm on my way." He flipped the phone closed and moved towards the door.

"Was that Billy?" Florence asked, impatiently.

Bunchy had forgotten about her just that quick. "Oh yeah. I'm going to get him right now." He thought for a moment. "Go grab him some clothes. You can roll."

Florence jumped up and ran to the house. Bunchy was in the Escalade when she dashed out the front door holding an armful of clothes and a pair of shoes.

Chapter Ten

"Billy ain't called yet?" Dubb asked, walking up the front steps. Lonnie Ray was sipping on a fifth of Hennessy sitting in his wheelchair next to the black iron screen door. "Damn, Lonnie Ray, it ain't even twelve yet and you sippin' already."

"Don't sweat my technique. If you wanna sip all you gotta do is ask," Lonnie Ray quipped in his harsh voice.

"I asked if Bru called, you ain't answered that!" Dubb answered smartly as Lonnie Ray turned up the bottle again. "Yeah, pass that shit," Dubb commanded, walking in front of the wheelchair and sitting next to him in an old stuffy lounger. He reclined in his brown khaki suit, flipping up the built-in footstool. The first sip of cognac turned his face screw.

Lonnie Ray's thin frame shook with laughter, showing missing and rotten teeth.

"What's so funny?" came the deep base of Ruff's voice through the screen door.

Lonnie Ray looked over his shoulder at a spot in the screen where he thought Ruff would be. "Youngster... Ey, Billy Bob call?"

"Naw. He 'spose to be coming through. I gotta holla at 'im," Ruff answered.

"'Bout BoDeen?" Lonnie Ray asked, turning back to look out into the street.

"That and some mo'," Ruff said, his voice fading as he backed away from the screen door.

Lonnie Ray snapped to attention at something he felt he was missing. "Give me that boy. You wasting good hooch." He grabbed the bottle with thin, eager fingers.

"That shit strong. Probably 'cuz it's early," Dubb admitted, salving his pride. He reached into his top pocket and pulled out a blunt. "Nigga be straight right now," he said, twirling the blunt in the air, then slipping it between his lips.

Lonnie Ray looked over at him. "Light that shit."

"You ain't got to tell me twice."

Dubb heard the beat first. The Game rapping over a knocking Dre beat. Then he saw Drak's Regal turn the corner on gold Daytons, gleaming in the early morning sun.

He was moving slow. Dubb could see his head through the front window as he crawled down the street, a lit blunt in his mouth. He pulled into the drive-way, the music competing with the excited barking of Kujo as he yanked at his chain in the middle of the dirt yard.

A familiar black van hit the corner, screeching its tires as the engine gunned.

Drak was just opening the door, the music still bumping, the dog's barking taking on a new urgency. The gun swung out the passenger window in slow mo-tion—it seemed to Dubb—and aimed at Drak.

"Drak!" Dubb yelled, rising out of his seat and pulling his heat from his waistband.

The van swerved to the curb as the gun popped in a methodical rhythm, piercing the air over the music and the barking. Dubb was running off the porch pop-ping off shots into the side of the van. It squirted off, the arm moving backwards towards him as it moved away. The loud shot of a 357 Magnum went off behind Dubb as he moved towards a fallen Drak. When he got to him, Drak was on the ground, his back against the Regal. His shirt was soaked wet. The red was muted by the black of his khaki suit.

Ruff had burst through the door, his large frame bounding down the steps busting shots at the van as it drove off. The shooter had done his damage.

The music was still playing. Dubb held Drak in his arms, willing him to open his eyes. There was a sound missing. Ruff was on the sidewalk watching the van hit the corner at the end of the block. He looked back into the yard. Kujo was laying on his side, his tongue hanging to the dirt. A small hole seeped blood over her tan hair. Her blood-red nose was wet, trying to take in breaths. Ruff was through the gate like he weighed 90 lbs. He scooped Kujo up in his arms and ran up the steps past Lonnie Ray, who looked asleep in his chair.

"Lonnie Ray!" Ruff shouted, holding Kujo in his arms.

Lonnie Ray opened his eyes. "Bitch shot me in the arm!" He grinned wickedly.

"Kujo shot. I'ma take her to the vet. You straight?"

Lonnie Ray nodded.

"Call an ambulance for Drak!" Ruff nodded his head towards the yard then disappeared inside the house for his car keys.

"It's too late," Dubb said to himself as he held Drak in his arms. He heard sirens in the distance. His mind was trying to figure out if there was dope in the house. The blunt was somewhere in the yard. His Glock. He laid Drak down gently and popped the gun compartment in the Regal. He got Drak's gun and put it with his in the trunk of his car. When he got back to Drak the first cop car was pulling up to the curb. It just missed Ruff as he pulled off with Kujo. Lonnie Ray looked asleep on the porch, the bottle of Hennessy slowly rising to his lips.

"In my draws, Bru! In my draws! Not even no shoes! I'ma smoke that pig, Bru. Serious." Billy Bob was still ranting and raving. Bunchy knew he was serious, but it was more than what the pig did. They still hadn't gotten Midnight. That's who Billy Bob wanted.

On the way home Billy Bob told Bunchy all that Big Red had said. About G-Rob and Maniac. Shit was crazy. Big Red was hot as fish grease. Florence had no idea what was going on. She looked at Billy Bob from the back seat with fear, awe, and a weird sense of attraction and pride that her man was truly with the business. She said a silent prayer that everything would be all right.

It was almost just past noon when they pulled into Billy Bob's driveway. "Barefoot in my draws, Bru!" he said, hopping out of the Escalade. Bunchy had to smile.

Elaine shot out the door when they pulled into the driveway. "Billy! What the hell is going on? Florence called me at work saying something about you getting arrested. I called the police station and they said you weren't there. Where have you been?" She was standing in front of him, keeping him from going into the garage.

"I'm cool, Ma. I'm hungry though," he complained.

Her little boy all over again.

Florence watched the contrast. How sweet and tender he was with her. And with his mom. He was just a kid, but a man all the same. She wondered if he even had feelings for all the drama around him. If he thought of the people that died the night before. Every now and then she would catch him in thought, but she couldn't tell if he was sad or planning his next move. He was one of the few people she couldn't read. This intrigued her even more. Reminded her after her long absence why she was so open for him. He was so addictive. All these things ran through her mind as she followed him into the house behind his mother.

"Let me see," Billy Bob said, tenderly touching her face. Florence had healthy swabs of Vaseline on the scar across her cheek. "Your lip not that bad," he assured her, kissing her lightly. They were at the kitchen table eating eggs and bacon.

Elaine poured more orange juice into Bunchy's glass. "Thanks Moms," he said.

"Billy, why that pig come snatch you up like that?" Elaine asked her son.

Billy Bob had a mouthful of food. He grabbed up the orange juice to buy more time and consider his reply. This was more for her benefit. She always acted like she wanted to know the details—to show her motherly concern—but he didn't feel she could actually handle it. She had to know what time it was with him and maybe was afraid to confront him for fear of losing him altogether. He looked over at Bunchy. The shit they'd been through together. Barely out of their teens and grizzled veterans of the game. Yet the game was closing in on them. The pig said the game was sour. "You know the pigs, Momma. They always got a reason to harass us." Florence couldn't wait to get him to herself.

"Was you worried about me?" Billy Bob asked Florence when they were finally alone. He was laying on his bed as she stood over him.

"A little," she answered with a coy smile, pinching her fingers together. She lay on top of him, searching his face. "Do you get scared?"

So close to her he could see the flecks of gold in her hazel eyes. He couldn't remember ever being scared. Was that normal? "Were you scared?" he asked, watching her eyes recognize and relive the fight.

She shook her head no.

"Me neither," he responded with satisfaction.

He was so clever, Florence thought as she began kissing him. "Billy Bob," she whispered as she rose over him. "I want you to check in college with me." She searched his face. It didn't register that he even heard her.

Someone was tapping on the window, interrupting Florence's valuable time alone with Billy Bob. "Yeah!" he screamed towards the window, thankful to be saved from what surely was going to be a serious discussion.

"Bru," Bunchy replied simply.

When Billy Bob got to the garage, Dubb was standing in front of the widescreen in a trance. "Tell Bru what happened," Bunchy said.

Dubb was shaking his head, not seeing what was on the widescreen. "Midnight came through the spot and dumped. Drak gone! Drak gone." He was choked up, trying to hold in his pain. His fists were clenched against his thighs.

Billy Bob watched him in silence, a murderous rage boiling inside of him.

Bunchy filled in the rest. "Lonnie Ray got hit in the shoulder. He at Mercy Hospital. You know can't nothin' kill that nigga. Ruff at the vet."

Billy Bob looked at him quizzically.

"Kujo got hit. She be okay though," Bunchy added.

Dubb came to life. "We gotta find that bitch, Midnight," he said, punching his fist into his open palm.

Silence filled the garage. Each absorbing what just happened. Each putting together in his mind what should happen next. All wanted to see Midnight first, but no one knew where to find him.

Dubb spoke up, "That bitch you beat down, Bru. The one set Box up."

"Naw, don't call them bitches," Billy said, stopping Bunchy from calling Tomika. He couldn't deal with that drama right now. "I'll holla at Milo," he said in finality.

Bunchy shut his cell phone thinking he should've thought of that first. He knew Milo knew everything and everybody.

Dubb was finally able to sit down. He was exhausted with sorrow.

Chapter Eleven

BoDeen had been running the streets all day, missing the violence erupting around him. He was opening up new spots and taking over old ones left open by the back and forth battles between Billy Bob and Midnight. The vicious cycle of revenge and retaliation left people dead and mothers crying in the street. BoDeen was beginning to feel his wings again as his pockets began to fill and his reputation began to renew itself with activity.

Dimp was at the dining room table talking on his cell phone to a 13 year old girl when BoDeen walked in the front door followed by Droop. Between the chicken leg in one hand and cell phone in the other, Dimp managed a 'hi Dad' when BoDeen proudly ran his palm across the curly mop of Dimp's hair.

Missy's attention was on the phone where Gwen

was once again having trouble balancing out the cash register in the beauty supply section of the hair salon. The problem was minimal and as she hung up she had to remind herself to apologize to Gwen for snapping at her. Other things were on her mind. And when she saw BoDeen come home trailed by Droop, it took all of her strength to control her temper. She didn't like to argue in front of Dimp.

"Get off the phone until you finish eating," she said to Dimp as she came out of the kitchen. She turned to BoDeen after acknowledging Droop with a fake smile. "We need to talk." She didn't mean for it to come out so harshly, but that's all the forgiveness she could master on such short notice.

"Is this what you plan to do?" Missy hissed, turning on him once they entered their room.

BoDeen closed the door behind him. "What you talkin' about Missy?"

"This!" She pushed her finger into his chest as if he were inadequate. He looked good enough in Sean John jeans and a button-down shirt, but she was talking about who he was and what he was doing. She'd been had issue with it, but she'd seen him return to his old ways, no matter that his mouth said differently. Now he was dragging one of his henchmen into her house. That did it.

"What?" He foolishly thought everything was cool. He thought once he got rolling and putting money in the house, she'd be cool. *I'm the same man she married,* he reasoned. *I know she don't expect me to do a 180 flip and switch overnight.*

"This! BoDeen." Now she waved her palms, which could have meant the whole world. "I already told you I ain't going through this shit. When you were locked up you talked about opening a detail shop and doing right. Now that you're home, you in the street just like before you left. What do you think is going to happen? Niggas dying in the street left and right. That ain't enough for you?" She suddenly became sad because she knew Billy Bob was knee deep in the business. She heard everything at the salon. The ghetto grapevine passed the business like a virus. She was glad Milo wasn't involved, except that his name grew to mythic proportions just because of that.

BoDeen was affected by the potential of him being taken away from her. Matter of fact he seemed to be taking advantage of the chaos. Tears began rolling down her face. She was beyond words and the ones that came were surrounded by grief. "We worked so hard for you Bo, and you treat it like it was nothing." Her face was streaked with tears drying because no new ones replaced them. "And you have the nerve to bring some nigga into our house like this is some sort of kickin' it spot! What kind of shit is that!"

"Droop alright," was all he could manage.

"He ain't alright! You don't think I haven't heard of him before?"

"You want him to leave?" BoDeen asked, flashing

anger through his eyes.

Missy was unbowed. "That's just a start! You know the rest. I ain't got no more to say." She looked defiantly into his eyes before brushing past him with a shove.

Haitian Jack's recovered from the shooting. A giant mural of Rolando was over the bar. His beefy face smiled immortal with 'R.I.P. BRU 1979-2007' inscribed under him. You couldn't help but see his picture when you walked in. In Rolando's place were two, armed, off-duty Sheriffs. They were kept busy ensuring that no gun entered through the front door.

Billy Bob reminded Bunchy to leave his gun in the truck. "Bru. I feel naked," Bunchy complained as they walked through the front door. It was barely seven on a Friday night and Haitian Jack's was showing early signs of the kind of night it was famous for. Beautiful, well dressed people mingled and laughed. Clinking glasses and shooting pool. Munching on Buffalo wings and sharing stories. The overhead DJ was mixing songs off of Jon Legend's new CD and some new Tweet. The atmosphere was cozy and the energy positive. The dance floor held a respectable amount of people while more occupied the seats lining the window overlooking the bar. Billy Bob scanned the video game section and the row of pool tables under the dance floor looking for enemies. Men glanced back at him with a slow nod while the women looked boldly.

HoodRich's reputation entered the room like a strong gust of wind. Some walked up on them cautiously to show respect and acknowledge the three of them so as not to be confused as a hater or enemy. Billy Bob, Bunchy, and Dubb wore the same powder blue khaki suit with their platinum diamond encrusted "HR" emblems swinging across their chest. They cut a disciplined, tight, and grizzled trio.

Sherrie was talking to Dread behind the bar when Billy Bob led them through the door. She met them in the foyer and motioned them towards the staircase in the back that led to Milo's office. She was only too happy to get them out of sight. She held Billy Bob's hand with affection as they walked through the V.I.P lounge. Kilroy was talking to three tall, shapely women. They looked to be talking serious business coated with a relevant joke to ease the tension. Kilroy broke away from the girls as Billy Bob entered the room to give him a hug and some advice. "Think three moves ahead." With a wink and eye contact with Bunchy and Dubb.

They were steps from Milo's office. The large shiny wooden door was closed in front of him. Billy Bob was only now aware of the hole he was in—measured against the ease, success, and security of the people he'd seen growing up on his block. He had a sickening feeling in his stomach about his own situation. There was a truth fighting inside of him. It was buried under the code of the streets he'd lived by all his life. It felt like merging traffic of duty and escape were meeting in his soul. He felt himself slipping away from having a genuine life to enjoy with his genuine friends—good people who wanted to see him live. Not just live but live rich and die ready. Legit. Free. He knew with a certain anger that he would be busting on somebody before the night was over. And his life wasn't promised in the morning. He would be in the street grinding while everyone else was partying, laughing, and having fuck sessions. He felt trapped, but couldn't reach the lock to set himself free from the depths of his lifestyle. He felt weighted by his duty of G-Rob, Rolando, and his homies. Midnight wouldn't let him ease up now to square up. Bunchy and Dubb were prepared to die for something that was making his stomach tight. Yet there was a certain pride he felt was with the business. Loyal to his friends. Grimy in his hustle. Paid by the hood. Where no where else he had power, he had power in the hood. And that must be defended and protected. He was HoodRich for life.

"We love you, Billy," Sherrie said, releasing his hand and opening the door to Milo's office. She sounded sad and hopeful for him. Like she wanted something different for him, but was not the person to reach him.

"Bru." Milo smiled broadly, genuinely happy to

see Billy Bob. He put away the file he was writing in. He rose to embrace Billy Bob.

Milo's office was immaculate. The hardwood desk and walls were gleaming with an air authority. Milo was dapperly dressed as usual in a single breasted midnight blue suit with a powder blue tie and pocket square. He'd matured well into his legit lifestyle. He greeted Bunchy and Dubb with firm handshakes and invited them all to have a seat in the leather chairs facing his desk.

Billy Bob felt the comfort of where he wished to be settle over him. The love he had for Milo was obvious. The same as the love Bunchy and Dubb had for Billy Bob.

"I heard about G-Rob. Is his mom straight?" Milo asked, looking through some files in his desk drawer.

"Yeah, I handled that. And Drak's folks said good looking out on them ends," Billy Bob answered.

Milo nodded.

It was rare that Dubb and Bunchy were able to spend this sort of quality time with Milo. Not because he wasn't accessible, but the daily grind just didn't allow it. They were quietly reassured that he was supportive of all Bru's even though it was he and Billy Bob who were tight. Milo was making it clear that he had love for them. Living and resting in peace. And to know that he sent Drak's family money and asked about G-Rob made them feel good about the business.

"You straight, Bru?" Milo asked pointedly, looking

into Billy Bob's hazel eyes. He was no longer the young boy who had a crush on Sherrie or the boy he'd see every night riding his bike to meet him when he went to see G'ma. He missed those days. He hated to see Billy Bob living between jail and death. Billy Bob hesitated at this question, returning Milo's pointed gaze. A secret communication was exchanged; when this shit is over I need your help to get to where you are. Milo gave a slight nod at this unspoken request.

Milo handed him a slip of paper he'd slid out of a manila envelope. "Everything you need is right there."

Chapter Twelve

Droop didn't know what to do with the information he received from the street. Word was that Billy Bob kidnapped his boy Maniac then Midnight got word where he was and went to get him, killing some minor HoodRich figures. Midnight was no doubt with the business. Droop had to call his man Bumper Jack from outta Watts to find out the intricate details of how Stutterbox put salt in the game and how under pressure Maniac told everything he knew. That's how the spot got burned down and that fine ass bitch Candi who danced at the Barbary Coast got burned alive inside. Shit was crazy. Then Bumper Jack told him about how Midnight domed Maniac at the beach for what he said.

"Damn!" Droop had exclaimed, shocked at the intensity of what was going on and at the loss of his boy Maniac.

He was coward at heart and used his mouthpiece to get around the drama whenever it was directed at him. It was his trademark to roll with the nigga who he thought was pulling weight. BoDeen was his ticket if he could keep the drama to a minimum. He felt he at least should go through Midnight's spot to holla about his boy Maniac. When he asked BoDeen to roll with him, BoDeen declined, saying something about how he needed to handle some other business. Droop rolled solo, something he rarely did, but what he really wanted to do was get a feeling for where he stood with Midnight and his hood because Maniac was his boy. And if shit got ugly he was prepared to dirty mac Maniac to save his life. He knew where to find Midnight.

It was almost 10 at night when Droop turned onto 81st Street. He'd heard Midnight was living with this broad name Marcena. The house was in the middle of the block. Word was that Marcena had the best brain on the West Side. She could suck a golf ball through a water-hose. In Droop's perverted mind, he pushed aside his misgiving about showing up unannounced at Midnight's spot in order to get at Marcena on the down low. First, he had to have a reason for showing up at her door. Midnight was it. As he neared the middle of the block he felt less sure about this being a good idea. Marcena's phenomenal brain pulled him in. A few cars sat idle at the curb in front of her house with heads dipped low in the seats. They watched him park and get out the car. He could see they were smoking blunts and drinking beer. A few thugs were standing out on the curb.

"What you doin' over here, Droop?" asked the gravel-voiced Black Kato. He watched Droop approach the gate and got up out his seat on the porch where he was seated with a thick light-skinned girl. Black Kato was Marcena's brother. He knew Droop in passing from the county jail. He knew about the rumors that Droop was a snitch, but no one was able to put any paper work together to confirm it. Still, his movement was limited.

"I need to holla at Midnight," Droop said.

Black Kato looked him up and down standing on the other side of the gate. "What about?"

"Maniac."

"Hold up right here," Black Kato said, moving towards the front door and disappearing inside.

It was too late to turn back now. He'd never be able to show his face again. Shit, the heads in the cars right behind him probably wouldn't let him leave. He thought he would feel safer in the vest that held a 9mm Glock under his leather P-coat. But he didn't. A head shot would do the trick.

Black Kato was at the front door waving him up. As Droop passed by him and moved through the front door, he felt Black Kato's distrust and violence just beneath his grimy pendleton shirt.

The living room was small. It looked crowded with so many people in it. A floor model TV right by the door was showing the updated version of Superfly.

Four grimy heads filled a couch on the wall to his right sharing a blunt. On the couch in front of him were two hoodrats sitting on either side of PeeBo, a doughboy he knew from Crenshaw High. Behind the couch in the small dining room, four more grimy thugs were playing cards on a filthy folding table. The house had the smell of french fries and smelly feet. Nothing looked clear. He could see into the kitchen from where he stood. Dirty dishes were piled in the sink. Frameless pictures of dudes in the pen stood side by side with pictures of kids taped to the walls.

"He in the room," Black Kato said, motioning towards the hallway. "To your left." The hallway was dark. A low light came from a cracked door to a room on his left. He knocked twice before opening the door slowly. The room smelled foul. A mixture of old socks and ass with weed smoke on top. A bedside lamp cast an eerie glow on Marcena and Midnight. She was under the covers, the blanket pulled up to her neck. Droop could see the outline of the curves of her body through the cheap blanket. Midnight was on top of the blanket next to her with no shirt on. Droop could smell his feet from where he stood. His socks were filthy. He wondered how Marcena dealt with it.

"What you want nigga?" Midnight asked with no respect.

"What's up Comrade?" Droop began, shook by the bold stare of Marcena.

"I ain't yo muthafuckin' rad nigga. What you

want?" Midnight asked again. His temper rising.

Droop did some quick thinking, the true coward coming out in him. "Cuzz! What that soft ass nigga Maniac did was some bitch shit. Who you need to holla at is Billy Bob. I don't see how he gettin' away for this long."

Midnight was losing his patience.

"He rest on 39th Street. Not a spot. Mom's tilt." Droop watched this info settle in. If Midnight already knew, he didn't let on.

A slow wicked smile broke across Midnight's acne scarred face after Droop left the room. It was made more menacing by the glow of the headlamp.

Chapter Thirteen

"Do you have to?" Florence asked, holding Billy Bob's hand as he was about to walk out of the room.

"I'll be right back," he answered with a kiss on her forehead. His hand slipped from hers in slow motion, feeling her tension 'til the break.

Bunchy handed the open cell phone to Billy Bob as he walked into the garage. "Ruff."

"Whaddup Ruff. Kujo still got his bark?"

"Yeah. She gon' be alright. Lonnie Ray got a sling around his arm." There was silence for two beats. "Billy. Sorry about what happened to Drak."

"It's a part of life. We 'bout to handle that right now."

"Be careful. Slide through and pick up these heaters," Ruff offered.

"Got all the heat we need. You know Hutch stay at

Big Bear so he know what the cold feel like."

"No doubt. Holla if you need me," Ruff offered.

"I got this. Don't trip," Billy said, closing the phone. He reached for the vest Dubb handed him. Stutterbox's Suburban was backed up to the open garage door. Dubb and Bunchy were already fitted with military vests that had grenades and extra clips. They loaded pairs of SK and AK-47s, MAC-10s and a box of grenades and clips into the bed of the Suburban.

Dubb led the two-vehicle caravan just after 10 at night. Bunchy and Billy Bob were in the Suburban. No music played as each were temporarily caught up in their own thoughts. Bunchy was thinking about Florence's question to him a few days before about where he planned to be in three years. He knew where he wanted to be. Larger than G-Unit. Touring the world. He wanted to be done with the hood struggle. That he was with the business was no doubt. He had nothing to prove. They'd stacked enough money to start their own record label and do it big. He held the fat chunky .45 Grizzly in his hand. Watching the dull metal reflect the streetlights in rhythm as they moved up Western to make a left on Manchester.

"If we get separated, Bru, meet me right there," Billy Bob said, pointing to a 24hr donut shop on the corner before making another left and pulling to the curb behind Dubb.

They were three blocks away from the address Milo gave them on 81st Street. About four blocks over was where they'd burned down that house.

"Let's roll on these cats. They on the left hand side of the street," Dubb said, hopping into the back of the Suburban.

Bunchy got in the back seat so he could open the door on the left side. He grabbed a handful of grenades and an AK-47. He tossed an SK-47 on the front seat for Billy Bob.

"HoodRich, Bru. Let's roll," Dubb said from the back, pulling down his ski mask. "The white house with blue trim. A gate out front with bushes."

Billy Bob pulled slow to the corner of 81st Street with the lights off. "It's a short block." He was looking through high-powered night goggles. "Niggas out front smoking. I got them. Bunchy, you lob the grenades when me and Dubb get off. It's some cats in the cars in front of the house. That's you Dubb when we roll up."

"Let's send these niggas to hell," Dubb growled.

Billy Bob turned the corner and gunned the engine. Bunchy put two Glocks out the side window busting at the curious heads who raised their guns as the Suburban came to a quick stop in front of Midnight's spot. Billy Bob jumped out and let off with the SK-47 over the top of the cars into the yard where men scurried for protection. The deep growl of Dubbs's AK-47 chopping through the cars lit up the block. Screams, broken glass, crunching metal, and knocked concrete filled the air. Whatever few shots were fired by the dudes in the cars were no match for the high-powered assault rifles. They were ducking on the sidewalk behind the cars, but the AK and SK-47 bullets were ripping through engine blocks and putting holes in the concrete.

Droop had just stepped off the front steps when the Suburban stopped in the street. He was momentarily glad that he was able to get out the house when he heard the first shots. He watched as someone jumped out the back and begin shooting. As he tried to duck down the path leading to the front gate, a grenade landed right in front of him. He didn't believe it was real. Couldn't be real, he thought as it exploded in his face. He was dead in the middle of the yard as more grenades passed over him onto the front porch.

Blood painted the windows of the cars as Bunchy and Billy Bob moved past them, installing fresh clips. They both let loose on the house. Bullets sailed through the front window opened by a grenade. People scurried inside the house, screaming in pain and fright. The bullets tore through what was left of the front door and wood siding on the house. Large chunks of wood flew off the house creating a new hole. Billy Bob and Bunchy stood on the sidewalk, dead bodies at their feet as their rifles fired into the house, emptying clip after clip.

The assault was massive and without mercy. The trio backed to the Suburban, hopped in and sped off. They left bodies littered over the asphalt. The air smelled of gunpowder and smoke. The house smoldered under the explosions of grenades and firepower.

As they hit the corner, the block was quiet where before it harbored the sounds of war. No one dared to come out of their homes. The explosions and rapid gunfire moved them away from their natural inclination to be curious. The chaos instead moved them far into their closets and bedrooms, praying to God that the violence would stop.

Billy Bob parked the Suburban behind the Caprice Dubb had driven. They unloaded what was left of the grenades, guns, and ammo into the car. Bunchy doused the inside of the Suburban with gasoline and set it on fire. When the Caprice hit the corner, the Suburban lit up the sky with a powerful explosion.

Chapter Fourteen

Florence had lain awake in bed waiting to hear the familiar footsteps passing by the window on their way to the garage. It was getting late. Then she heard them. They were heavier this time. Weighed down with heavy iron and duffel bags filled with the metal of guns and bullets. And arousal crept through her loins at the thought of what Billy Bob must have been doing out there in the streets. The uneasiness she felt about the possibility of him not returning was replaced by a thankfulness for the sound of those heavy footsteps passing by the window. No sounds as hushed voices accompanied their march from God knows what or where to safety. Home. Her body warmed as she waited for the tap-tap of feet minus one pair to pass by going the other way. Then she would hear the back door close, feet on carpet, and the bathroom door opening and soon after the shower coming on. She waited, her body tingling with anticipation.

The returning tap-tap of feet never passed by. She instead heard the heavy boots come down the hallway towards the bedroom. Her heart raced. What happened? Was something wrong? She opened her eyes in the darkness, listening for the footfalls. The bedroom door opened suddenly, letting in the aroma of gas, metal, and rubber. The smell was pungent. Charged with activity. Billy Bob jumped onto the bed beside her, landing on her leg with his heavy boot, making her cry out.

"Sorry, baby," Billy Bob whispered, not making a move to get off her. Instead he lay fully on her with his bulletproof vest still on. The smell was all over him. Her head was buried in his neck.

"You wasn't sleep," he whispered over her. His voice was electrified with adrenaline. The power of life. His body hard.

Florence could only breathe him in. If the city night had a smell, it was on him.

"You know I wasn't sleep. How could I?" she mumbled into him.

He hungrily kissed her on the mouth. He'd bitten the inside of his lip while busting the heavy gun. She could taste the tart heavy metal of the blood that oozed from the cut with the effort of the kiss. She sucked his lip, causing him to wince. Feeling his retreat, she chased his lip and sucked harder only to let him free to slowly trace her tongue over the softness of his raw lips. If Billy Bob was a drug, she felt like she could overdose. Her body was pressed under the vest. She wanted it off. Wanted him undressed. Her hands worked of their own accord while she continued to kiss him on the mouth. Trapping his tongue, sucking the truth from him. Penetrating the violence and unspoken malice that his tongue held.

The vest snapped off heavy, giving her access to the body she knew well. The tender skin. The soft soul. Unprotected. Unarmored. She pulled the thick wool sweater over his head. His body was warm. She touched him in places that made him jump with pain. She had no way of knowing that were it not for the vest he'd be laying in the street on 81st. Where a bullet hole would have been, a deep bruise was raised as a testament to his survival. Her body heated as her fingers rubbed across his bruised ribs and chest as a salve against the pain. Billy Bob sighed with the pleasure and the pain of her touch.

He slowly eased under the covers next to her. Florence lay naked and warm welcoming. His body was hard against her softness. She rolled on top of him and kissed him on the forehead. She slowly worked her way across his face; eyes, ears, nose, mouth, chin. She slowly moved over his chest and shoulders, placing wet lips on his hot wounded skin in appreciation of his life. She eased over his navel, kissing the core of his strength. His hardness pressed against her body, a pendulum waiting to be swallowed. She kissed the tip of the swollen head, wrapping her lips around the meat. She slid her mouth down its length, hungrily sucking the natural flavor. Wetted and slippery, she bobbed up and down on it, feeling his temperature rise in her mouth.

She wanted to feel him inside her. Just when she knew he could take no more, she rose up and put her hips over the shiny pulsing pendulum swinging in the air straight up. She slid slowly over it, covering the wetness with her own tight warmth. With him fully inside, she ground down on him while laying her breast on his chest. "Is that it?" she whispered in his ear. He answered 'yeah' in a hoarse moan. She could've meant anything with her question he knew, but whatever it was, he was ready for that to be it.

Chapter Fifteen

Billy Bob slept hard. Deep in sleep he was released from the pressure of the trap he was in. His mind worked to gather the pieces and movements necessary to direct his energy in a different direction. So much time and energy had been devoted to hustling, shootouts, grinding and staying alive. Living to die instead of dying to live. He didn't realize how heavy the burden was until he decided he didn't have to carry it. Dope in one hand and a pistol in the other was a powerful magnet for jackers, haters, snitches, pigs, and enemies gunning for you. The added weight of representing HoodRich was like honey for bears who wanted to eat with no hunger. Deep in sleep HoodRich forged a new meaning. He could handle the bears and was willing to carry the honey. This came natural. Success through adversity was sweet. Just like honey.

He woke up to the smell of fried eggs and bacon. A rap followed him from his nocturnal thoughts. 'HoodRich thick like molasses / rollin' with ambition smashin'/ thick pretty bitches with firm titties small waist and fat asses.' He smiled with the peace that covered him, stretching like a cat under the covers.

It was Saturday morning. Elaine had the small television on in the dining room listening to channel 7 news while she set up the table. Florence was standing still, holding an empty plate and glass in her hands as she listened, captured by the morning headlines. Billy Bob walked into the dining room trying not to seem too interested in the newscaster's report of a gangland massacre in a residential neighborhood. The camera panned across a house that looked like it belonged in Baghdad, suffering a major assault by Allied Forces. The bullet-riddled cars out front could have easily been placed on any street in Fallujah. The front of the house was burned and blasted through. The newscaster found a resident who looked both confused and reluctant to talk. She was mesmerized by the devastation. The newscaster had to get her attention and urge her to tell what she heard or saw.

"I didn't see anything." Her cotton floral print robe was pulled tight although the sun was beginning to break through the morning mist. "All I heard was loud explosions and loud guns. Sounded like machine guns." Her eyes were wide with intent hoping that might clarify her situation.

The cameraman focused on the black anchorman. "Obviously the scene behind me was a calculated and determined plan to murder, kill, and destroy all the occupants of this—what's left of—this single family home. It's obvious that there were bodies in the two cars just behind me. How many I don't know. Residents say that on any given night any where from 15 to 25 young men could be seen hanging around this house selling and smoking drugs and drinking beer. Whoever did this—and they have no one in custody at present for this horrific act of violence—whoever did this knew who they were after. Witnesses say that this area is home to Dirt Gang Crips, a local gang here and the occupants of this house may very well be members of this gang. This wasn't your normal drive-by." Someone attracted his attention off camera as the picture wavered.

Now Elaine stood watching next to Florence shaking her head in a barely noticeable motion. Billy Bob noticed because he was looking at her. A pitcher of orange juice in her hand.

"Joining us is Lieutenant Grigsby from the 77th Division police department." The cameraman now included both distinguished, professional, uptight black men on the screen. Behind them, crime lab technicians worked through the debris of mayhem. "Lieutenant Grigsby, can you tell us how many people were murdered here overnight? And a possible motive or if any arrests have been made?"

Lieutenant Grigsby furrowed his brow in concentration and determination. "What happened here was a senseless act of violence. Our investigation is ongoing and no details can be released at this point. What I can say is that this will not be tolerated and the criminals will be brought to justice. Any persons with information about this incident are encouraged to come forward."

The TV filled with the newscasters neutral expression. "Thank you, Lieutenant Grigsby. That's the situation here. I'll have an update in our half hour report. To recap—"

Billy Bob turned off the TV.

"I'm starving, Mom." He sat down and reached for the orange juice.

Elaine handed her son the juice afraid to believe he made the front page. That he might be responsible for what happened. Before heading back to the kitchen she caught Florence's glance. A shared communication of women who loved a man they dare not try to control for fear he would truly be out of control. Any control should have started a long time ago. Now, all they could hope for was that he made it home every night. Elaine's glance said 'welcome to Billy Bob, just love him with all your heart.' They both knew that there was no loyalty, dedication, or love better or stronger than what Billy Bob shared for his family and friends. That he was no punk was a welcome bonus. Elaine was happy to go get the bacon and eggs to feed her man-child. Lord knows he must be hungry. The thought tapping at the back of her mind.

Elaine didn't know Bunchy and Dubb were asleep in the garage. She quickly cooked up some extra breakfast and gave it to Billy Bob to take out to them. She didn't want to look in their faces and secretly wondered what happened to Stutterbox. She hadn't seen him around in a while.

Billy Bob woke Bunchy and Dubb with the smell of breakfast. The comfortable living space came to life as the sun was peaking in the sky. The Documentary CD by the Game was thumping, making their heads bob. Billy Bob rolled a blunt as he watched Saturday morning cartoons on mute. Bunchy produced a pair of powder blue dice and began to roll in front of the leather couch. No cocaine was being measured or cut this morning. Bunchy sensed a change in Billy Bob. No one spoke on the events of the previous night. These things went unspoke of so as to make it a habit. Each knew where the other stood. Their union was solidified with a mutual understanding and trust. Each could hold his own plus one more.

"D.R.A.K." Bunchy shook the dice and rolled. "Seven for my Bru." Four and three showed as he picked up the twenty Dubb had thrown down.

As Dubb and Bunchy were taking each other's money, every roll dedicated to Drak's memory, Billy Bob was watching a dropped Durango on 22' rims turn slowly into the driveway behind his Navigator.

Then he backed up and parked along the curb. "Ruff here," he said, barely above a whisper, surprised that the big man was here. He rarely came over. *Something is on his mind*, Billy Bob thought.

Bunchy and Dubb were now sitting on a short couch, watching Ruff push Lonnie Ray in his wheelchair. They were navigating the tight squeeze through the gate into the backyard. Lonnie Ray's arm was in a sling. Dubb was smiling, thinking 'that nigga ain't gon' never die'. He was happy to see Lonnie Ray.

"What's up, Bru," Billy Bob said as Ruff approached with Lonnie Ray. They exchanged dap.

"My niggas make the front page," Ruff said, quoting Pac. "That was some Iraqi insurgent type jump off. I'm glad I ain't got funk with you," Ruff added with a deep laugh, giving Billy Bob dap again.

Billy Bob's answer was a slight head nod. He didn't like being acknowledged for his activities. Oddly, he was shy in this way. He looked down at Lonnie Ray. "You straight folks?"

"Yeah. Goin' to take more than a punk ass bullet to keep me from talking shit." Lonnie Ray smiled an ugly grin, creasing the scars and burns from the battery acid on his face.

"Y'all drinkin'?" Billy Bob asked, motioning to the tiny fridge in the garage.

"Don't threaten me with a good time," Lonnie Ray piped up, urging Ruff to push him into the garage, out of the peeking sun.

Dubb, Bunchy, Lonnie Ray, and Ruff were giving each other dap and situating themselves inside the garage as Billy Bob watched Milo's Lexus turn into the driveway. *Damn, did somebody call a meeting?* he thought to himself, glad Milo stopped by.

"Y'all got a stove in here?" Lonnie Ray asked, finding a spot to stop his chair, looking at the empty plates of food on the glass table.

Ruff glanced quickly at Billy Bob. Same old Lonnie Ray.

Billy Bob knew Ruff would never leave the house without eating a full meal. "Where Kujo?' he asked, missing the bark of the red-nosed Pit Bull.

"She at the dog-spital. Got a cast on her leg. Can't walk around too much. She be alright though." Now Ruff watched Milo push through the gate followed by Hutch, dapper as usual, as he dipped into a leather chair. Ruff's weight took a beat to distribute itself evenly and settle.

Billy Bob was the first to meet Milo. "'Sup, Bru," he embraced his mentor, not surprised at the softness of the expensive cream two-piece linen suit. "'Sup, Hutch," he said to the beefy-faced always present Hutch.

Milo and Hutch were the perfect pair. Life had been good to them because they got out the game when the time was right. Billy wanted the same for his crew. They were both smiling at him. Obviously they'd seen the morning news.

"Young Bru. That business was some serious work," Milo said, pride in his voice.

"Yeah. How's the wifey doing?" Changing the subject and asking about Jody. She was finally pregnant after years of trying.

"She at the casa. Staying off her feet," Milo answered, moving towards the garage and a man he knew of and respected. "Ruff. What's going on man? Sorry to hear about what happened to Kujo."

"She be alright," Ruff answered, still seated, giving Milo a heavy fisted dap.

"Make your way down to the lounge. Let Kilroy V.I.P. you for the night on me."

This got Ruff's attention. He knew what to expect from V.I.P treatment at Haitian Jack's. He'd heard some good stories from some of his partners who'd been privileged enough to receive an invitation from Kilroy or Milo.

When Elaine saw Milo park in her driveway and get out the car with Hutch, she shook her head and 'unh unh unh'd under her breath. She still had a crush on Hutch even though she had a few years on him. And Milo was growing into a fine man. It was all she could do to restrain her excitement (I'm a grown ass woman) and not run out to say hello. They were here for Billy Bob. Let him accept his guests. So, she waited a respectable amount of time before getting herself presentable and encouraging Florence to follow her lead.

Everyone was seated in a semi-circle sharing light laughter and revelations when Elaine and Florence walked into the garage with plates of fresh fruit and pastries. Elaine offered Hutch a plate of pastries with a smile, reminding him of her crush on him.

"That's what I'm talking about!" Lonnie Ray was the first to show how happy he was to be eating. He held his hands out to receive the plate of pastries from Florence.

The atmosphere was rich. Where most people had hidden agendas even amongst friends, this group had real love for one another and Florence could see this immediately when she walked into the gathering. She was impressed by the sight of Milo and Hutch seated together on a short leather couch. Both well fed and groomed by women who loved them. They didn't have a hungry look about them that men not satisfied had. She smiled with a small wave as Milo waved her over to him. Milo patted a small space between he and Hutch and motioned for her to sit between them. She looked over at Billy Bob and noticed his expression of openness and comfort was unlike any other time. It was obvious to her that Milo represented more than a friend to him. They shared something more deep. And to have Milo next to her made her feel welcomed. And Hutch was just adorable. She loved the smell of him. Sitting between them she quickly understood how anyone could feel protected by them and honored to have a genuine friendship with them. She wanted the same for Billy Bob.

"Is this the one, Bru?" Milo asked Billy Bob, nodding towards Florence and tapping the leather behind her head, his arm over her.

"If it's cool with her," he answered humbly.

"I like her." Milo gave his appreciation. He looked at Billy Bob with a strong bond of brotherhood. He loved him so much it pulled at his insides. He was so innocent yet had the heart of a lion with loyalty to match. Whatever he needed, Milo was prepared to give. This wasn't the first time Billy Bob had come to his aide. The first was when he was gunned down. Billy Bob came through in a clutch to save his life and commit his first murder. Ever since then it seems that his reputation had been solidified by his nonchalance and heart. Milo was sure that Billy Bob had yet to see what an impact he had on people. Once he did, he would be able to successfully transform his life and be a legit success. He wondered if Billy Bob had bad dreams. He wondered if killing affected him in any way. It didn't seem to, as he watched him laugh and joke with Bunchy and Lonnie Ray. Billy Bob looked over at him now.

"We gon' start a record label. Bru," Billy Bob announced.

Elaine was by now sitting on the arm of the couch damn near in Hutch's lap. She took this opportunity to hug her arm around his thick neck with good news. Florence was smiling, glancing at Milo who she could never tire of. He was so youthful in his enthusiasm and optimism.

"Is that right?" Milo asked, looking over at Bunchy, then Dubb.

"HoodRich Entertainment. That way we can branch out into movies and stuff," Billy Bob added.

"How much you got saved up?" Milo wanted to know.

"We got enough to bubble. Trust that," Billy Bob assured him.

It was a festive occasion. Milo offered any help they needed. Ruff gave them some contacts he had for bodyguards 'so ya'll ain't got to do the dirty work', he said with a wink. Hutch knew someone who could give them studio time right away for their demo or first single. Milo waited to see how excited they got at Hutch's news then said that he was damn near sure he could get them an audience with Dre. And if they were any good get them signed. Meanwhile he invited them out to Chatsworth to iron out some details to get their own label started.

Florence stayed true to the end. School would be starting in a week. She looked forward to Billy Bob taking her to the UCLA campus for registration. Now all she had to do was get him to take some classes. It would be too cool if Bunchy and Dubb took some classes. In her mind, she saw them seeing each other on campus. Hanging out between classes. She felt like a princess.

Chapter Sixteen

The vacuum came at the perfect time. Word was that Midnight was either dead or on the run. No one knew for sure since his body was never recovered and the police investigation wasn't giving up any information. Some even said that Midnight was so shook that he was under witness protection. All his people, even his mother couldn't be found. The police were under federal pressure to keep the investigation sealed and put a lid on the brutal murders being carried out on the city streets. Ironically, the streets had been quiet for the past week. The only thing happening was some minor shootings at drug spots. Evidently someone was consolidating the spots vacated by Billy Bob and Midnight. Their workers were left to fend for themselves against a crop of hungry thugs directed by BoDeen. In one week he'd locked up the hood and solidified his power.

Missy went about her daily routine numb to his growing stature. What she was seeing was a repeat of what she saw just before he went to prison. She didn't know how long it could all last. She was glad that he was staying away. It had been a week and every day at the salon she heard a new story of where, who, and what BoDeen was doing. She took the stories in stride and never fed into them with a smart remark, as many hoped for. She stayed silent, but this didn't keep her patrons from sharing what they heard or saw.

Missy would later recall sensing headlights roll across her bedroom curtains in the early morning. Gauging by how sleepy she was at the time, she figured it had to be about two in the morning. She thought that it might be BoDeen at the time making a rare stop home. She remembered thinking how she would pretend to be asleep if he woke her coming through the front door.

She was never awakened after the lights crossed her bedroom window. BoDeen never came through the front door. When she got up that Saturday morning she made Dimp breakfast and sat him down to eat. She had a hard time of it because he was trying to hold two girls on his cell phone at the same time at eight in the morning. She'd laughed proudly inside at the early signs of a HoodMac in her nine- almost 10-year old son. "They're just my friends, Mommy," Dimp explained, deciding to compromise with his mother by telling one of the girls that he'd call her back.

Dimp was at the dining room table, fork in one hand and cell phone in the other. Missy stepped out the front door to see if the morning paper had been dropped off yet. *Was BoDeen sleeping in his car?* she'd asked herself when she saw him sitting in his brand new C300. The dew on the windows obscured a clear sight of him. Her heart began to beat faster and the hollowness in her stomach widened as she approached the foggy driver's side window. The closer she got, she noticed more clearly the spider web of cracks in the window. A neat hole was in the corner. Her heart jumped. BoDeen's head was slumped on his shoulder facing away from the window. She was too shocked to scream. Missy looked around her afraid that someone was near. Then she looked towards the front door to see if Dimp was there, glad he wasn't outside to see his father dead in his car.

HoodRich lived in the studio. True to his word, Hutch had a studio lined up with a nice producer. And on the fifth day of recording Milo walked into the studio with Dr. Dre while Billy Bob was laying down serious vocals for his first single, "Sour". Billy Bob was in the sound booth with Bunchy by his side singing the hook. A smile spread across Billy Bob's face every time the hook came because he could still not get over the fact that Bunchy could sing his ass off. He had the throaty sound of Nate Dogg and the sweetness of Snoop. This made Billy Bob emphasize his rhymes so as not to be outdone. Billy Bob had a smooth straightforward style.

When Milo walked in with Dre, Billy Bob was finishing his last bar. "Fake charmers chasin' a dream / spendin' precious time focused on cream / runnin' the streets / prayin' for that gangsta lean / thinkin' your game is sweet / sour after hour / Tag Heuer ticking on that power / game over team sour."

By the smiles outside the sound booth, Billy Bob knew that they liked what they heard. The following Monday they were headed out to Dre's recording studio to meet Eminem and The Game. Dubb couldn't get over the fact that Eminem wanted to guest on their album. Dre promised they would have full access to all his beats, even some from the first Cronic album that he never used.

"I'm about to do this album. You know this, Florence. I ain't goin' to have time to be going to school," Billy Bob said as Florence was putting the last of her enrollment papers into her leather Coach briefcase.

"Just sign up for one business class. Or at least something related to music. One class. One night," she pleaded, looking over to Bunchy for help as he lounged on the living room sofa.

Billy Bob gave it some quick thought. He'd hoped that this little protest would work, but Florence wasn't having it. "Alright. That might work," he agreed. "Let's get rolling. It's almost too late."

"Okay." She rose quickly, remembering something she forgot to put in her briefcase. "I'll be right out. I have to grab some papers and my PDA."

"Hurry up. We'll be outside." Billy Bob slung the Coach bag over his shoulder and followed Bunchy out the front door.

"Bru. We gon' be on a college campus fucking all the educated honies." He looked back at Billy Bob. "Well, not you but me fo' sho'. I'm gon' put this HoodRich into effect. They ain't goin' to be able to stand it." Bunchy was excited as he moved towards his Escalade parked in the driveway.

"It's only one day a week, Romeo," Billy Bob quipped. "But knowin' you, that's all you need."

"No doubt. Different honey every week." Bunchy laughed as he opened the door and popped the latch for the rear door.

Billy Bob was at the back putting Florence's bag into the rear compartment. Bunchy's gun was in full view. Billy Bob picked it up. "You rollin' with this?" He held it out for Bunchy to see, looking around the side of the truck for his answer. Bunchy's attention was on something coming up the street outside of Billy Bob's view.

It sounded like an M-80 firecracker. Billy Bob instinctively ducked his head, the gun rising in the air. The loud popping sound went off a few more times. The bullets crashed into the metal of the truck around him as he fell to the ground to see who was shooting at him. Bunchy screamed out in pain as he slumped against the side of the truck.

As Billy Bob pointed the gun at the moving car, he heard Florence scream his name from the porch. The popping sounds continued, bullets going through the amps and speakers just above his head. He gripped the chunky weapon in his hand and forced himself to steady his aim against the bullet coming his way. The arm holding the gun was moving towards the front porch where Florence was yelling his name. Billy Bob's first shot hit the tire of the Cadillac. The arm moved back in his direction as the car swerved. Billy Bob rose to his feet letting off shot after shot from the fifteen round clip as he moved towards the Cadillac. He felt his leg shoot out from under him as the black gravel rose to meet his face. He felt the burning in his chest and leg as he lay on the ground struggling to get up.

The Cadillac was trying to right itself, struggling with the blown tire.

Billy Bob looked over towards the house, his cheek pressed to the street. Bunchy was laying on the grass next to the Escalade with blood blending through the colors of his striped button down shirt, tinting maroon the platinum of his chain. Florence was standing in the middle of the grass watching the scene in horror. Her eyes locked with Billy Bob's as he rose from the ground, her hand over her mouth willing him to stay down. Billy Bob rose against her will and gave chase after the hobbling Cadillac. Behind him he heard the familiar chirp of a police siren. The Cadillac crashed onto the sidewalk, ramming into the low black iron-gate surrounding the house Milo grew up in, across the street from the store he still owned.

The door flew open, squirting Midnight onto the pavement. He stumbled, dazed into the street trying to gain his balance to run. He moved right into Billy Bob's line of fire. Billy Bob was in pain and barely able to run with a bullet in his leg. He began firing the .45 Grizzly into Midnight from about 20 yards away, twirling him into the middle of the street. The police siren chirped dramatically behind Billy Bob as he stumbled towards Midnight shooting whenever he could find the strength to lift the gun. It was only when the clip was empty and he clicked the trigger several times at Midnight's prone body did he fall to the ground having accomplished all that was on his mind.

The Cadillac's passenger door tumbled open. Fatboy emerged from the car wide-eyed. He raised a .9mm Glock at Billy Bob as he lay in the street exhausted. The chirping stopped replaced by a commanding voice to drop the gun! Big Red stood in the middle of the street pointing his revolver at Fatboy. Fatboy got off one round before Big Red caught him two times in the chest, making him bounce between the doorframe of the car before slumping to the ground.

Billy Bob was losing consciousness as the sounds of sirens and a woman crying filtered through the haze clouding his senses. A pair of strong, desperate arms pulled at him. His head was cradled against a familiar breast, vibrating with tears and pleas. His mind was a flashcard: Milo on the ground as he stooped next to him on this same patch of asphalt; Florence going back into the house to grab her PDA; in the studio with Bunchy rapping over a fat track; his mother pouring orange juice into a glass. The arms that cradled him rocked back and forth. He felt the warmth and the tears falling onto his face. He lost consciousness as new hands fought to take control of his life, pleading for someone to let them help.

Chapter Seventeen

The first time he opened his eyes "Cheaters" was on the TV situated on the wall at the foot of his bed. He'd glanced to his right and left where more beds held broken bodies with tubes running into holes made small by needles and those normally meant for bodily functions. His eyelids were heavy with medication, giving him enough time to look back at the TV where a white girl was confronting her black boyfriend followed by a camera crew, before they shut again.

Billy Bob was awake again, but kept his eyes closed, listening to the sounds around him. The TV was muted, the color beams showing brightly through the room of 10 beds. The guy in the bed next to him was laughing at a joke told from two beds over. The smell of iodine and open flesh wounds prevailed over the flowery perfume the nurses introduced whenever they came in to hand out medication or change wound dressing.

"Nigga, how I'm gon' run! The pig bucked me!" the guy next to Billy Bob answered seriously.

"Tweety Bird. Nigga, before he capped yo' ass, why you stop?" the guy two beds over asked.

"Nigga was stuck in the headlights!" someone shouted from further down the row, chuckling.

"Fuck you, Bam!" Tweety Bird growled.

They started laughing again. Billy Bob opened his eyes slowly, looking down his body to his toes. He was covered with a thin cotton sheet. He was naked under it, wrapped in an open backed hospital gown. He had to shit. Walking to the bathroom was out of the question. He relived the pain of the doctor shooting a dye into his hip that ran through the veins in his legs to see if their was serious damage to any arteries or muscle. When the dye moved through him it felt like he was cumming on himself. The bullet went straight through his leg. He looked around for something to shit in. He grabbed a bedpan from the table next to him and raised his hip to slide it under him. The smell of shit quickly shot through the room.

"Nurse! Nurse!" Bam shouted, the smell reaching him. "Nurse! Damn! Nurse!"

Billy Bob lay back after putting the shit heavy pan on the table. The smell didn't bother him. Where the others had accepted the fact they were in the jail section of General Hospital and would soon be transferred to Central Jail, Billy Bob was sick with captivity and fresh gunshot wound. The smell of shit was the least of his worries.

"Oh my! Who's responsible for the defecation?" a rosy cheeked, steel gray haired white nurse asked. She was pushing a cart with dinner plates of foods and juices.

Billy Bob opened his eyes at the sound of her voice. He watched her park the cart at the foot of his bed, crinkling her small nose. She was moving along the side of his bed towards the source of the odor. "I would appreciate it if you would call for someone to help you to the restroom, Mr. William Mason. You're new here so I'll let this go," she lectured, holding up the heavy pan for his inspection. "But next time you'll begin accumulating hole time," she finished with a menacing stare intended to exclamate her warning.

Billy Bob barely comprehended her meaning through the medication, fatigue, and annoyance with the fact he couldn't move. He was trapped in a room with people he didn't know, telling stories they made up as they went along. Tweety Bird told a story about this fine girl he had, only to have Bam come with one better about his having a bigger ass and sucking dick stronger. They laughed at their own comedy, barely able to conceal their fraud. Billy Bob found no humor in it. And the nurse called him by his government name. Like she knew him. His mother didn't even call him William. Not even when she was mad.

Billy Bob endured more tall tales through a dinner of instant potatoes and a chicken patty. Everything tasted like cardboard. It was obvious to Billy Bob that Tweety Bird and Bam considered this the best meal. Oh wait, the lasagna was the best.

The ten- bedroom held a couple of pisas and a white boy. An old man near death was next to him. For some reason, Tweety Bird and Bam did all the talking. The less Billy Bob said, the more they conjured up absurd stories of having the most cars, killing the most niggas, and doing everything big. They talked too much about it for any of it to be true. Billy Bob had never heard of either of them. By the time the after dinner pain medication took effect he was ready to shut them niggas up through sleep.

The next time he opened his eyes, Saturday morning cartoons were on the television. The sun was shining in brightly through the barred windows. He wanted to get up and walk out this stale ass room. He pushed the bedside call button for the nurse. He had to shit and needed some privacy against them niggas who never seemed to shut up or go to sleep. They watched him tediously move to the bathroom with a male nurse's assistance.

Billy Bob had his eyes closed, listening to Bam regale Tweety Bird with a bogus story about how he was spending $40,000 a month on weed alone. How he had an Escalade on 26" rims and a 740 on dubbs. They were parked at his momma's house.

Tweety Bird answered with an occasional, "Is that right?", and "Yeah", waiting for his turn to tell his lie.

In mid-sentence about a time he went to Vegas and was sure to end with him winning a fortune, Bam stopped talking. When Tweety Bird didn't fill the silence, Billy Bob eased his eyes open. Standing at the door, escorted by an L.A County Sheriff was his mother, flanked by Milo, Hutch, and Florence. A dual feeling of warmth and sadness moved through his immobile body. He was far removed from them as they stood in the doorway smiling down at him like emissaries from an abundant place of luxury and freedom. Neither he could get to.

Elaine was the first to move away from the halo of Florence and Milo towards his bed. Tears welled up in her eyes, dripping over the rim and racing down her brown face. "How are you, baby?" she asked between a quivering smile, tears dropping from her chin onto the thin sheet covering his stomach. She rubbed her hand across his chest, the coldness of the diamond tennis bracelet on her wrist made goose bumps flash across his skin. Her hand moved to his jaw and across his ear as he worked to keep his emotions in check. Through his mother's emotion he realized the seriousness of the situation.

Tweety Bird and Bam watched the scene in silence. Calculating the measure of Elaine in expensive jeans that hugged her apple bottom shape. She was weighed down with gold and diamonds hanging from every possible hole and limb. They watched Florence move to the other side of the bed—must be his girlfriend—with a feminine grace they both unconsciously licked their lips to. Milo and Hutch stood at the foot of the bed looking like they were coming from a Black Men Magazine photo shoot. They quickly realized that the skinny quiet nigga was somebody important. They listened with interest, trying to replay all the frivolous conversations they'd had.

"How you feelin', Bru?" Milo asked, smiling for assurance.

"Better when I can walk outta here."

Silence. Everyone hoping he wouldn't ask the question and knowing he would.

A cold chill moved through Billy Bob. He looked from one face to the other afraid of what he felt. "Where's Bunchy?"

His mother's grip tightened around his hand. Milo returned a stone-faced stare. They didn't have to tell him. Billy Bob closed his eyes against the truth. Then he broke down, screaming, "No! Bru! No! Let me out of here! I gotta get out!" he yelled. Flailing against the surprised grasps of Elaine and Florence. He snatched out the I.V. and swung his bandaged leg to the floor. Elaine jumped back at his aggression, watching him fall to the floor in agony. Between his screams and shouts, sobs of pain erupted. Grief escaped through his voice.

Milo rushed to pick Billy Bob up from the floor. He held Billy Bob to his chest absorbing his tears and shouts of 'why?' When Milo lay Billy Bob back on the bed he was exhausted with grief. Billy Bob fell asleep as the nurses reattached the I.V. and redressed his wounded leg.

Chapter Eighteen

Milo was functioning on remote control. Handling business without the usual flair and gratification of doing things big. At home, Jody tended to him with care, hoping that his despondency would break and the brightness glow on his face once again. Only when she mentioned anything concerning their unborn child would a glimmer briefly show in his eyes; to fade again when the grief of Rolando's death and Billy Bob's situation took up residence in his heart and spirit.

Milo was handling Rolando's death with all the strength he could muster. But to think he gave license to Billy Bob getting hurt weighed on his conscience. Crippling him like a vicious virus. Death was all around like a curse. As if payment was due for the prosperity he'd enjoyed for the past five years.

Missy was in the kitchen cooking gumbo. This

was therapy. There was a natural migration of those closest to them to Missy's house. It'd been a week since BoDeen's cremation. The nights found Milo and Hutch hanging tight, moving like the last ones left, stopping at Missy's for a moment and heading out again. Restless. Gwen and Jody stayed close to Missy, providing comfort and companionship in a time of loss.

Jody watched Missy through hazel eyes as she stirred the pot of gumbo. She knew the pain Missy felt. And thanked God that Milo had come through this ordeal still alive. Lord knew she'd had her share of pain.

"How are you feeling, Jody?" Missy asked suddenly, as if escaping from thoughts of herself.

Jody instinctively rubbed her swelling stomach. The grief she felt was for Missy and Milo. She responded with a sympathetic smile.

Missy returned it knowingly and let out a deep breath, as if releasing the power of her sorrow. Trudging through the pain. "What's next, Jody?" she asked, turning to her sister-in-law. Her voice was laced with indecision.

Jody felt her pain. "Live life," she answered simply, offering a supportive rub across the shoulder.

Missy sighed, trying to offer a smile in appreciation. She sounded so much like her brother and father. She moved towards Jody. They held each other in a warm hug, exhaling against one another.

"I'm jealous," Milo exclaimed, standing at the kitchen archway. He watched his wife and his sister disengage from their hug. They both extended an arm out to him with a smile. He moved into their outstretched arms and embraced the two most important women in the world besides his grandmother. As they stood in the middle of the kitchen supporting one another Milo felt a small body trying to wedge between he and Missy. He looked down at the curly mop of hair atop Dimp's head. Dimp looked up at his uncle with tears in his eyes, releasing the sorrow felt by the whole family for the loss of his father. Milo glanced up at Missy. She mouthed that this was Dimp's first time crying. She rubbed her son across his face.

Missy appreciated the support of her family and friends, but she had a need to numb the pain. BoDeen was her first love. She stayed down for him all those years while he was on death row. She thought of things she could have done differently. As she replayed her pleas and demands, she realized she'd done all she could. BoDeen was insecure about his lot. He was intent on reclaiming a former glory. Trying to relive the '90s when he commanded privilege and respect in the street.

She walked Milo and Jody out to the Lexus. The brisk air felt familiar, like the morning she found Bo-

Deen slumped in his car in the same spot Milo's car parked. She trembled at the memory as her brother held her in his arms.

After she tucked an exhausted Dimp into bed and having answered his questions of whether his father was in heaven, she trudged to the den. The house was quiet. She opened a bottle of wine and filled a glass. Reclining on a sofa in the dark, she sipped through her first glass before a tear fell from her eye. The second glass of wine was like a coat of Novocain over her heart. The emptiness filled her. The third glass of wine gave her a false sense of optimism as she mumbled affirmation to herself. The fourth glass erased all thought from her mind and made her pink lips twitch and her eyes glossy under closed lids. The glass slid from her hand, spilling a corner of red liquid onto the sofa as she nodded off. Drifting, images of BoDeen sitting in his car with a hole in his head moved across the back of her eyes.

"I hope Missy's okay," Jody said, bringing Milo out of his own thoughts. She wanted him with her. This was the best way, she'd learned, to know how she could support him. It was a gentle manipulation. Working most of the time.

"Yeah, me too," Milo answered, turning down the volume on Mary J. Blige. It had worked. Over the years, time and time again Jody proved him right in his estimation of her. And to think he was in love with Bobbi Wilkerson. Jody played him close, waiting for the opportunity when Bobbie would play herself out. "Bo-Deen got caught up in his own image," Milo observed. He had a strong suspicion that Big Red had something to do with BoDeen's death, thinking back to what Billy Bob said about Big Red's comments.

Jody was patient. She listened more to what he didn't say than to what he said. From the first time she saw him, she knew they would be good for each other. She smiled to herself with the memory of him seeing her make love to another woman and even seeing her perform at a strip club all those years ago. Now she was carrying his baby.

"What are you smiling about?" Milo interrupted her thoughts.

Jody turned to him in her seat. "When we first met." Watching his profile. A slow smile opened the corner of his mouth.

"Is that right?"

"Yep. You thought I was a hoochie huh?" She watched him contemplate. This amused her.

"Not really." Pleasantly he remembered the strong tug she evoked from him when first they met. The drama she caused in his thoughts. Friction. Love.

"I still have mad love for you," she reminded him.

The words were filled with an appreciation she felt in her bones for his survival and strength.

"You had me open," he began, going back to her question. "I wanted to take care of you, but didn't know we'd end up married." He looked over at her with a sly grin. "You had this planned all along didn't you?" Milo asked with a smile she knew well. His thoughts were pure, untroubled by death. A welcome respite.

"You ain't mad. You know I'm the best thing that ever happened to you," she teased boldly.

"Cocky aren't we?"

"What? Say it ain't so. Just say it." She pinched his ear, pulling it at an odd angle.

Milo laughed despite himself. "You're going to make me crash," he warned through the laughter, forcing Jody to let go of his ear. Milo lightly placed is hand over her swollen stomach, feeling the small mound under his fingers. "You're my earth and I wouldn't have it any other way."

Jody needed that. "Thank you."

"You're always welcome."

"We'll see," she said seductively.

The Chatsworth cul-de-sac was quiet with sleepy non-activity of the early morning when Milo turned into it. Seemed like long ago when Missy breathed hard into his chest and asked, "Who killed BoDeen?" He wished he could've answered her question. Better yet, that he could save her from the pain. This was only an hour ago. Jody offered to stay with her, but Missy assured them she'd be okay. Little did Milo know Missy was well into a drunken stupor.

Milo was happy to see Jasmine's champagne colored Dodge Magnum parked in the driveway. He knew she'd have stories to tell about her trip to Switzerland. Her game was international, far removed from her days of identity theft and fraud. She now offered her services as a consultant to large corporations to prevent corporate theft and image control.

It was no surprise to Jody or Milo that shopping bags were strewn across the living room couches and on the floor from foreign stores, some with names they couldn't pronounce. Jasmine was thoughtful as ever. No telling what the morning would bring. Jody headed upstairs as Milo checked the downstairs master bedroom where his grandmother slept. He stood at the door long enough to watch her breathe a few times under the comforter. Satisfied, he checked the game room and the door to the sunroom. Scanned across the pool in the backyard and made his way back to the kitchen to pour two glasses of cranberry juice.

Upstairs, he peeked into the guest room. Jasmine's long thin body was spread under a thick comforter. Her pale skin glow under the light seeping in through the windows, peeling through her long black hair fanned out over the pillow.

Jody was coming out of the restroom dressed in a lace pink teddy with a sexy grin on her face. Her round stomach a reminder of her condition. She was filling out nicely. Her already shapely body was made more sexy and plump with pregnancy.

Milo couldn't hide the arousal made evident by the look in his eyes. "Are you serious?" he asked, handing her a glass of cranberry juice.

"As a heart attack," she cooed, then rubbed her legs together like butterfly wings.

"I'm horny," she admitted, blaming the baby.

There was peace in her arms. In her touch. These same fingers dressed his gunshot wounds. Peace in her eyes. The same eyes that called to him. Beckoned him to a future with her. Peace in her embrace. The same embrace that grew on him. Held him. That grabbed him excitedly when he'd been away too long. Peace in her kiss. Her lips that hungrily searched his face that was so familiar. Every turn and ridge. The planes and rounds of his face shaped to her every caress. Together their love was forged through a time of war. Forging a trust and tenderness that held through many a crisis. This night of lovemaking was testament and declaration of the strength they'll need to rely on for the coming trying times.

Jody was warm underneath the hard muscle of Milo. She opened to him willingly as he carefully entered her, arching his back to make room between them for their unborn child. Their baby, barely out of its first trimester, lay between true love. Trapped with the rocking motion of mother and father. A gentle swaying and caressing. Whispers of admiration and love moved between their bodies for the baby to hear. To witness a love supreme. A rising heat rubbed over the blessing in a wave after wave of peace, pleasure, and love.

Milo stroked her gently, her pussy made hot with pregnancy. Made full with arousal. They climaxed gently into and onto each other. Milo rolled next to her and held her close, his hand gently rubbed her stomach. She scooted back into him as she did the first time they lay together after a wicked game of dice. She smiled with the memory as sleep settled over her, fully sated.

Chapter Nineteen

Billy Bob was numb through processing. He barely felt the needles puncture his skin to draw blood, filling the vials attached to them. He watched the bright burgundy liquid swirl against the plastic looking unlike any blood he'd seen shed as a result of serious wounds or prelude to death. This blood coming from his veins was alive and moving where he felt dead and comatose. He was hypnotized by the filling up of the life force, barely hearing the nurse ask questions from a clipboard. Cardboard questions asked a million times over. How could the fat faced nurse expect him to talk while he watched hypnotized with a needle in his arm. Do you have a venereal disease? Have you ever-attempted suicide? Do you have any enemies? No. No. and No. He could not picture the face of any enemy that was breathing. The needle pulled out slowly, leaving a drop of blood bubbling at the hole in his skin. He watched dully as the fat white lady wiped across the blood with a cotton swab, leaving his skin shiny. More questions followed. How old are you? Is there a history of diabetes in your family? Have you had the chicken pox? Measles? 20. Don't know. Yes. Don't think so.

Billy Bob was well enough to walk with a cane. He was moved to the medical ward of the county jail. Everything was white walls and grey steel. The only color other than that were the orange jumpsuits. The beds were a thin cot on steel. The water was cloudy liquid. The food was bland and most times indistinguishable from something left for a dog. And everywhere stunk of flesh wounds, funk, and fear.

He was lucky enough to be in a one man cell by himself. Billy Bob's only view was of a dirty wall outside his cell. If he pressed his face to the bars, he could see to the front of the row where another gate was closed, leading to a long hallway. He licked his ashy, chapped lips and realized he could improvise the antibiotic ointment he was given to spread over his leg wound, to moisturize his lips. He lay back on the bunk and closed his eyes against the harsh florescent light in the ceiling. He wondered why there was no light switch and then when will they turn it off. Damn.

An intercom crackled to life. "And for your listening pleasure," a deputy drawled too close to the mic, trying to be funny. A country song began playing through a speaker high on the wall outside Billy Bob's cell.

At first he wished he could turn it off, but after awhile the sad songs started making sense to him. He submitted to the wailing as he lay on the bunk with his eyes closed. The odd scent of the hamburger that lay uneaten on the steel desk by his head wasn't as strong as it been an hour after dinner. His thoughts wandered. Scenes and remembrances walked across his mind as he lay in solitude for the first time since Juvenile Hall.

Billy Bob relived the moments right before the moment that would change his life. Wondering if: What if Florence hadn't forgotten her PDA? What if Bunchy didn't have the gun in the truck? What if Big Red hadn't turned onto the block? What if he just stayed in bed with Florence that morning?

His thoughts tumbled over themselves as the many possibilities played themselves out until he ended back at reality. The thought that he couldn't make love to Florence, shoot dice in the garage, or see his mother made him sad. His thoughts turned to Bunchy and the realization that he'd never see his Bru again turned his stomach hollow and forced his eyes open.

It was dark inside the cell. He couldn't tell what time it was or how long ago the country music was turned off. Bunchy's face collaged with faces of his life: Milo. Hutch. Dubb. And Drak. Damn! Drak was dead too. Rolando was dead. Shit was fucked up. He wondered how it all happened so fast. Never did he think he'd end up in a cell alone feeling helpless. There was nothing to occupy his mind or ease the bluntness of his situation. He was alone.

The tier was quiet. He tried to move his eyes beyond the cell and see what was happening at home. He could envision his mother making a dinner that he couldn't get to. Florence was at the table keeping her company. Maybe they were waiting for Saturday so they could come see him. *What day was it anyway? Thursday. What kind of day will tomorrow be? Do I have to stay in this cell all day? Doing nothing but staring at the wall listening to the people in the other cells holler back and forth about nonsense? And wait for the nurse to bring my medication? The pigs hand out mail and chow? And any other bogus interruption to mark the time of day with and break up the long stretch of time?*

The thought of doing this day after day sent a cold shiver through him, making him shake in his lonely cell. He shut his eyes again with the realization. A cold tear escaped his eye and ran down the side of his face. It was a silent pain that no one else would see and no one else could comfort. It would dry on his face without a word or notice from anyone in the darkness of the dank cell. No other tear would accompany it to keep it company. It was alone in its journey just like Billy Bob was alone in his.

Jasmine crept through the bedroom as Milo and Jody still lay in the position they'd fallen asleep in. Spoons. She eased onto the bed and cradled her body against Milo's, making him the middle of a sandwich. She draped her arm across both of them, rubbing Jody across her stomach. She was prepared to lay there until she thought of something more provocative to do.

Milo stirred. "What's up, Jas," he whispered.

"Mmmmmm," she moaned. "Don't move, you're so warm I just want to lay here," Jasmine whispered.

"What time is it?" Milo asked.

"Almost seven. I'm on half a world away time. Want me to go away?" she teased.

Milo smiled. He felt Jody move her butt into him. She was awake. He understood her perfectly well. She wanted to make love. "We'll be down in a minute. You cooking?"

"Sure." Jasmine answered, rubbing Jody's stomach. "I know you up, girl. You just want me to leave so you can get your freak on. You nasty." She giggled as she rose from the bed.

"I love you, Jasmine," Jody whispered.

"Backatcha." Jasmine was closing the door behind her.

When Jody heard the door shut she reached her hand behind her under the covers to stimulate what she wanted inside of her.

Milo grew hard and strong with an early morning erection. Jody arched her back as he entered her smoothly. He lay on his side going in and out of his wife with a gentle motion. She ground against him, her caressing his thigh, feeling the tension move through him until he released himself into her.

"Good morning, honey," Jody whispered. Satisfied.

Milo's answer was a gentle caress and kiss on the back of her neck. He grabbed her to him tightly as his dick grew limp inside her, then hard again. He felt her smile and move against him again, urging him on.

They didn't make it downstairs for another hour. Jasmine knew better and timed breakfast perfectly. Milo was happy to see G'ma up sipping tea. He sat next to her at the kitchen counter and gave her a kiss on the cheek. "Good morning, G'ma."

She smiled a toothless grin at her grandson. "Sleepy head." She rolled her eyes teasing.

"You are absolutely glowing sister girlfriend!" Jasmine exclaimed as Jody rounded the corner behind Milo.

"Hey!" Jody smiled and made a curtsy bow. "Girl, I have missed you so much. I started to come wake you up last night." Moving to embrace her friend.

"No, she didn't," Milo interrupted.

"OK, I didn't, but I'm glad you're back."

"Me too," Milo added from his seat.

"I can't tell. Where's my hug?" Jasmine asked Milo.

"You got it in bed remember?"

"I wish." Jasmine teased with a giggle.

"How long you here for this time?" Jody asked,

having a seat next to Milo as Jasmine placed fat chicken and broccoli omelets on their plates.

"Well... I terminated my overseas contracts. I'm going to look for something closer to home. I might just chill for a year," she said, placing the plates in front of Milo and Jody. "Plus I miss y'all and I gotta make sure you give my god-daughter a good name. Something like Jasmine." She laughed but looked serious with the suggestion.

Milo perked up, his mouth filled with omelet. "A daughter?" he choked. Everyone laughed but him, knowing he wanted a son.

Missy woke up on the couch to the touch of Dimp's shaking hand. She could see in his expression that she must have looked exactly how she felt. She rose up on the couch groggy with a foul iron taste in her mouth. Her head was spinning. She resisted the urge to reach for the bottle of wine to see if there was any left in it. Dimp was watching her closely. Gauging the promptness of her movements. Marveling at the effects alcohol had on his mother. He quickly surmised that she was at a disadvantage and knew he never wanted to be like that.

"Come on, Mom. We're going to be late!" Dimp

said with a tad less respect due to his new realization.

Missy gave him a sharp look to remind him that she was still his mother. He declined her the satisfaction of redeeming herself at his expense by turning his back and walking into the kitchen to pack his school lunch.

It was almost noon by the time Missy walked through the glass doors of her hair salon. After dropping Dimp off at the K. Anthony private school (late) she went back home to get something for her headache. A glass of wine. She fought against the voice in her head that said, 'it was way to early to be drinking liquor.' She'd responded blithely that a glass of wine was good for you. She discounted the voice with the suggestion her headache would be cured with a nip of the cause.

"Hey, girl," Gwen said from behind the arrival desk. She was becoming increasingly worried about her friend. Missy was coming in late more often and her face was sallow, losing the glow she was known for. She was taking BoDeen's death hard, Gwen reasoned, even though she was putting up a good front. But Gwen knew her better than most, and she didn't like what she saw.

"Good morning, Gwen," Missy answered from behind huge Fendi shades and Altoids.

"Afternoon," Gwen said more sharply than she intended.

Missy looked up from the appointment book sharply. "Who works for who?" she asked venomously.

Gwen didn't answer and instead returned the kind of stare friends reserved for friends when their feelings were hurt only because they showed concern.

"We've got a busy day huh?" Missy asked, as if her last comment and Gwen's reaction was of no consequence. She pushed the appointment book back towards Gwen and quickly glanced at the many waiting people in the lobby seated on two long leather couches. They flipped through magazines and watched Bind Date on the plasma screen against the far wall.

"There's someone here to see you about a job," Gwen said, nodding her head towards a light-skinned man in the waiting area.

"He fill out an application?" Missy asked. When Gwen pulled the application from a drawer and slid it to Missy, she asked, "How long has he been here?"

"Since nine," Gwen answered smartly.

Missy would have normally read over the application before interviewing people for jobs. There were two reasons why she invited the man to her office. One, to read anything other than the appointment ledger would hurt her bloodshot eyes. Two, she felt sorry for the handsome fella who'd been waiting over two and a half hours for her. He must have needed a job bad. When she turned to wave him over, he was already up out of his seat heading her way. He caused an immediate reaction in her. He was broad shouldered and tall. Hazel eyes and a neatly trimmed low cut beard.

His walk was sure and confident, hardened by years in prison.

"Hi. My name is Keashon Ford. I'm interested in your security guard position."

She knew he at least had to be 35 years old if not older, though he looked youthful. Hair cut close to his scalp. His multi-colored, striped Phat Farm button up shirt was crisp and his dark green slacks hung loose over long legs.

"Do you have any experience with security work?" Missy asked, holding his application to the side. She still hadn't taken off her shades.

Keashon hesitated with a small glance to each side of him, giving Missy a chance to consider their lack of privacy. She took the hint. "Come back with me to my office."

As Keashon followed her through the knee high wooden partition, several women under bright light in various stages of hair management looked their way. With styling chairs on both sides of her, Missy led the way to her office while responding to several 'hello's and rumor induced stares that spoke of concern or validation of what they'd heard.

At the last booth just outside the door that led to her office, Missy was held up by the flamboyant LaMonte. He had trouble keeping his eyes off Keashon while he complimented Missy on the fuchsia color of her Baby Phat track suit which he'd seen before. His eyes darted back and forth as he relayed the latest gossip about a trifling new hairdresser at booth three. Word was she knowingly passed on a venereal disease to spite men for one giving it to her. There was at the moment a huge blow-up about whether or not she should get tested for HIV. She refused, saying that since there was no cure she was going to keep on 'giving niggas what they deserved. If they didn't want it then stay away'. That was going to be hard to do since she was stacked like a bookshelf.

"I'll talk to her," Missy assured him, noticing LaMonte's blunt interest in Keashon. She looked back at Keashon for an instant before opening the door to her office. She couldn't be sure if LaMonte made him nervous or if he was being unnaturally distant as if afraid to be found out. The wine was clouding her judgment.

From her leather chair, Missy could see through the one-way mirror the entire salon area and through to the front door. She still hadn't taken off her dark shades. "Do you have a gun permit?" Missy asked pointedly, the voice one used to asking direct question and getting what it wanted.

Keashon looked as if he misunderstood her, afraid at this point to answer no.

"You need to be able to carry a gun to work here. A nightstick won't do you any good if someone comes up in here heated trying to rob us. You have a criminal record?"

Keashon wished he could see her eyes. From the looks of her she was paid in a major way. Platinum rings and earrings with sparkling diamonds on every finger and at least five holes in each ear. Platinum tennis bracelets slid along her thin wrists with each motion. She was mad to walk the streets like that, he thought. There was something about her. A reason she felt comfortable flossing the way she did. "Yeah. I just got out the joint," he admitted.

"What you get locked up for?"

"Robbery."

Missy didn't flinch or make to conceal her worth. This gave him pause. It was obvious the job was out of his reach. He wanted to get to know her. The woman who could obviously set him straight just getting out of the pen. She came across as untamed. A challenge. An exciting challenge. If he could knock her he'd be straight.

Missy was looking through the one-way mirror. Milo was pushing through the wooden partition, leaving Hutch at the reception desk chatting with Gwen. "I'm sorry I can't offer you a job right now," she said dismissively. "Let me walk you out." She rose to her feet.

Keashon followed her gaze. Missy appeared to know and react to the broad shouldered, black man. He wondered what the man's connection to Missy was. He walked down the aisle like he owned the place. *Probably her nigga*, he thought to himself. Everyone seemed to know him.

Missy was thanking Keashon for coming when

Milo met them in front of LaMonte's station, who was giddy like a peacock with so much activity in front of his station. LaMonte let a blow dryer hang limp in his hand as he became absorbed by the presence of Milo and Keashon. The gray haired lady in LaMonte's chair, whose mane was in disarray, silently wished the three would disperse so LaMonte could get back to work on her hair.

"Don't I know you from somewhere?" Milo asked, trying to remember why T-Man had said Keashon couldn't work for them.

Keashon started to ask if Milo did time, but instead said, "Probably seen me at the red light."

"Naw." Milo snapped his finger. "You interviewed for security at Haitian Jack's." He remembered now. T-man said he didn't have a pistol license. "Sorry we couldn't help you out."

We? Keashon was puzzled. "You work for Haitian Jack's?" he asked.

"Jack was my father," Milo answered simply, choosing not to go into detail.

Keashon nodded his head slightly in understanding.

Missy was watching and listening behind dark shades, measuring Keashon against her brother's presence. Milo gave her a funny look when he walked up. She welcomed the interruption. She knew Milo was sure to comment on her shades. "This is my brother, Milo," she said to Keashon. The connection and answers to his unasked question passed across his face.

Milo shook his hand. "I'm always looking to help a brother out. Get a pistol license and holla back."

"Good lookin' out. I'll work on that."

"You have to get your record expunged first," Missy offered.

This was new information for Milo, though not surprising.

"Awright. I'll get back to you," Keashon said more to Missy than Milo. He couldn't tell if she caught his meaning behind those shades.

LaMonte smacked his lips when Keashon neared the partition. "I would just eat him up girl." Then he looked at Milo with arched eyebrows. "You too. Don't get me started," he quipped with a laugh.

Missy turned to head into her office, but not before telling LaMonte he'd eat anything put in his mouth.

"That's right, girl. As long as it passed government inspection. Bitch ain't tryin' to get no bad meat." He laughed harder this time, enjoying himself.

Milo was only too happy to get away from the skinny blonde haired LaMonte and into Missy's office where he could see what was up with those shades. He wanted to say something when he first saw her. He stretched his long, comfortably dressed limbs on the familiar wooden chair against the wall facing the one-way mirror. Hutch looked up from the counter when Keashon came through the wooden partition and passed by him. He then went back to talking to

Gwen with the same smile before the interruption. It was just like they just met, Milo thought to himself as he watched them. He turned to his sister. "What's up with them glasses?" he asked suddenly.

She stared at him silently, mocking from behind her shades.

Milo resisted smiling at her antics. "Take 'em off. Let me see your eyes."

"When are you going to see Billy Bob?" Her glasses still on.

"Tomorrow. Take off your glasses."

"Are you going to help him get a lawyer?" She staring at him still. Making no motion to take her glasses off.

"I got Rubin for him."

This was the same lawyer that got BoDeen off death row.

"That's good."

"Glasses." Now Milo was serious.

Missy removed the Fendi shades slowly, watching the expression of fright and concern register on her brother's face. Her eyes were puffy and red. She wanted to cry at the hurt on his face.

"What are you doing?" Milo managed. "Are you drinking?"

Tears slowly filled over Missy's eyes. Milo got up to give her an embrace. She sobbed heavily into the velour of his Sean John tracksuit. Probably her first real cry since BoDeen's death. He wondered if Billy

Bob's situation just added to the drama. And Rolando's death was no doubt heavy on her heart. She sobbed steadily, releasing her grief into her brother.

Chapter Twenty

"How they treatin' you, Bru?" Milo asked through the glass with the phone to the side of his face. He'd watched Billy Bob maneuver himself with a stiff leg onto the wooden stool.

"They 'spose to be moving me to the mainline in a minute. They say I'm well enough." Billy Bob looked gaunt. His normally healthy gleam was dulled by the non-reflecting gray walls of the county jail. His lips were chapped and his fingernails were dirty. Without the platinum chain slung around his neck, anchored heavily with the diamond pendulum, he seemed naked and light. For the first time since Milo had known Billy Bob, he looked vulnerable. Milo hated to see him like this.

"Rubin say we'll try to get you a bail. Even if it's a mill ticket, we got you. Don't worry," Milo promised.

Billy Bob hated the way he must have looked to Milo and Hutch. They were dapper as always in custom tailored two-piece suits. "You talk to my mom?" he asked.

"Yeah. She got your bread scooped up. Ruff slid her a few stacks too. I didn't know you were breaded like that. When we get you outta here, we're back on track. Don't trip," Milo assured him.

"Man, this place is dirty. And they played country music all night," Billy Bob groaned.

Milo was smiling. Glad that Billy Bob found some humor in it. "Your Moms and Florence will be through here tomorrow. You got you a down girl, Bru. Hold on to that one."

"Bru, when I get outta here, I'ma marry her."

Milo nodded his head. "Yeah. This place will give you some perspective I know."

A guard appeared at the end of the row signaling that the visit was over. The phone went dead.

Milo got up from the stool and pumped his fist over his heart as the guard escorted Billy Bob away from the window and out of his view.

By the time Billy Bob got back to the row, word spread that "that rich ass nigga Milo" had visited him.

"Yeah, the one that own Haitian Jack's." The gossip included a complete bio on his feuds and murders and his relationship with Billy Bob. The gossip spread fast and furious through the county jail; and with that, the knowledge of who William Mason truly was and the drama and circumstance of him being in jail.

"He chased that nigga Midnight from Dirt Gang down the block and shot him two times in the head."

"Is that right?" came the incredulous replies to the gossip.

So now when Billy Bob passed by a cell he caught involuntary 'what's ups' accompanied by strong head nods and odd stares from people looking to either provoke him or answer to Midnight's murder or any of the other bombings, burnings, or shootings he'd been a part of.

Billy Bob lay back on his bunk reliving the short visit with Milo and looking forward to seeing his mother and Florence in the morning. Someone was calling his name from a few cells over. He didn't answer. The calling soon stopped, leaving Billy Bob to his own thoughts. He could see the hurt and worry on Milo's face as he sat across from him on the other side of the glass partition. Now he understood what freedom was. He tried to imagine where Milo and Hutch were now as he lay on a hard bunk in a dreary cell. *What music were they listening to*, he wondered. Soon the overhead speaker outside his cell would pump the inevitable country. He realized that even if he wanted to, he couldn't walk for more than eight feet in any direction. He wanted a blunt and knew he wouldn't have one.

What will his mother cook for dinner tonight? It didn't matter because he couldn't eat any of it. Would

Florence sleep in his bed? It didn't matter because he couldn't sleep in it with her. And he would never see Bunchy again. He wondered when would he get used to jail and the time when these recurring thoughts would stop running through his mind. Sleep was the only thing that saved him from the loop of his thoughts.

Milo was still thinking of Billy Bob when he walked into the house. Jasmine was coming down the stairs when she saw him on the entrance landing. She quickly called to Jody who was in the kitchen. She went to Milo and embraced him in a tight hug.

"How is Billy Bob doing? I know he hates being in that hell hole," Jasmine asked, holding Milo's hand as they walked into the kitchen.

"I can't even speak on it, Jas," Milo responded.

Jody was closing the oven, a tray of red snapper fish in her hand. She looked up when she heard her husband's voice. "Hi, baby." She smiled.

"Smells good," Milo said. "Where's G'Ma?" He'd looked forward to seeing his grandmother. She was asleep when he left that morning. She'd been sleeping more and more lately.

Jody exchanged a knowing look with Jasmine before telling Milo that she was taking a nap.

A knowing sadness passed across his face. He silently said a small prayer for his grandmother.

"Here. Sit down. Let me fix you a plate. G'Ma will be up in a minute," Jody tried to reassure him. "And after you eat, call Mr. Rubin. He left a message for you."

Milo grabbed the phone off the wall as he sat down before the plate of rice, broccoli, and fish Jody set in front of him at the kitchen counter.

Missy barely had the strength to make dinner for Dimp. She popped a couple of burritos and macaroni & cheese into the microwave. She knew he'd take his food into the den and play Xbox while he ate. She wondered where he got the extra hand to call one of his girlfriends at the same time. Missy grabbed a bottle of wine and went into her bedroom.

She lay sprawled over the bed covers trying to convince herself that she would only drink one glass of wine. Her hands shook after she drank the first glass. She then told herself that two glasses weren't much. Half of America drank at least three glasses with salad and dinner. This just made it easier for her to pour her fourth glass. She still had her clothes on when she passed out on the bed.

Elaine's eyes were red and swollen. Billy Bob could tell that she'd been crying. She was sharing the round wooden stool with Florence. Her hand was pressed against the glass partition while the other held the phone to her ear.

"How's my baby doing?" Elaine asked, struggling to hold back the tears.

Billy Bob had just endured a long walk down the row towards the visiting room. Now everyone knew to associate his last name with the now infamous 'Billy Bob'. He was an instant reputable from what everyone now took his hood to be called HoodRich Hustlers. Someone had called this out one of the cells. He didn't know where the 'Hustler' part came from. He felt like a celebrity who had fame and haters. "I'm doin' awright, Momma," he said, then looked to Florence. She was looking beautiful in a sheer print dress. Her hair was pulled back in a wavy ponytail. "How you doin', angel?"

Elaine handed the phone to Florence. "Do you need anything?" Florence asked when she got the phone on her ear. Before Billy Bob could answer she had to hand Elaine back the phone to cover her face with both hands to hide the tears.

"Milo said that Rubin is a good lawyer. I'll be at your bail hearing at the end of the week. And don't worry baby, you're going to get out of here. That pig that arrested you, they talking about he might be under federal investigation." Elaine gave him a knowing look and rubbed her fingers together, mouthing the words 'money' and 'protection'. "So don't worry, baby. You just be strong. Did you get the magazines we sent you?'

"Naw. Not yet." He looked over at Florence who was recovering. "I love you," he mouthed through the window. The phone went dead before Florence could get the phone from Elaine and say something back. She mouthed the words, 'I love you, too' through the glass as a deputy appeared to escort Billy Bob back to his cell.

When Billy Bob got back to his cell there was a folded note thrown onto the floor. He was warned beforehand by a young tan-skinned brother a few cells over who had told him to look on the floor as he passed by. Billy Bob picked up the note and struggled to unfold the intricately tucked and folded paper square. He read by the light coming in from the tier; 'Billy Bob. First of all I send my respects. My name is Elijah and I'm in here for selling dope. My man Drak (RIP) who served me proper was your folks. I'm a young rider. I know all about you. Drak had a lot of respect for you. Ruff is my peeps too. You got some haters in here, but I'm with you. I'll be going to the mainline soon so hopefully we'll go to the same module. A smoker shot me in the foot so that's why I'm on this medical row. Let me know if you need anything. I'm down with whatever you want to do. Holla Back. HoodRich Hustler for life. Elijah.'

Billy Bob cracked a smile as he tried to match the original folds of the letter. When he couldn't, he threw it in the toilet and lay back on his bunk to relive the visit with his mom and Florence. Maybe he could think of Florence until he fell asleep and then dream about her. Even better, maybe they would make love in his dreams.

Chapter Twenty One

The scene was becoming sadly familiar. Missy popped into the salon later than usual donning the same dark Fendi shades to hide swollen eyes treated with Visine. She was all titties and hips as she was losing any fat around her neck and waist. The drinking was robbing her of the usual vitality and sharpness she was usually equipped with.

Gwen was staring at her with a communication better left unsaid when she stopped to look into the appointment book. "Ms. Barlow has been waiting for you for 30 minutes. Your early appointments left already," Gwen said as she placed her pale, jeweled hand between the pages of the appointment book. She nodded towards the waiting area.

Missy prided herself on being prompt and taking care of her customers. Instead of hearing Gwen's statement as a warning to check herself, she took it as an insult. Her judgment was clouded with drink. Missy looked for the pretty brown face lady who would be wearing a fashionable wool apple hat. Before she got to Ms. Barlow at the end of the sofa, a familiar face was looking at her with inviting eyes. Behind the shades she pretended not to notice as she called Ms. Barlow's name. She motioned the beautiful woman to the back showing no reaction to the rolled eyed and haughty attitude.

Missy was almost to the wooden partition leading into the salon area when Keashon gently tapped her on the elbow. She furrowed her brow as if trying to remember who he was.

"How you doing, sister? Remember me? I'm Keashon Ford. I interviewed here last week."

Ms. Barlow was now standing next to them obviously annoyed at the interruption because Missy wasn't saying anything. She was waiting for Keashon to continue.

He gave a quick glance at Ms. Barlow. "Missy, if you don't have plans for lunch I'd like to spend some time with you." He looked at his watch. "Tell you what. How about I come back in a couple of hours. Say one o'clock?"

Ms. Barlow pressed her lips to the side of her face and gave a low sigh.

"Lunch huh?" Missy contemplated, looking Keashon up and down in a different light.

She was being careless. "I'm going to be busy today. Come through tomorrow at noon, OK?"

"No problem." He offered a gratuitous smile and turned with a slow stride through the glass door.

"Missy!" Gwen said louder than she meant to. "Are you serious? You don't even know him and he just got out of prison," Gwen finished, staring through the dark shades into Missy's eyes.

"Since when did I start paying you to plan my personal life. Concern yourself with the appointment book. Or do you have a problem with that?"

Gwen was shook. Missy had never spoken to her this way in the nine years they'd worked together. Though Missy was the boss, she'd never pulled rank and considered Gwen an equal and friend. It became quickly apparent to Gwen that Missy was caught up in a tornado of misery, spiraling towards self-destruction. She was looking at Missy, incredulous at the way she was getting at her.

When Gwen didn't answer, Missy took her silence as being correct. She spun towards Ms. Barlow. "Follow me. Sorry to keep you waiting."

Ms. Barlow was embarrassed at being a witness to the disrespect. She avoided Gwen's steely gaze as she passed by and through the wooden knee-high swinging doors.

When Missy was out of sight. Gwen held back tears as she picked up the phone to call Jody, hoping Milo was at home so he could know how his sister was

JOY DEJA KING & PETER MACK

acting and get some background on the dude that was taking her out to lunch the next day. She knew Milo would feel her after the situation with the guy she had been dating before she married Hutch. He ended up shooting Milo and would've killed him if Billy Bob wasn't on point and gunned dude down in the street. She learned then that they had to be careful of who they let have access to the family.

Milo was watching G'Ma closely. She was in a rare energetic mood, commandeering the kitchen to make a brunch of chicken and mushroom omelets. The sun was shining through the pristine powder blue and stainless steel kitchen. The rays bounced off the walls and through the crystal plate ware matching the brilliance in G'Ma's demeanor. She seemed to gain energy from the sun. Her shiny skin was pearl black on a face smiling a toothless grin as she set a plate of food in front of Milo. Jody was at the refrigerator getting cranberry juice when the wall phone rang. It made Milo happy to see his wife moving alongside his grandmother. He was even happier to see G'Ma out of bed and in good spirits.

"Hello," Jasmine answered the phone, coming into the kitchen in pink sweatpants and a white t-shirt with Jessica Rabbit on the front. When she wasn't working she dispensed with the high fashion. Even in sweats she put most women to shame. But not Jody. Milo found this funny and satisfying because he loved Jasmine equally for introducing him to his wife. "Hi, Gwen. Yeah, they're both here. Hutch is on his way to pick you up for lunch." She looked into the living room. "At least he said he was. He's still in the living room watching some ancient boxing match on TV. Oh. Hold on," Jasmine handed the phone to Milo. "It's Gwen." She raised her eyebrows and enunciated in a way that meant something important needed to be said.

"What's up G.W.?" Milo asked as he forked a healthy piece of omelet into his mouth. His chewing slowed down more and more as he listened to Gwen. His face grew pensive and he stopped chewing altogether. "No doubt, Sis. I'll look into it," Milo said into the phone as he peeked into the living room where Hutch was engrossed in the fight. "He's on the way. It's going to be okay. Don't worry," Milo finished and handed the phone back to a worried looking Jasmine.

"Something wid Missy?" G'Ma asked, looking concerned. Her Haitian accent pronounced with worry.

Milo didn't want to ruin a good day for G'Ma. "Missy is fine G'Ma. That was Gwen complaining about Hutch." Milo leaned off the kitchen counter and yelled into the living room. "Bru! Your wife's waiting on you!"

Jody was watching Milo as he watched Hutch raise his beefy frame off the couch in a hurry to grab his stingy brim hat and plaid Burberry blazer. Hutch managed to tone down his dress code. Instead of a fully tailored three-piece suit he now sported designer baggy jeans, tailored boots from London, and a blazer with tailored 1,000 thread count Egyptian cotton button ups.

G'Ma managed to shake her concern, but Milo knew that as soon as they could, Jody and Jasmine would corner him out of G'Ma's earshot and demand to know what was up with Missy. Milo had to make a few calls and get to the sports bar to do what he had to do, but not before eating the rest of the brunch G'Ma had prepared and enjoy her company while she was up and about.

Billy was pacing back and forth in the cell after the deputy made his midnight module count. The idle chatter on the row slowly subsided, leaving everyone to face their own thoughts. He was lost in the recesses of his mind, pacing to gain strength in his leg. He was glad that he had his own cell. He'd heard that it would take about a week to move him to the mainline. And then he would be in either a four or six man cell; depending on what module he went to. Milo had said something about a bail hearing. That would be cool. A million dollars. That sounded like a lot. *What is that... 10%... $100,000 and property? I might have to put up at least $250,000 cash.* Billy Bob became giddy with the idea that he could bounce from this filthy motherfucker on a million dollar bail. He laughed out loud as he made a sharp U-turn at the front of the cell. "Like a fuckin' movie star! Bounce up out this bitch!" he growled low, clenching his fist.

"You alright over there?" a low graveled voice whispered.

Billy Bob stopped in the middle of the cell looking at his frozen shadow out on the tier. Whoever that was had to be watching his shadow pace back and forth. He'd seen an old man get escorted in last night. A tall, thin, light-skinned man that walked slow. The guard was patient with him.

"My name is Cecil. I just got here last night," the old man drawled in a southern accent.

He had his head at the bars as he sat on the floor. The voice was low to the ground. Billy Bob looked for his shadow and found it at the bottom corner of the cell next door. Billy Bob got on the floor and pressed his face to the bars. He was less than a foot away from Cecil. They were separated by a concrete wall and bars.

"Hey, Mr. Cecil. You okay?" Billy Bob asked respectfully.

"Well... I'm still here ya'know. Look like you got a bit on your mind. Pacing and what not the way you are," Cecil said. His voice was extra low and raspy against the silence of the tier. "Let me ask you a question. If you could start your life from scratch would you take the pain off your back?"

Billy Bob thought about this for a minute. He couldn't imagine his life being any different. He lived the way he wanted to and was afraid of what he would be like if it was any different. "Naw Mr. Cecil. I'm cool. I wouldn't change nothing," Billy Bob admitted, thinking of chopping up pounds of cocaine, smoking massive amounts of weed, fucking mean bitches, rolling in a squatted navigator, chilling with Bunchy, and seeing Milo's face the day he got out the hospital. Billy loved everything about his life. The good and the bad.

"You wouldn't change nothin' huh?" Cecil asked sadly.

"Would you?" Billy Bob asked, looking out at Cecil's shadow.

Cecil let out a strong breath and got quiet. Billy Bob wasn't sure if he was even going to answer his question. "I wouldn't have murdered my own son," came Cecil's reply followed by a deadly silence.

Billy Bob couldn't imagine the old man killing his own son. He sat with his head against the wall saying nothing. Every now and then he looked out onto the tier for Cecil's shadow. He was still in the same spot on the other side of the wall. No movement. Silence. Except for the hum of the overhead florescent light.

Chapter Twenty Two

Missy had become a master at disguising the effects the alcohol was having on her. Although everyone noticed and whispered about the way her once filled out track suits and sweaters now hung off her like wet clothes; she was now adept at using Visine to clear up the redness and ice to keep down the swelling. Now she was looking like she didn't get enough sleep. The dark Fendi shades were replaced by gold rimmed Carolina Herrerra glasses.

She was late for her 10 o'clock appointment due to a hangover and the rest from a confrontation with her nine-year-old son, Dimp. It had become obvious that Missy's drinking was affecting the people around her in different ways to everyone, but her.

Missy had no idea that Dimp was watching her so closely until this morning. When she opened her stinging eyes, fully dressed, sprawled across the comforter atop her bed, Dimp was looking at her with disappointment. Missy masked her embarrassment at his indictment with anger. She'd yelled at him for coming into her room.

He then asked her a simple question, "Are you an alcoholic?"

"Hell no! Get the fuck out of my room!" Missy had screamed. A new sickness folded itself over the already hollowness of the morning hangover thanks to her screaming tirade against her son. Saying things she immediately regretted. She was upset and annoyed with herself for cursing and screaming at her son and the fact that her grief and dependence would not prevent her from sliding down the ride again. As she drove Dimp to K. Anthony Elementary she tried to apologize. Dimp was mannish. Not responding to her vane attempt at forgiveness and her bogus explanations. She still hadn't answered his one simple question.

Missy made an effort to amend her earlier treatment of Gwen. The reactions she was getting to her odd behavior further depressed her. When briefly free of the influence of alcohol, she made an attempt at apologies and niceties. She was like flip and flop; Jekyll and Hyde. Jody called her the night before, before her first drink and jokingly called her the Phantom of the Opera, suggesting that she get help. Missy had a strong feeling that Milo would be showing up soon. She almost became defensive with the thought. Caught up in her ego and success; like nobody could tell her anything.

Dimp's challenge earlier that morning kept her from taking that wake-up call of Moet. She was glad of it when Gwen called her in the office to announce that Keashon was in the lobby to take her to lunch. Missy was excited both at the risk of going out with someone she didn't know and the prospects of it. "Thank you, Gwen. I'll be right out," Missy replied into the phone.

Keashon rose from the leather sofa when Missy pushed through the wooden partition. She avoided Gwen's disapproving stare as she greeted Keashon. "You get points for being on time," she said, then turned back to Gwen who was pretending to flip through the appointment book. "Gwen, Ms. Stacy will be here at one, if I'm not back ask her to wait for me. I should be back in time though." Missy smiled despite Gwen's obvious nonchalance. *We gon' have it out*, Missy thought to herself before heading out the door.

Missy was gone for no more than five minutes when Milo and Hutch pushed through the glass doors of Missy's Magic. Gwen was too happy to tell Milo who his sister just left with. "Missy just left with the jailbird for lunch," she offered.

Milo was mildly disappointed, though he played it off. "That's cool. I'll holla at her tonight. Thanks for letting me know what time it is."

"Yeah, but she already mad at me. I'm just trying

to look out for her," Gwen replied as she picked up the ringing phone. She wrote down a scheduled appointment and hung up the phone, glad to get back to Milo.

"You did right. There are some things about this cat she should know about," Milo warned.

Gwen looked from Milo to Hutch, trying to read any expression that might give her a clue to what Milo was talking about. She couldn't read anything in their faces. They were keeping it gangsta, she thought to herself with a smile intended for Hutch. She hated when he did that. She knew he would say it's not their business to discuss and not even the most unbelievable blowjob could get him to go against his first word. Still, she loved that about him.

"My brother used to date a girl that was the manager here," Missy observed as the waiter seated her at a window booth. She looked around briefly at the sharply dressed professional looking crowd. *In an hour all would be back at work*, she thought to herself with satisfaction.

Keashon was looking up at all the celebrity photographs on the walls, nodding his head. "I've never been here before. It's cool that Magic Johnson is putting his money back into the neighborhood. But he still charging us though. This stuff should be free," he said, half jokingly.

"I'd rather give it to him than to a white man," Missy answered.

"When it comes to money, don't matter who gets it if the prices are too high," Keashon challenged.

"You think the prices are too high?"

"It is kind of expensive." Keashon looked the menu up and down.

"When was the last time you were on the streets?" Missy was looking him in the eyes to see just how serious or stupid he was.

Keashon silently gave her points for her directness. He liked that about her. "I like those frames. You had me worried a little with those dark shades last time I saw you."

"I hate to think what you would have been if I didn't have them on," Missy said seriously, looking at the menu.

"Why? You had pink eye or something?"

"Or something," she answered evasively.

A freckled-faced redhead appeared at the table. "Welcome to Friday's. You two ready to order?"

"Yeah. I'll have the chicken sizzler and salad with ice tea," Missy ordered. She wanted a white wine but the look on Dimp's face was still fresh in her mind.

The busy lunchtime crowd was barely noticeable as Missy and Keashon enjoyed each other's company. Missy was impressed by his knowledge of current events. He was informed about the need for leadership in the Black community and the power of circulating Black dollars before spending them outside the community.

"It's been all theory up until now. You can't imagine how it is to be locked up and steadily gaining knowledge about things that you feel you could be a part of and prosper at."

"Well, now you have your chance. Just have to take one step at a time. Remember, baby steps lead to grown up steps," Missy advised.

This wasn't what Keashon wanted to hear. He wasn't telling her all this so she could talk to him about baby steps. He needed cash. That was a more interesting conversation. "Freedom ain't free. And I'm trying to get free. Sure, I could work a nine to five and try to save money, but the system is designed in a way that I'll be chasing my tail for the next 15 years making 10 dollars an hour. A slave to my next paycheck."

Missy understood exactly what he was talking about. People complained about it all the time at work, while others worked extra hard with small businesses on the side that with time grew large enough that they could quit being the slave Keashon talked about. "Like I said, baby steps. Get something started on the side. Selling t-shirts or anything. I wouldn't be mad at you if you got a bunch of girls together and started a bikini website. There are a bunch of ways you can start small and over time new ideas will present themselves to you."

Keashon appreciated what she was saying, but he wasn't trying to start small. He knew she was cashed out. A little thrown his way could go a long way. "Is that how you started? I mean you do own Missy's Magic right? So what, you started hairstyling renting out a booth at somebody else's spot? Baby steps?"

Missy smiled. "No. My daddy bought my salon for me as a graduation present from college."

Keashon's eyes lit up. "Like that? The whole spot? Fully loaded?" He nodded his head. He wanted to ask how did her father come into that kind of loot. "I guess he gave your brother Milo the sports bar huh?"

Missy noticed a bit of envy in his voice. She'd heard the edge before from people who resented what looked like an easy ride to success. They didn't know the half. She didn't like discussing her brother's business with people, but she did offer a little insight. "After my brother was almost killed, he opened the bar. So what about you? What are you plans?" Missy asked, quickly changing the direction of the conversation. She was really glad she didn't have that drink.

All types of thoughts were running through Keashon's head. Her father was breaded. Her brother almost got killed. How? Why? Where did he get the money to jump and open a bar? He wanted to ask more questions but knew it was way too soon. He didn't know what his next move was, he thought he was making it right now, but Missy saw him coming at every turn. "Right now I just have to get my foot in the door somewhere. Then I can start thinking of saving a little cash and start something on the side like you say."

"Sounds good," Missy said, resisting the urge to give him any clue that she'd help him out if he put his foot forward in the right direction. She liked him from what she could tell about him. There was an air of cleanliness and dignity about him. He exuded a manliness and a certain sexual aura that she was attracted to. She was watching him closely. His light brown eyes, the way they reflected the sun. His large hands, the way they gestured when he was making a point or the way his head tilted back when he laughed. She liked his lips, the way his facial hair was trimmed around them.

By the time the waitress came with the check Missy was open to seeing Keashon again. As the conversation had progressed, Missy's reservations about him just getting out the joint were replaced by her attraction to him.

"So when will I see you again?" Keashon asked as he slid two twenties into the leather bill carrier.

Missy thought about this for a hot second, having made up her mind some time ago. "I don't know. What did you have in mind?"

You don't wanna know what I have in mind, he thought to himself before saying, "Whatever... I know you're a busy lady. I just want to spend some time with you whenever possible."

"I think we might be able to arrange that," she assured him with a gap tooth smile.

The youngster Elijah from a few cells down went out to an attorney visit earlier that morning, Billy Bob had thought about him just before dinner, but decided to wait for him to holla. After dinner when most of the tier was quiet, sated from the inadequate food, and there was no movement, Elijah attached a piece of soap to the end of a line of twisted string. He slid it down the tier making it stop in front of Billy Bob's cell.

"Pull it in, Bru," Elijah whispered down the tier.

Billy Bob smiled when Elijah called him 'Bru'. He really wanted to be down, he thought to himself as he pulled on the string. A sealed envelope came tumbling down the tier. Billy Bob pulled it under the cell door into his hands.

"I got it, Bru," Billy Bob said in a low voice, pulling the envelope away from the string.

Elijah pulled on the string, making the line disappear back down the tier, the soap knocking against the cement.

Billy Bob moved to the back of the cell and ripped one end of the envelope open. He pulled out an oddly torn piece of yellow paper and read the note written in small plain letters. 'What's up, Bru. The pigs tell me I'm moving to the Twin Towers across the street. I'll try to get you pulled over to where I'm at. You don't want to stay in central. Too many haters to knock down. I got this tweed this morning. Enjoy. We'll chop it when we meet up. Much Love. Hood Rich.' Billy Bob immediately threw the piece of paper in the toilet and flushed it. He turned the envelope up and out tumbled a tightly bound ball of weed wrapped in cellophane followed by a book of matches and pack of zig zags. A smile spread across his face. Good lookin' out. He went to the front of the cell and yelled out to Elijah, "I feel you, Bru. Good looking out."

"No problem, Bru. For life," Elijah responded.

Billy Bob was beginning to like Elijah. He moved back to his bunk and quickly rolled a small joint and lit it. He inhaled two quick times and smacked his lips, tasting the cronic roll around in his mouth before he let it go down. His body jerked, making him cough up the smoke. He couldn't believe that a small joint made him choke when he used to smoke blunts on a regular basis. More than that, he began to feel the effects immediately. He licked his lips and smiled as his eyes became hooded. Nothing on him belonged to him. The orange jumpsuit and the jail shoes that looked like cheap Vans were all county jail issue. The plain white boxers were ill shaped and rode up his thighs when he walked. It felt weird not being able to wear his own clothes.

After the first joint he began to feel alive. He began to feel like his old self. A reminder of what it felt like to be free. The only sad thing was he was alone in a cell with no one to kick it with. He sat back on his bunk and let the bud run through him. He was higher than he could ever remember being. He was feeling good, letting his mind take him places. He was in his garage listening to Ludacris' Red light District CD. Bunchy was next to him on the couch. Dubb and Drak were shooting dice on the floor. Cronic smoke was thick in the air. Billy Bob smiled to himself with his eyes closed in the dark as he was transported in time and place. All of his troubles were far away.

Milo had intended to stop by Missy's house at about six, catching her right after work, but he got caught up at the sports bar with an employee dispute. A new waitress claimed that his bartender sexually harassed her. She threatened to put Haitian Jack's on blast if Milo didn't address the issue, preferably by paying her off for her silence. Milo knew that Dread wouldn't harass anyone, he got too much pussy as it was. So much that he turned down more than he got. Milo set a trap for the skank. He set up a video camera in the VIP room and had T-Man take her in there to talk. What ended up happening after a few drinks and a blunt of some Hawaiian bud was more than she cared to repeat or look at when the tape was shown to her. Plenty of dick sucking, pole dancing, reverse cowgirl fucking, and finger banging was all on the tape. After the showing of the tape, she could barely hear Milo when he told her she was fired because of all the crying and tears and basic disbelief at being caught at her own game. She couldn't help but to respect the game and Milo for still paying her wages for the rest of the week.

By the time Milo stepped into Missy's house, Dimp was already in bed. Missy was in the den drinking red wine. An empty bottle was next to a freshly opened one on the end table. Missy was slumped in the leather loveseat watching Lifetime on cable.

"Wassup, Sis?" Milo asked, coming into the den and reaching down to kiss her on the forehead.

He took a quick glance at the bottles of wine and a look into her glazed eyes. He took a seat in the leather lounger next to her. BoDeen's picture hung over his trophy case looking down on them. Missy's hair hung long and swirled silky, touching her collarbone.

"How you doin', brudda?" Missy slurred in her drunkenness.

Milo relaxed his long limbs and extended his long legs away from the chair. Hands folded over his stomach. "Hear you got a new boyfriend," he said in a low voice.

Missy took a sip of wine, wetting her pink lips. "Is that a crime?" she asked pointedly, on the edge of her temper.

"It is when nobody know him or where he from," Milo answered, still calm.

"You mean when you don't know him, and if you want to know where he from, ask him." Missy hissed, buoyed by the liquor.

Milo erupted. "The nigga just got out the joint Missy! You don't even know nothin' about him!" he glared. "You know how in school you get a failing grade if you miss so many days? Well, that's like being in the joint. He's missed too many days. His attendance is lacking. You man got a failing grade."

Missy stopped him. "Who authorized you to give out grades!? Who died and made you head nigga in charge?" she yelled, her body contorting and neck rolling with each word.

"Do I have to say?" Milo responded after a few beats of silence. His voice was low again, letting her remember that Mom and Pop were dead and all they had were each other and G'Ma.

"Why y'all fighting?" Dimp said from the doorway, awakened by the yelling.

Milo jumped up. He was afraid to let Dimp see Missy stand up. No telling how the liquor would affect her walk. And he didn't want Dimp to smell her. "It's alright nephew. We're just having a discussion that's all. Everything's OK," Milo assured him as he walked

Dimp back to his bedroom.

On his way back to the den, Milo debated whether or not to tell her what he'd heard about her new boyfriend. By the time he reached her, he decided to get more confirmation and find out where the cat was from and if anybody of note knew him. When he saw him he'd ask himself.

"So when am I going to meet him?" he asked Missy while standing at the same spot Dimp stood just moments ago.

"Never, if I can help it," Missy slurred, not looking at her brother. The second bottle of wine was empty now.

"You're killing yourself. You need to check yourself."

"Get out my house!" Missy hissed, her temper taking over.

Milo looked on at her silently, knowing she was unreachable with the mix of her temper and red wine. He left her there to slump where she sat.

Jody saw the strain on his face as he undressed, preparing to get in the shower. "She's taking BoDeen's death harder than I thought," Jody said, wanting Milo to talk about his visit with Missy. She didn't like the look on his face.

Milo stopped at the bathroom door and looked back at Jody as she lounged on the bed. "Yeah. It probably don't help that no one know who killed him. I have a feeling who did it, but that doesn't help."

Milo let the cold water run over his head as he took deep breaths under the spray. The weight of death, jail, Missy, and G'Ma's health was heavy on him. In the solitude of the shower, all the pieces of his life seemed to be cracking. G'Ma slept all day. He had a sick feeling she wasn't long for this world, but she was smiling every chance she got. He had a baby on the way at a time when so much grief was in the family. And Missy was off the hook. Everything was going so smooth right up until Rolando's murder. Milo felt like he could cry, but knew it would do no good.

The shower door opened slowly, catching Milo unaware as his head was bowed under the water. He blinked under the spray. Jody was standing at the door naked, her beautiful toffee-colored body making room for the growing body inside her stomach. She stepped into the shower, braving the cold therapeutic water. She hugged Milo around the waist, her swollen breasts were pressed against his back. They stood like that for a few minutes in a comfort zone. Milo then turned around to face her and took her into his arms. Jody was his rock in a swirling wind. She whispered her confidence in him into his wet chest. He was once again assured of why he fell in love with Jody in the first place. She possessed a quiet strength and devotion that went beyond the superficial and moved deep into genuine loyalty.

Billy Bob had no idea how long he was in a trance. He sat on his bunk, transported from place to place. His dick got hard and soft several times as he spent time with Florence, laughing and clowning on several different occasions. He soft chuckled to himself while memories of Bunchy slapping some broad in the mall for touching his braided hair passed through his mind.

"Youngster... youngster.." a low gravely voice whispered from nearby, pulling him back to reality.

Billy Bob resisted being pulled away from his trance. He kept his eyes closed, holding onto the image of his mother standing at the back door calling for him to come in from the garage and eat.

"Youngster... ey... youngster.. You up?" the voice called again.

It was no use. He needed to smoke another joint. Billy Bob opened his eyes to reality slowly. The dark cell was depressing as ever. It had to be late because the tier was quiet. It had to be well past the ten to midnight block when everyone rebelled against the quiet of their own minds.

"I heard you laughing over there," Cecil observed.

Billy Bob was up, taking a piss. The stream hitting the pool of water hissed against the quiet. He shook his dick and flushed the toilet. "What's up, G'Pops?" he said from the back of the cell. He moved to the bunk to roll another joint.

"They moved Elijah out of here awhile ago," Cecil informed him. "He called down here to you, but you musta bin asleep."

Billy Bob looked out onto the tier for Cecil's shadow to see where he was. He wasn't surprised Cecil was at his usual spot sitting on the floor with his back against the wall. Billy Bob lit the joint and moved to the floor at the front of the cell. "I was out of it. I didn't hear him leave."

"He's a good youngster. I see he did something good for you before he left," Cecil whispered through the bars.

"You smoke?"

Billy Bob was looking out to the tier when the answer came. Cecil's pale beige arm was crooked through the bar with his finger pressed together like a pair of roach clips. Billy Bob took a good pull to fill his lungs and passed the joint over to Cecil. He listened to Cecil pull on the joint and stifle a ragged cough. Then there was silence.

"That's some good stuff," Cecil admitted after he recovered from his fit. Then he asked with the boldness of the weed. "What you in jail for?"

"Murder," Billy Bob answered as he rolled another joint. "Why your kill your son?" he asked in return as he lit the joint.

Cecil sighed before he took another good pull off the sticky. After he blew the smoke out, he prepared to answer. He'd given this some thought, but Billy Bob was the first person he could actually tell it to. His wife was still upset with him and the rest of his 10 kids didn't know how to approach him for fear of upsetting or disrespecting their mother. "Well son... I suspect it was a variety of reasons. I didn't wake up the morning thinking I'd kill my son before the sun set."

"What he do?" Billy Bob interjected.

"Oh..." Cecil sighed. "I don't know if it was anything that he did. We had a little argument and things got out of hand," he admitted, although he'd worked out in his mind the real reason. He took another pull of the joint and went over the situation and reasoning in his mind. He'd raised 10 kids and fought in World War II. His wife of 50 years was a Jehovah's Witness. *It was time that I did what I wanted to do,* he reasoned to himself. *No one bothered that I wasn't religious or that I went to the horse track on the weekends. Then all of a sudden crack was in the same neighborhood where I was a respected storeowner. The city took my store to build a park, but that's no excuse. But too much time was on my hands. Still should have been no big deal.* Cecil was conflicted in his thoughts, sitting on the floor with the bud flowing through him. *Ain't I entitled to live a lit-*

tle after fighting and supporting my family? Having fun with a strawberry or two? But I'm sure it was embarrassing to my son to see me around the neighborhood buying crack tricking with strawberries, but that gave him no right to come into my house and disrespect me.

Cecil sighed deeply with the end of his contemplation. He took another hit off the joint, careful not to burn his lips on the hot tip. "I guess it just boiled down to disrespect," he answered Billy Bob sadly, blowing out smoke.

"I feel you," Billy Bob agreed, understanding how disrespect can make you kill a man. *Maybe his son felt disrespected for something too*, he thought to himself. There was always two sides to a story.

The cronic smoke was working on them both as they sat back to back on either side of the concrete wall. The silence pushed them inside their own thoughts buoyed to new heights by the weed. Far away from home, they were connected in their sorrow. Someone was dead for as little as disrespect and no doubt as a consequence of the life they were living. These assurances played out like a revelation seeking repentance as they sat on the floor in a cell at the county jail dressed in orange jumpsuits. The only thing waiting for them was a hard bunk and an indescribably bland breakfast of powdered eggs, bread, and juice. No warm hellos or genuine smiles. No BET or RapCity videos. No shiny new Escalade waiting in the driveway to floss. No fresh dry cleaned clothes or platinum chains to hang around your neck. No horses to bet on and no strawberries to tempt with a couple of rocks of cocaine. No wife to say 'I love you' to. No kids or grandkids to quiet down because you can't hear the TV. No friends to greet as they pulled into the driveway. No one to hold. No money to count. No refrigerator to open. No one to make love to. No choice to go outside and mow the lawn. Disrespect and murder. On a cold cell floor with a stranger sharing smuggled weed. The best that it could get.

Chapter Twenty Three

"Wait... wait... not so hard," Missy whispered. "You're going to wake up my son." She pressed up against Keashon to slow his motion.

Keashon was banging her back out. "Damn baby, you got the best pussy in the world," Keashon whispered in her ear hoarsely.

"How would you know?" she asked playfully.

He answered with a slow long stroke trying not to make the headboard bang into the wall. He was satisfied that she got the message for making him wait so long to fuck. He knew she wanted it when first they met, but she was bullshitting, it seemed like to him. Missy was the most real piece of pussy he'd had since he got out the joint. Keashon had fucked an old girlfriend, but she felt like she'd been ran through by half the neighborhood. Then there were a few young tenders that he met at a pool party that just wanted to get hit from the back. None of them had the class of Missy and he was anxious to show his appreciation.

Missy was rebelling against every sense of duty and responsibility she'd lived by. Half of her rebellion was due to the grief she felt for the loss of Dimp's father and the resulting deterioration of her moral center by alcohol; the other half was simply to spite her brother in her defensive stance. She knew he was right deep down, but to give in was harder than stopping a moving train. She allowed a man she'd barely known into her home late night, compromising this fact with the notion that Dimp was asleep. She didn't want to think of what it would feel like if Dimp should wake up and walk into her room at two in the morning.

It wasn't until 4:30 a.m. as they lay after an exhausting night of marathon sex that Missy remembered he had to be out before Dimp woke up. She wanted to let Dimp know ahead of time that Mommy had a new friend. Then the meeting could take place anytime during the day light hours. But right now Keashon didn't have to go home, but he had to get the hell outta Missy's house.

Billy Bob's leg was getting better. He was glad of it.

At least he could put weight on it enough to squabble. With the visit his spirits rose. He spent the max at the store and put some money on Cecil's account so he could go to the store for him. His single man cell was stocked with zoos zoos and wams wams. He was on his way to getting his weight back. Billy Bob shadow boxed into the wee hours of the night, when everyone else on the row was asleep. There was a period between 10 and midnight when the row was filled with chatter by those afraid to spend time alone with themselves. He waited until it quieted down before he exercised his leg and threw punches like a boxer in training. The more he thought of his dead loved ones, the more life filled him and his motivation to survive. In Bunchy's memory, he did an extra 500 push-ups when he thought he could do no more. In Drak's, memory he threw an extra 100 sets of one-two combinations when he thought his arms would fall off. In Rolando's memory, he did an extra 300 back arm lifts off the sink when he thought his elbows would surely fail him.

Before he realized it, a deputy was at the front of his cell calling his name for court. He looked surprised to see Billy Bob up, fully dressed, eating a cup-o-noodle and trailmix. Inmate William Mason was looking very different from the emaciated boy who was transferred over from the county hospital.

Billy Bob couldn't remember if being in court was such a dreary and intimidating event. In juvenile court there was a certain measure of chaos and predictability. The chaos was not really knowing if you'd be sent off to camp or youth authority. The predictability in being that you're a juvenile and if nothing major was done, a parent can come and get you and take you home. Where in juvenile court people milled about with expression formed by the duties of expediting children; here there was the grave burden of law and minimum sentencing requirements that rendered a staid seriousness to the proceedings. One that a parent merely appearing for a wayward child could not solve.

Billy Bob found comfort in seeing the rich, smiling faces of Milo and Florence flanking his mother in the first row of wooden benches. The silver-maned attorney, Mr. Rubin, had to whisper into Billy Bob's ear to stop him from turning around in his seat to look into the audience. Billy Bob had expected to see Big Red in the audience. He hated that his mother had to see him escorted from a side door with his feet and ankles cuffed with chains and bracelets. He'd tried to return her look of confidence. Nothing but support shown on her face.

"I understand the people have opposition to bail being set at this time," the chocolate colored judge boomed from the raised platform. He peered over small reading glasses towards the district attorney, standing up at the table across from where Billy Bob sat.

Billy Bob felt out of place. The D.A. and the Judge were both black. He had a hard time believing it. Maybe I should have a black lawyer, he thought to himself as he watched the thickly shaped D.A. in the tan blazer and shirt shuffle through some papers on her desk. Long hair. Carmel freckled complexion. French tipped nails. Billy Bob paid attention to her every move and detail, wondering what could she possibly have to say.

"If it pleases the court," the D.A. began in a professional, distinct tone, arching her chin up. Her voice was like honey. "The defendant, Mr. William Mason, in this case is answering to an execution-style murder and attempted murder. He is further being investigated for several other murders, including torture." She looked down at some papers on the desk. "Kidnap, arson, possession of military ordinances including grenades, night scopes, and automatic weapons." She looked over briefly at Billy Bob, then turned back to the judge. "The defendant is alleged to be involved in a drug ring. The leader no doubt," she finished, curling the edge of her pretty mouth.

The Judge bristled. "Is this a count in the complaint?" he interrupted.

She was caught. "Umm... no, Your Honor."

"Then dispense with the allegations and get to the point."

The D.A. closed the file in front of her. "The people oppose bail pending the outcome of a continuous pending investigation into Mr. Mason's criminal activities," she tapered off and sat down in her seat slowly.

The Judge looked towards Billy Bob. "Mr. Rubin?"

The well-dressed lawyer stood. "The notions, suppositions, and hearsay the people refer to are a product of the words of a detective who is currently being investigated by the Federal Anti-Corruption Agency for racketeering, murder, intimidation, kidnap, perjury, and a host of other crimes. If proven true, my client will be left to answer to none of the charges listed on the complaint. We respectfully request a modest bail," Mr. Rubin finished.

The Judge seemed to weigh both sides of the argument. The audience was quiet. Billy Bob watched the Judge with interest as he looked down at his desk. When the Judge looked up, Billy Bob was glued directly to his eye as they peered over those glasses right back at him.

"It's obvious to me," the Judge began in his booming voice. "Very obvious that the defendant is a very interesting character and may or may not have been in bed with this rouge detective. However, the charges here seem to hinge on the outcome of an investigation without a due date. As much as I'd like to expedite this matter, I don't feel at this time bail is prudent. I'll make an order for a report from the investigating agency." The Judge looked over at the D.A. "The people move for a trial date?"

The D.A. stood triumphant. "The people request a continuance pending the outcome of the court's order."

"Is this OK with the defense?" the Judge asked Mr.

Rubin.

"Yes, Your Honor."

Billy Bob was confused. He didn't know if he was free or not. He looked behind him at Milo, his Mom, and then at Florence for any indication that they understood what he did not. He read the same confusion on their faces mixed with disappointment. He turned back to Mr. Rubin. "What happened?"

"Bail was denied."

"I can't get out?" he asked urgently.

"Not right now. Be patient. I'll come talk to you."

Billy Bob was upset. His understanding was little as to why he couldn't get a bail. He slowly realized that the deputies were leading him back through the door from which he'd come. He was behind it when he noticed that he didn't get a chance to say 'bye' to his family. He didn't see his mother shed tears or when Milo quickly approached Mr. Rubin and grabbed him roughly by the arm. He didn't know that Florence watched him all the way through the door. He was alone again. On his way back to that cold lonely cell.

"Mom, is it ready yet?" Dimp yelled from the den where he played Madden 2005 on his PS2. Missy was in the kitchen thinking of how to approach the subject of her having a new friend with her son. Dimp was so aware and smart, she knew she had to be straight up with her man-child. She was making his favorite dinner of baked fish, broccoli, and wild rice. "I'm making your plate now. Go wash your hands and come into the dining room."

The table was set when Dimp came into the dining room wiping his wet hands across his t-shirt.

"Use a towel boy!" Missy argued, silently admiring his growing form. He had broad shoulders and even at nine years old his chest was defined. He was wearing his hair in a short curly afro. The big curls cut in half before they could fully form on his head. His dark eyes were like a bottomless well with thick lashes. *No wonder he was juggling girls non-stop*, Missy thought to herself.

Dimp plopped down onto the seat. "My favorite. What I do?" he asked wide-eyed, preparing to pick the fish apart.

"Say your prayers, Dimp. One for your father." Missy looked on at her son with pride, savoring the moment of his youth.

Dimp cupped his hands quickly under his chin and said a silent prayer. Quickly.

"Dimp," Missy interrupted his resumption of digging into his dinner, making him look up at the tone of her voice. "I'm going to start dating again."

"That mean you're going to have a boyfriend, right?" he asked.

"Yes."

Dimp shrugged his shoulders. "No way I'm calling him Dad. My friend Mark's mom made him call her new boyfriend Dad."

"How does Mark feel about that," Missy asked, interested to know since Dimp obviously had strong feelings about it.

He shrugged his shoulders again. "He says it, but he really means dipshit."

"Dimp!" Missy said, shocked. Then had to laugh at it. Dimp smiled. "Fair enough," Missy said, recovering her composure. She looked intently at Dimp while he ate, wondering what his secret word would be for Keashon.

Chapter Twenty Four

Milo was headed towards Haitian Jack's banging that Rhythm & Gangster by Snoop Dogg. He was tripping on how mellow the tracks were. Snoop Dogg had matured and his music grew with him. Milo could appreciate the smoothness of a player doing it big and by his own rules. It was motivating and uplifting. Rising from nothing to something and staying strong through all adversity. He remembered how his father had lived in Haiti before moving to the states. All those early years of hustling moved across his mind. His father was larger than life, maneuvering through the streets to feed his family and leave something for his children.

Now it's my turn, he thought to himself as Jody flashed across his vision. She would be having his child soon and he wanted shit to be straight for his seed. And he wanted shit to be straight for Dimp. A sour expression impressed upon his face as he thought of his sister and her drunken ways. He made a mental note to check her boyfriend out. That situation had to be attended to. He knew it was going to cause some friction, but for the sake of protecting what they had, Missy was going to have to be mad for a minute.

Hutch was at the bar when he walked into Haitian Jack's. It was barely after five and the after work crowd was just filing in for happy hour. The music was thumping inside the glass wall on the overhead dance floor. A few people sat on the stools that lined the glass wall overlooking the foyer. Underneath the dance floor, the pool tables were being put into action by a large group of pretty, young, boisterous females who'd obviously just left an office building where they worked. They were a mixed group, dressed professionally in attire that doubled for club wear. Naturally they attracted an equal amount of men over to their general area, sniffing the air, suddenly interested in shooting pool.

"Kilroy got that info for you," Hutch said, taking a sip of Hennessy.

Milo took a seat next to him at the bar. A cranberry juice appeared in front of him. "The pig or Missy's boy?" Milo asked as he sipped the juice. He was looking around at a new group of smiling, pretty women that pushed through the front doors.

"The pig. He say the boy's info be here in a few," Hutch assured him. He tipped his hat to the smiling, pretty girls that took seats next to them at the bar.

They quickly ordered drinks to get their night started. "Kilroy upstairs and you already know he's breaking in a new piece of sweetness. Nice work too. Ass like that." Hutch puckered his lips, making them fat.

Milo welcomed the smile. A gleam not long exercised shown in his eyes. He'd been playing grown up for a while and all the new pressure needed a release. It had been all business. He and Hutch didn't go out or chill like they used to. He welcomed a small distraction. He'd get to the info on the pig in a minute; but right now he wanted to be entertained and where better to be entertained than in the V.I.P. section of his own club. Kilroy had a fresh tender upstairs that gained his interest. He peeled off the stool with a fresh drink in his hand. "Let's go see," Milo motioned to Hutch with a playful smile.

Milo screwed his face up (DAMN!) when he saw the honey caramel woman going through her motions on the pole atop the small wooden platform. Her ass stood at least a foot away from her small waist. Her long silky black hair hung in long Shirley Temple curls down her back. Her eyes were large and doe-like. Her lips were shaped like a perfect heart. She looked as fresh as baby milk, but her moves on that pole said she was a grown ass woman.

Kilroy was leaned back on a velour love seat pulling on a fat Cuban cigar. A large bottle of Remy Martin was on a glass table in front of him. He looked pleased with himself. His smile pushed his freckles across his tan face towards his gray eyes. His flaming red hair hung loose over his shoulders. He was smiling at Milo knowing that not much could get that kind of uncensored reaction from him. "Take a load off, Bru," Kilroy advised, nodding to the couch on the other side of the intimate room.

Hutch followed Milo to the leather couch opposite Kilroy. He stretched out and took a sip of his dark-colored drink. Hutch took his cue from Kilroy and looked towards the stage for the private show.

"Hi, Milo. Hi, Hutch," the sweet syrupy voice of the girl-woman acknowledged. "My name is Betina," she purred. No doubt she knew who Milo and Hutch were. She was very appropriate and cast a seductive shadow over the whole room. Like anything was possible and whatever happened you would enjoy it. She glanced at Kilroy before she moved to circle the silver pole slowly and seductively in a transparent linen skirt. The red g-string teased through the material. Her large pert breasts were propped further by a half bra.

Ludacris' Red Light was pumping through the speakers with a mellow horn section silhouetting his smooth delivery. Betina closed her eyes and shimmied across the pole, spreading her legs and rocking from side to side as if warming up her hips for seduction. She turned around and bent over swaying her large ass from right to left. She moved slow and deliberate, teasing them with her motion. Slowly, her long nailed fingers unsnapped her skirt, releasing that almighty ass from its imaginary harness. She looked back at Milo for his reaction. Satisfied, she smiled in return. Not a blemish, wrinkle, dimple, or stretch mark was on her eggplant colored body. She was as tight as guitar strings. Betina squatted briefly and performed stunts on the pole all the while checking their faces for approval.

Milo watched in awe. He for the moment was able to forget all his problems and worries. It had been awhile since he was simply able to enjoy himself. Ludacris was flowing. Kilroy looked satisfied. Hutch was eager to touch Betina. Milo nodded his head to the beat and watched Betina swing around the pole and make her ass clap to the beat of the music. This got a body jerking reaction from Hutch as he tapped Milo's arm to make sure he saw and heard that. This is what it was all about. Why he switched up the game. Chilling in his own spot with friends he'd known since the beginning. True friends who he knew would ride or die for him. Milo was happy to be where he was. But soon it would be back to business. If the info Kilroy had for him was correct, the pig was about to see how a gangsta hand is played without warning. No telling how long the investigation would take. And he wanted Billy Bob out of jail to enjoy what life really had to offer. Something had to give and Milo wasn't prepared to do the giving. Some taking had to be done.

When Billy Bob finally made it back to the county jail and after waiting in holding cells alone for hours before he was escorted back to his cage, he felt like he'd boxed 12 rounds, ran a game of full court basketball, and played 11 games of chess. He was physically and mentally exhausted. The words said at court had grown feet from walking through his mind all day. He tried to decipher the meaning of the legalistic jibber jabber. And what did it exactly mean for him that Big Red was being investigated? How long would it take? And hearing about all the stuff he was being investigated for. He remembered it all, but couldn't believe he was as bad as they made it sound. Arson. Multiple murders. Kidnap. Torture. Drug trafficking. That shit sounded crazy, like something you'd read in a book or see in a movie, or on America's Most Wanted. He watched the cell door close trying to see himself from the outside. He must have looked like a child monster to the court and the people who heard those things about him, Billy Bob thought to himself.

Now he was back in his cell. It seemed like the noise and chaos of the day shut itself off with a heavy thud of metal meeting to close the iron door. He sat on the bunk, feeling small inside his orange jumpsuit. Increasingly, he felt like he had no control over anything that had to do with his life. This was a scary thought for someone who did what he wanted and when he wanted to with no regard for the cost and brave enough to handle the consequences. But these were expensive prices and dire consequences and the weight of the penalty began to weigh on young Billy Bob. He felt like he could cry, but rebelled against the emotion, clenching his fist and punching into the air with a grunt that sounded loud against the silence of the tier.

"How'd it go youngster?" Cecil asked from the next cell over. He was at his usual spot on the floor against the bars.

"It went," he answered shortly from the back of his cell. Billy Bob lay on his back looking up at the ceiling. He was wrapped up in his own thoughts. They were the same thoughts appearing at the front of his mind over and over again hoping to be thought of differently each time around.

"Don't' let them rattle you. No matter how bad it sounds you got to keep a positive attitude," Cecil whispered.

Billy Bob didn't respond.

"Yeah..." Cecil exhaled loudly as if wishing he'd taken his own advice as it came to him. "You gotta move from a position of strength. People will try to make you seem wrong and weak so they can get the upper hand on you. And you know what happens when people get the upper hand? They do what they want with you. It isn't until it's too late you realize that you should have been stronger to be in a better position. Whatever you did, at the time you were working with the best mind you had. Now you realize you made some mistakes because you didn't think things through. The reason for that was you were influenced by something... maybe a girl, drugs, money, revenge, ego, reputation... whatever... and all of these things really don't matter. They give a false sense of self worth. You gotta learn to be worth more than what is influencing you." Cecil's voice trailed off. He'd retreated into his own thoughts. As the words came out of his mouth, his own influences flashed before him. The circumstances of his situation made him sad because now he felt like he could have avoided it had he employed the same position that he was speaking on.

Billy Bob's attention was caught at "self worth". He remembered Florence telling him that he couldn't love her more than he loved himself. And how she wanted more love and by that she wanted him to love himself more. Hearing Cecil and remembering Florence's words suddenly made what was once cloudy clear. He listened for Cecil to start talking again.

"You gotta think of it like this... Is a million dollars worth me losing my life? Is driving a nice car and wearing nice clothes worth more than my life? You might say that these things make life better, but how can they when you put your very life in jeopardy to get things that supposed to make it better? That's like going out into the rain with an umbrella and not opening it until you get all the way wet. Or how about chasing the finest girl in the world and getting her and she gives you AIDS. It all comes back to self worth. You chased the girl to make yourself feel good about yourself, without having to have her, she wouldn't have been the type to attract your attention."

This made sense to Billy Bob. He had to laugh a little. "That's right," he said, still chuckling.

Cecil was glad to get a laugh out of him. "There's a reason why doing wrong is so easy. The devil is very swift and quick to send help when you think of what wrong you want to do. The minute you think of a scheme, ain't it surprising how easy it seems and how fast you can find help? But when you want to do good, God is slow to answer. Seems strange I know. Seems like God would be quick to help. But that's where patience comes in at. The girl that it takes a long time to fuck is usually the one that you want to keep. She's usually the best one for you right?"

Billy Bob was nodding his head before he actually said, "Yeah."

"And the fast girl is the one that got the crabs or give you the drips."

Billy Bob laughed out loud, rising from his bunk to move to his spot at the front of the cell. "That's real, Cecil."

"God say be patient and all things that are good will come. But in order to be patient you have to believe that good will come. As soon as you don't believe, then you don't have patience and the easy way is right there for you with the devil's help. And this is because you have no self worth. You don't believe in yourself and that good things will come to you. Like you don't deserve it. You see how it all depends on each other, youngster?"

Billy Bob was staring blankly out onto the tier. It was all so clear to him. And he was mad that he didn't know this before.

"Don't' blame anybody," Cecil said.

Billy Bob blinked his eyes. Just as Cecil said this he was going over the people in his life who helped him do whatever he wanted to do. Hutch with the guns. Milo. Big Red. Even Mom.

"You only get what your heart desires. Your family and friends love you and only give what help you request. Just because you come to the realization that you were wrong doesn't mean everybody else is at fault. Ain't nobody in that cell but you. So you got to start with you and only you," Cecil advised. "Stay positive, that's all."

Cecil was silent. Billy Bob was absorbing what he said. His thoughts were doing flip-flop backs in his skull. He was chewing on rough meat and with every shredded thought the meanings became more and more clearer to him. He got up from the floor and moved back to his bunk. He lay down and crossed his legs at the ankles with his arms folded behind his head. He understood clearly now why he was in a lonely cell.

It had nothing to do with crime. It had everything to do with self worth. The jewelry, cars, money, clothes, girls, weed, and the sheer activity of selling dope and stunting seemed ridiculous. All these things, he knew now, were used as props like price tags on merchandise. Without the price tags, the merchandise was without value. But things that are worth a lot have no price tag. Even though Billy Bob had a high price tag, he was worthless. He put his own life in jeopardy just to be able to paste price tags on his body. He closed his eyes against the realization and pain of it. His body shut down with misery and a silent prayer for forgiveness.

Haitian Jack's Sports Bar & Lounge was starting to jump. Milo could feel the energy seeping in through the cracks and hinges of his office door. Hutch was seated across from him as he leafed through the manila folder Mr. Rubin had provided him with. It had detailed information on the pending federal investigation and the alleged charges against Big Red. It had exact records against him dating back to when Milo was a boy and Big Red was in his father's back pocket. The file moved through the years all the way up to Billy Bob. Milo shook his head slowly in dismay at the level of involvement Big Red had with so many people. Instead of taking them to jail, he set people up for murder and accepted payment from others for protection. For more than 20 years, Big Red had his hands in all manner of crooked dealings that went on in the hood.

Milo closed the manila folder and picked up a powder blue folder that Kilroy had waiting for him. This one had Big Red's personal residential address, a Big Bear cabin address, a Montana ranch address, a boat dock address and all of his credit and banking information. Big Red was a multi-millionaire with property all over the place. From the paperwork in the folder Milo learned that Big Red had been divorced twice and had two kids from his first marriage. His oldest child was a girl. She was currently a sophomore at Stanford University.

The other was a boy who was currently in a drug rehabilitation center in the valley. He was younger than his sister by two years. There was a black and white picture of a dark, statuesque, ebony-colored woman crossing the parking lot of a small specialty grocery store called Joseph's. The attached note described her as the owner of a flower shop in Culver City. She was Big Red's mistress. A divorcee with no children. She was pretty, Milo thought to himself. He wondered why she was giving Big Red the time of day when he flipped over a computer generated printout of the woman's personal tax records and property receipts. The flower shop was in Big Red's name as principal owner. She was listed as the beneficiary and co-signee for the loan of the property. Her house in Gardena was paid for after only six years since the purchase date. Milo understood perfectly. Big Red was her sugar-daddy. Service rendered; services paid for. That's some expensive pussy. You go sista, Milo whispered under his breath. There was also a list of Big Red's watering holes. The casino he liked and the bars he visited most frequently. Milo was surprised when he read what Big Red's favorite foods were. He arched his eyebrows at Hutch.

"Very thorough," Hutch agreed.

"Arizona Ron don't play," Milo said, closing the folder. "He still push that black Yukon?" Milo remembered with fond memories. Ron was one of his father's best friends.

The one he called on when he needed some heavy lifting done.

"With slow grooves on," Hutch added with a knowing smirk on his fat face.

Chapter Twenty Five

BoDeen's stern expression looked down from the large portrait. He stood in front of a squatted Silverado truck dressed in Khakis and white t-shirt. The muscles of his arms, chest, and legs bulged in rebellion and expression of manhood. A manhood raised by the code of the streets and educated in the ways of the dope game after a failed bid at a professional football career.

Missy sat in the Lay-Z-Boy looking on as Keashon and Dimp played each other in basketball on the PlayStation. Reminders of BoDeen were everywhere. Where before BoDeen's constant gaze was comforting, now it spoke of condemnation. He spoke words that only Missy could hear or thought she heard through the haze of remorse and a weird feeling that BoDeen was still in this house. She closed her eyes against his indictments. She responded: What you expect me to do? You left me here all alone. What the hell am I supposed to do?

"Mom! You see me slam dunk on Keashon?" Dimp asked excitedly, his eyes locked on the big screen where Keashon was advancing the ball up the court.

Missy opened her eyes, interrupting her private conversation. She looked over at her son's smiling, intent face. He was concentrating on defense, trying to keep Keashon from scoring. Dimp had successfully built a thin wall of aloofness around him, meant to convey the fact that though Keashon was around, not to get it confused with him replacing his father. Still, Missy enjoyed the fact that Keashon was willing to play his part.

"Bam! On your head. Posterize!" Keashon shouted, having paid Dimp back with a reverse dunk of his own.

"That should have been traveling!" Dimp complained as his fingers worked the controls to get his man down the court.

Missy was conflicted in a way that she'd never been before. She'd always been sure of herself and one never to waiver between two points. On the one hand, she wanted what was best for Dimp and on the other, there was a selfish desire to please herself, something she felt she'd been denied while taking care of every one else. An untapped resentment was seeded deep within her at seeing those closest to her involved in committed relationships, married, and building families for themselves. And the man she loved the most ended up self-destructing and dead in her driveway. Sometimes she felt like driving into the desert and disappearing for good.

"Get that out of here! You can't come into my house with that!" Dimp shouted, his hand feverishly working the controls after blocking a shot put up at the three-point line by Keashon's point guard.

Missy smiled, broken from her solitude. She sensed a little too much bravado in her son. She watched his serious expression, looking just like his father. He was being territorial too, letting Keashon know whose house he was in.

Dimp was Missy's reason for holding on to what little strength she had. He was her world and knew her heart would burst, killing her instantly, if anything happened to her precious son.

Later that evening, after Dimp grew tired enough to call it quits and go to bed, Missy and Keashon snuggled close in the living room. Heather Headley was playing low on the surround sound as they sat talking. It was late and Missy hadn't decided yet if Keashon would be spending the night. Although Dimp was receptive to her having a boyfriend and seemed happy enough that they played video games together, she wasn't sure if it was time for Dimp to wake up and find Keashon walking around in his boxers. At the same time, she didn't want to ask Keashon to leave before morning.

"What did you think of me the first time you saw me?" Missy asked, looking down into Keashon's face. He lay across the sofa with his head in her lap.

"I wanted to tackle you."

Missy laughed, "Seriously. What did you think?"

He looked up into her dark eyes for a couple beats. "You were a mystery that I wanted to solve."

"My brother would rather I stay a mystery to you," Missy said as a passive challenge.

This sparked his interest. He'd wanted to know more about her brother, but had decided up until now to let it roll. "You and your brother pretty tight, huh... he don't like you to have boyfriends?" He was still in her lap, looking up into her face.

Missy let out a deep breath, thinking of her brother. They'd been through so much together. "He's the beat of my heart. He just wants what's best for me."

"He think I'm not good enough for you?"

Missy rubbed Keashon across his cool forehead and over his close cropped scalp. The bristles of his hair were like Braille under her fingers. "He doesn't know you. If I left it up to him you'd have to pass a background check and come with references." She gave a short laugh.

"Sound like you dig me more than I know or you just trying to get back at him for something."

His comment cut across the fat. Missy thought about this. Her private thoughts had tumbled and dried this over and over. Now that Keashon had put them on the line, she was forced to fold them. *Why am I mad at Milo?* she asked herself. "I like you more than you know," she assured Keashon, bending down to kiss him. "You staying the night?" she asked, making up her mind.

Milo turned into the cul-de-sac and was glad to see Jasmine's champagne colored Dodge Magnum parked in the driveway. He forgot she said that she opted not to renew her overseas contract and would look for something closer to home. There was no question about her finding her own spot to live. There was more than enough room at his house and Jody was way too real to be threatened by Jasmine's presence. After all, she was the one who introduced Jody to Milo and single handedly put the playbook together for Jody to win Milo's heart. Milo had his three favorite girls under one roof, which was cool by him.

It was almost three in the morning. Someone was in the kitchen cooking what smelled like waffles. Milo closed the front door and walked into the lit kitchen. Jasmine had just sat down to pour syrup over a stack of waffles.

"You pregnant?" Milo asked, surprising Jasmine with his quiet steps.

Jasmine jumped, startled. "You scared me, Milo," she said, clutching her hand to her chest, still holding the female shaped syrup.

"What you doing up so late?" Milo sat his leather laptop case on the counter and went over to the fridge to get a glass of milk for Jasmine.

"I was just about to get some milk. You are so thoughtful. I just couldn't sleep. I went to Missy's salon today and saw Gwen. I still haven't met Missy's new boyfriend." Jasmine took a sip of milk. "Thank you."

Milo was sitting next to her at the counter. "Yeah. I stopped by there earlier, but she wasn't in. She's spending a lot of time with this character. He hasn't done anything crazy yet, he just got a crazy record. There's something about him that I don't trust."

Jasmine held a slice of waffle on her fork just below her chin. "You think he'll do something to Missy or Dimp?" Jasmine asked.

Milo was afraid to answer this question because the truth was that he didn't know. Anything could happen when you deal with people you had no history with. It would be different if they didn't have so much to lose or didn't work so hard to achieve success. Putting trust in people was an expensive business. "Naw," Milo answered to ease Jasmine's worry. "I just wish she'd find someone in her own league. Maybe somebody that we know something about or at least could put a hand on."

Jasmine gave Milo an endearing shove with a low

chuckle. "You are something else. So protective. Sherrie told me how a long time ago when you two were sitting in your SS Impala how you said that anybody that she dated had to pass inspections. You need to lighten up. You think?"

Milo remembered that memory fondly. It was the one-year anniversary of his father's death. They were smoking a blunt. It seemed like so long ago. Before Jody and Haitian Jack's. Before a lot of shit... murders and total chaos. Milo suddenly turned sad with the memory of Marcellus. His easy laughter. Suddenly he missed having him around. He turned to Jasmine. "Tell me something. Why you used to give Marcellus a hard time every time he came through?"

Milo's question was a surprise. Her face registered calculation as she tried to remember her impression of Marcellus. She put her chin in her palm and thought for a minute. "Marcellus," she said wistfully. "He was cool people. I don't know... maybe... I liked him... if I let myself like boys that much. He was cool. It was exciting messing with him because I knew all he wanted me to do was like him." She looked over at Milo. "All that seems like yesterday, but so far away," she said, remembering all the drama of that year.

Jody appeared suddenly at the corner of the kitchen entryway. "What y'all looking so sad for? Or do I wanna know? Hi, honey." Jody moved over to Milo and gave him a hug. She sat next to him and looked into his face, trying to read what was going on.

"It's nothing girl. One comment led to a memory and all of sudden we were living in the past. And you know that's foul," Jasmine said, stabbing at her just warm enough waffles.

Milo cheered up. "How's my baby doing? And my little man," he asked, rubbing her stomach through the satin gown.

"We're fine. Glad you're home. How's everything at the lounge?" Jody asked.

This conversation would normally be held in their bedroom as Milo was getting ready to get into the shower or just getting in the bed.

"Everything's cool. What are you doing up?" Milo wondered, looking Jody up and down. "You feeling okay?"

Jody leaned her head onto his shoulder and grabbed a hold of his hand. "I was just missing you. I woke up and thought you were here. I felt you honey. Deep in my bones. If you weren't in the house I would have been scared." She sounded like a little girl. Purring against Milo.

"Well." Jasmine interrupted the private moment. "Sound like a date to me. Y'all be careful not to hurt my baby." She laughed at her own joke. She raised from her seat to put her dishes in the sink.

Jody was smiling. "Jasmine, grab me a basket of strawberries and whipped cream out the fridge please."

Jasmine swooned her body as she opened the refrigerator. "You sure hubby is up to this after a hard day's work," she teased.

Milo was looking between the two of them, embarrassed and hoping Jody wasn't that horny, though he wouldn't be surprised.

"No, girl." Jody laughed against Milo. "I just have a strong craving for whipped cream and strawberries. But... you never know," she hinted, taking the cold good strawberries and cream from Jasmine and pulling Milo out of his seat.

"I'll be right up, Jody. I have to check on G'Ma," Milo said.

Jasmine watched Jody turn the corner and head up the stairs. "At least something good came out of it," Jasmine said, speaking of the year Milo met Jody and Marcellus was killed. "You owe me big time," she added.

"No doubt. Come with me to check on G'Ma. How was she today? She sleep much?" Milo asked as they walked towards the downstairs master bedroom hugging each other around the waist.

"She took a nap around two, but other than that she's cool," Jasmine responded, opening G'Ma's door slowly and walking in lightly.

Milo bent low over the bed and kissed G'Ma on her warm cheek. She didn't move. Her breathing was light and even.

Before Jasmine went into her own bedroom she suggested to Milo to be patient with Missy. "Give her some time. She might make a mistake. Just be there for her like she was there for you," Jasmine reminded him.

Milo remembered how Missy was in his face when everything was falling apart around him. She was in his corner 100%, helping him see that the dope game was not his field of work. She didn't want him to end up dead or in jail for having to do something to some hater who didn't feel him.

When Milo walked into his spacious master bedroom, Jody was sitting in the middle of the king sized bed. She'd turned on the plasma screen. She was watching the original Shaft with Antonio Fargas and Richard Roundtree. She had her legs crossed with the bucket of strawberries in her lap. She was spraying whip cream on a strawberry when Milo noticed what she was watching.

They would put the original gangster Shaft on at three in the morning," Milo laughed, excited at the notion of watching it with Jody.

"No respect," Jody agreed as she took a delicious bite of her cream covered strawberry. "Want some?" she asked, raising a half-eaten strawberry up to him as he moved onto the bed next to her.

He let her put it in his mouth. He sat down on the bed with his back to the backboard. Milo slipped off his Cole Hahn shoes and took off his blazer. He took a deep breath, happy to be home and in his bed. He had little energy to get up and take a shower. He reached his hand out to the middle of the bed and rubbed Jody across the small of her. Feeling his touch, she scooted back a little so he could rub her fully from the neck down. They knew each other like the palm of their own hands.

"Those were the days. When brothers were real. Look. They got the afros and Shaft wasn't a snitch. He played the pig all the way to the end," Jody commented.

Milo was silent, listening to the sound of her sweet voice. He wanted her to keep on talking.

Jody slowly scooted back on the bed and rubbed her hand across the leg of his slacks and up towards his lap. She moved slowly, sedating him. Relaxing him as they watched the movie together. Shaft was getting ready to get some pussy from a sister he knew and was helping him. Jody moved her hand across Milo's zipper and pulled it down, making the fabric spread. She pulled his belt loose and unsnapped his pants, revealing the dark blue silk boxers she bought for him. Jody deftly undid the single button on his boxer and reached for the heavy meat hidden there. Milo gasped at her touch. She pulled it out and began to stroke him softly, making him grow slowly inside her small hand. Jody filled her mouth with whip cream and bent over Milo's lap to take him into her mouth.

The cream was cold on his dick, making him jump at first. Jody's mouth soon warmed him and extended him to his full length. She sucked on him hungrily. Pleasingly. She looked up into his hooded eyes all the while she massaged him with her mouth. She moved her tongue around the tip of his swollen meat with a familiarity of love and duty. She sucked him hard and strong until he came into her mouth. Even then she moved her full lips over the length of him until she was sure he was satisfied, then she popped her lips off of him creating a loud smacking sound. "Now go get in the shower," she whispered to him in the dim light of the plasma screen.

Milo lay with his back against the headboard for a minute trying to get his motion back. Jody sucked all life from him, rendering him motionless. "You know I can't move girl," Milo complained.

Jody let out satisfied laughter, scooting up next to him against the headboard. She placed her hand over the spent meat. "You really can't move?" she asked, moving her fingers gently over his dick, bringing it slowly back to life.

All Milo could do was grin as Jody moved over his legs and straddled him reverse cowgirl style. She gripped his knees and lowered herself over his now hard dick. She slowly slid down its length, satisfied that Milo let out a soft moan. She moved up and down slowly over him, grinding in circular motions. "You like this hot pussy daddy?" she asked.

Milo grunted when she ground down on him.

"This hot pregnant pussy feel good to you daddy?" she taunted as she slid up and down in a faster rhythm. "You not going to answer me? Is it too good?" her words echoed her more involved gyrations.

Milo tried to grip her hips and guide her movements, but Jody had other plans. She bucked on top of him. Shaking his grip loose, and moved her body up making his dick stretch downward while inside of her. He groaned with the sensation of being pulled and gripped tightly as she continued to slide down on him.

Jody moved off of Milo and took him into her mouth. She slid her lips over as much of him as she could for as long as he could until he motioned for her to roll over on all fours. Milo entered her from the back gently and slid inside of her to the hilt. "You trying to put it on me huh?" Milo asked as he moved inside of her.

"Do what you do then," she moaned, looking back over her ass at him. She moved against him, meeting his thrusts.

Milo felt himself growing hot at the tip with her movements. He jerked into her quickly and exploded, gripping her hips tight.

"There you go, baby," Jody whispered, working her pussy muscles around him, squeezing what was left from him. "Now we can go take a shower."

Milo collapsed onto the bed, pulling Jody on top of him. She kissed him tenderly. "Well, maybe we can lay here for a minute until you get your breath back," Jody teased.

Milo smiled against her lips as she kissed him, happy to lay under her for a minute. Not to mention the fact that she faded him. He'd never admit that he couldn't move if he wanted to, but was sure she knew as much. She giggled over him as she lay over his prone body. Satisfied with herself.

Chapter Twenty Six

Missy was enjoying waking up with Keashon next to her. As she rolled over in bed, she watched him get dressed for work. He'd found a job driving a delivery truck for Red Bull. A one night sleepover quickly turned into a regular affair.

"You look cute in uniform," Missy said in a pre-dawn sleepy voice.

"Don't start nothing you can't finish," Keashon playfully warned.

"You the one late for work." Missy stretched like a cat under the covers.

Keashon pulled his Red Bull cap over his head. "I'd love to stay and play, but poppa gotta go to work." He leaned onto the bed to give Missy a kiss. "See you later."

"Mmmm hmmm," she moaned in response, listening from her bed as Keashon closed the front door and started his car in the driveway.

Missy couldn't have been sleep for no more than two hours. The sun was barely over the horizon when Dimp called her from the open bedroom door. "You want me to make breakfast or are you about to get up?"

Missy rolled over to look at the time. 7:40 a.m. *Perfect*, she thought to herself. I'm getting better. I might even make it to work on time. "I'm up right now sweetie. I'll make us breakfast. Give me five minutes," Missy said, getting out of bed.

When Missy walked into the kitchen, Dimp was at the counter breaking eggs into a large glass bowl. "Grab the cinnamon, Mom," Dimp instructed.

Missy looked surprised, feigning laughter. "You cooking? You should have said something. I would have stayed in bed." She was at the spice rack grabbing the cinnamon.

Dimp twisted up his face and rolled his eyes, letting his mother know that he knew better than to believe she'd allow him to cook alone. "Naw mom, I was just getting it started for french toast." Dimp sprinkled cinnamon over the mixture of eggs and milk.

"Almost baby. Almost," Missy promised, rubbing her fingers through his curly mop of hair. "I'm glad you were being thoughtful." Missy moved to the stove to heat up the pancake grill. "You want turkey bacon?" she turned around to ask, moving towards the refrigerator.

"Yeah," Dimp answered, intent on mixing the eggs. "Hey, Mom." He looked up. "Is Keashon going to move in?"

This question caught Missy by surprise. She turned to face Dimp. "I hadn't planned on it. Why? You like Keashon?" she asked, interested in his answer since he brought up the subject.

Dimp shrugged his shoulders. "He always spending the night. Where does he live?"

"He has his own house," Missy answered, wanting to pull every thought out of her son's head, but knew that he would only give so much at a time. So she resolved herself to be patient.

"Why he always spend the night over here then?"

Missy had yet to become accustomed to Dimp's aggression and directness. He was growing up fast and forming his own opinions about how things should be. "Why?" she asked. "You don't like him spending the night?" Realizing he hadn't answered her first question.

"What kind of house does he have? Is it big like uncle Milo's?" Dimp pressed.

Now Missy understood. He was trying to place Keashon, using Milo as the measuring stick. "No. His house isn't that big."

Dimp was persistent. "Does he have a lot of money?"

"How much is a lot of money?" Missy challenged her smart son.

Dimp thought for a minute. "Enough to buy a Lexus and own a house, not rent it," Dimp responded, reasonably satisfied with his estimation of what a cool amount of money was.

"How much money a person has is not important. What's important is that they respect you and motivate you to be the best person you can be."

Dimp seemed to absorb her answer, giving it some thought as he leaned against the counter. He watched his mother dip the pieces of bread into the egg mix and place them on the hot grill. The turkey bacon was sizzling on the top half of the slab of steel. "So, you'll date a bum?" Dimp ask suddenly.

Missy had to laugh at this. "Of course not Dimp."

"Do you love him?" Dimp wanted to know.

Missy had to glance at her son to make sure the words were coming from his mouth. "Yeah. A little I guess," she had to admit.

"So does Keashon have enough money for you?"

"I don't really need his money."

"Does he need yours?" Dimp asked deadpan.

Missy was in the middle of flipping a slice of bread. Dimp's question caught her off guard, making her flip the toast onto the rows of frying bacon. The phone rang. *Thank God*, Missy thought to herself as she picked up the phone.

Dimp watched her cradle the phone to her ear as she flopped and fumbled the french toast. He listened to her end of the conversation. By her tone, a familiar one of attention, he knew Milo was on the other end. Dimp tried to guess what they were talking about, but it was no use. Missy was doing most of the listening and her answers were short and cryptic.

"Yeah, he's right here trying to turn a double play with his grown questions," Missy said into the phone as she looked over her shoulder at a smiling Dimp.

It made Dimp feel good that Milo had asked about him. When Missy handed him the phone, he acted like he didn't notice her warning look.

"Hey uncle Milo. How are you?" Dimp asked into the phone as he watched his mother turn to grab a couple of plates out of a cabinet. "Mom," Dimp said excitedly. "I'm going to Milo's this weekend? I want to see G'Ma and Jasmine. G'Ma say she'll cook something special for me."

"Yep. That's where you're going." Missy answered over her shoulder.

"What else are we going to do?" Dimp returned to his conversation with Milo. "It's the same if you tell me now." He urged the secret from his uncle. "Okay. Bye. Love you, too." Dimp handed the phone to Missy's outstretched hand.

"He wouldn't tell you what else you were going to do?" she asked, putting the phone back in its cradle on the wall.

"No. He said it was a surprise." Dimp's mind was quickly transferred to the upcoming weekend. It was Thursday and he quickly calculated that Saturday would be here in no time. He abandoned his probing questions satisfied that he'd approached his mother's last nerve. He didn't want to overdue it. He was happy to sit down to breakfast and get the day started so Saturday could get here even quicker.

Haitian Jack's Sports Bar & Lounge was pulsing. The energy inside the building could light up a small city. Just to be able to plug into the excitement was a rare pleasure that Milo succeeded in offering every Friday night. A quick glance around the room and it was only right that the tall men who played for the Los Angeles Lakers could be found shooting pool under the dance floor. At Milo's invitation Melyssa "Jessica Rabbit" Ford came through with a bevy of beautiful women. They occupied one of the leather booths situated on a raised platform on the side wall opposite the pool tables and dance floor.

Obie Trice and Sly Boogie just passed through on their way to the V.I.P room where Betina made a name for herself. Milo was seated with Sherrie at the bar taking in the excitement of the evening. Gorilla Black was the guest MC for the evening and with him came the entourage of moneyed thugs and beautiful women. A smaller venue with less attractions would not be able to hold the many celebrities and egos that were in Haitian Jack's. Security was tight and Milo had a reputation of creating a prosperous and peaceful environment.

Ever since Rolando was murdered only a few feet from where he now sat, Milo doubled his effort to make sure no guns got into his establishment. He personally went on a PR campaign to restore his reputation and that of his business. It didn't hurt that word quickly spread on the street about how the fallout from Rolando's murder was swift and brutal. Billy Bob was a legend and he hadn't turned 21 yet. No one wanted that kind of retaliation for acting stupid in Milo's club.

"There he is. On my God!" Sherrie gasped, gripping Milo's arm.

Milo looked in the direction that held her gaze. Through the front door stepped Arizona Ron. He moved like a mythic figure through a crowd of women who had to stop their conversation just to look at him as he passed by. His slim, dark figure moved with effortless ease like he was moving on slick snow. His olive colored tailored suit fit his slim frame perfectly. He was cut to the butt and cut in to the game. Milo smiled at the man he'd known all his life. It had been years since he'd seen him, but he hadn't aged not one bit. His cold, small, dark eyes canvassed the room as he made his way towards the bar. His angular, pock marked face testified to a sinister possibility.

Arizona Ron was from the old school. He didn't

do any unnecessary talking and never repeated what he heard. If he didn't see it he wouldn't say it. He was a legend to those who knew him. If you didn't know him it was better that way. He wasn't the type to make new friends.

"Mr. Milo Sempier. You sprout like good oak. From good folks no doubt," Ron whispered in his hoarse voice next to Milo's ear as he took his hand in his. He kissed Milo on the cheek.

"Good to see you, Ron. You remember Sherrie?' Milo motioned to Sherrie, who was seated next to him.

Ron smiled, showing his platinum grill with the diamond in each of his front teeth. "Ms. Sherrie. You are more beautiful today than you were yesterday," Ron said, repeating his handshake and kiss on the cheek with her. Ron stepped back and looked at them both with the same sincere smile. "Jack would be proud of you Milos." He waved at the room around him. "And you, Ms. Sherrie, he loved you with all his heart as he did Milos' mother. Right Milos?" Ron asked Milo out of respect.

Milo nodded in agreement.

"How have you been Ron?" Sherrie asked. The last time she'd seen him was a year before Jack was killed. They had been best friends and she remembered how Jack used to tell her that besides his family, Arizona Ron could get his last breath if he needed it. And Jack didn't take things like that lightly.

"Beautiful. The reward is in the struggle," Ron answered, landing his cold, dark eyes on Sherrie. A gleam show in them when she smiled.

"I'm sorry to hear about the loss of your wife," Sherrie offered, feeling close to the man Jack was so fond of.

"Thank you. You share my pain. Maria was the most beautiful woman in the world. I'm sure God missed her as soon as he sent her down here for me," Ron responded. "And what about you? Milos has kept the dogs at bay?" Ron joked.

Not very many people called Milo by his full name. Even Jody rarely called him Milos. And then it was when she had beef with him. Milo felt warm inside that Ron called him Milos. It reminded him of how close Ron and his father were. The gleam in his eyes for Sherrie was born of respect and a gentleman's courtesy. Now he was hinting about what Sherrie's status was. Milo knew that Sherrie was absorbed in her work and that not many people could come close to meeting her standards.

Sherrie laughed in her sexy way that spoke of unfettered sincerity because it was almost the truth. Seeing Ron brought back so many memories of Jack and the way the three of them stayed up late playing three handed poker. Jack and Ron's friendship was so strong and sincere that it was joked at times that both were Sherrie's protector. Ron without the intimacy. "You know Milo," Sherrie said. "Not many can bare the standard of his father."

Ron turned wistful. "No man can turn a spade into a heart like Haitian Jack. Some may appear to come close, but upon closer inspection there is revealed some flaw that Jack has mastered," Ron observed, staring deeply into Sherrie's eyes.

"He used to say, 'You know better, you do better' with the cigar puffing." Sherrie chuckled, happy with the memory.

"My Bru was a true believer in manifesting success in perpetuity," Ron said this as he glanced around him at the scene.

"Let's get to a place more private," Milo suggested, leading the way to a sunken V.I.P. booth against the far wall secluded in the shadows. It was roped off in anticipation of Arizona Ron's arrival. Later they would head up to the V.I.P. room and spend time with Kilroy.

"So what have you been doing with yourself lately?" Sherrie asked, sliding into the cool booth, waiting for Ron to sit beside her. Milo was on the other side of her. He and Ron formed the ends of the horseshoe while she was positioned in the middle.

Ron settled into the soft leather. "Same lavish habits, two rings twenty carats," he said, splaying his long dark fingers over the table. On his pinky finger was a large diamond crusted ring radiating brilliant colors in the shadows, catching all available lights. "Still rocking the Isley's."

Sherrie was more comfortable than she imagined she would be. It was as if Ron was filling a void left open especially for him.

Milo looked on with a grin at Ron's nonchalant flamboyance. The interesting thing was that Ron cared nothing about these things, but it all came so natural to him. Where others had to make an effort at chivalry, he made no effort at all. He was a seamless piece of cool. Unchinked and as smooth as a newborn's ass.

Yet Milo knew the calculating steel menace hidden beneath the velvet glove. Killing a man is like spraying a can of Raid on a hive of roaches to him. One life held no more value than the other. Ron was the type to regularly practice being uncomfortable as a form of self-discipline and mind control. He exercised these muscles the way others exercised their biceps and legs to make them stronger. So that when others found a cold shower unbearable, Arizona Ron relished the opportunity to practice his discipline. Where others became impatient in long lines, Arizona Ron took it as another opportunity to strengthen his nerves and will his body to conform to his mental wish.

He'd developed through this method of personal discipline and control the ability to find weakness in others. He was a meticulous observer of people's characters and would often promote unease in others by his silence, watching them slowly break down. To be in his presence was to be drawn to a strength that emanated from a source more powerful than any man. Arizona Ron was plugged into the never-ending power of power.

Milo looked on as Sherrie engaged Ron in a memorable conversation about a time long ago when he'd flown in to assist Jack in a personal matter. They shared a laugh at the memory of Jack providing Ron with a car that only played country music. It was funny because after a night in that car Ron had taken up to singing a particular country song that complimented his lazy drawl. Once again, he'd turned what others might have taken as a negative and turned it into a virtue of power and control.

"Whatever happen to that car?" Sherrie asked, recovering from her giddy laughter.

Ron thought for a second. "Well, first the radio had to come with me," he answered with a smile. "Believe the rest was donated."

"You mean you kept the radio?" Milo asked, unbelieving.

"Of course. It played my intro to country."

They were enjoying themselves together. Sly Boogie came strolling by coming from the V.I.P. lounge. "Yo', Milo. That Betina got me open. I'ma have to slide back through," he lisped in his trademark twang.

"I feel you. I dig her myself," Milo answered, then watched another satisfied customer walk away from their booth into the main floor of the lounge.

"Kilroy mentioned something about a new player under contract. Say she a franchise draft pick," Ron interjected.

Sherrie sensed her evening being interrupted.

"Well, if that's what you like," she teased.

Ron lightly placed his dark hand over hers on the table. "Just theatre. Live theatre. It only makes the moment better. After all, don't you like sports?" Ron asked in a whisper.

"What kind?" Sherrie wrinkled her freckled nose.

"The kind where one player can make a difference."

Sherrie looked at him with a blank expression. This was not the first time he'd said something that made no sense to her. And she began the process of working on what he said like a complicated riddle that had the potential of folding out in layers to reveal a precious gem of insight.

Milo was grinning when he rose from his seat, signaling to Ron the staircase to the V.I.P. lounge.

Betina's petite, thick frame was shaped by a sheer pink ankle length negligee. She was casually seated next to Kilroy in obvious deep conversation. Well, Kilroy was doing all the talking—better yet—instructing in a low voice. Key words and phrases were accentuated with graceful splaying of his long tapered fingers. They were the only two in the room. Kilroy looked up when Milo led Arizona Ron into the room. Sherrie excused herself from their company to take care of some business in her office.

"Long time family," Kilroy said, rising from his seat with a smile. He hugged Ron with a familiarity that went back over decades. They were the same height and build, except one was dark and the other tan with freckles. Where Ron's head was shiny and bald, Kilroy had a flowing mane of flaming red hair that draped over his shoulders in Shirley Temple curls. Both were dressed impeccably in finely tailored suits.

Ron was pleasantly surprised to see Betina. She was darker than him, something that didn't seem possible was. Where he was a dry black, she bordered on purple, and eggplant black with a sheen. Her long silky hair hung loose over firm breasts, creating a river of dark strands between her cleavage. "Franchise," Ron said with a smile, breaking from Kilroy to approach Betina. "We must have the same mother because I can feel your heart beat," Ron said as he extended his hand to Betina.

"Is it beating fast?" she asked, placing her soft hand in his. Letting it rest in his dry palm.

"In rhythm with my own," Ron responded, showing his platinum framed porcelain façade.

"Then we must be family." Betina smiled a thousand watts. She felt him immediately as someone important and unlike any one else she'd ever met. She wondered where he came from. Kilroy seemed to have spokes in every corner of the globe.

Hutch appeared in the doorway, his stout body filling the frame. He was dressed casually in a leather peacoat, brushed suede pants and thousand eyes boots.

Milo was wondering when he'd arrive. "She finally let you go?" he asked, knowing Gwen would make him keep their ritual Friday night date. "Where y'all go?"

"Some new joint called DC3. It was on top of a fancy hotel. Cost me a car payment," Hutch answered, not complaining, just stating the facts as he looked around the room. He knew Arizona Ron when he saw him.

"You know Ron," Milo gestured.

Hutch moved towards the assassin.

Ron rose from his seat. He extended his hand. "Your name is like a government check. Good. See you've grown like hard math." Ron smiled, taking his seat.

Everyone was seated, saving the real talk for later when they were alone. Kilroy served everyone their drink of choice and signaled Betina to take the stage. She rose with feminine grace, uncrossing her legs and striding with knocking hips to the raised wooden platform. The lights dimmed to a soft mixture of a blue, red, and yellow glow. Betina was the center of attention as the long time friends sat back to enjoy a private show by a franchise player on a number one team. She moved with the certainty of a rare cat, basking in the knowledge she was in rarefied company. As she looked out into the room she was pleased that she had their full attention without the antics of those not used to seeing a beautiful woman and respecting her just the same.

A smooth Jamaican rhythm beat softly and hypnotically through hidden speakers. The soft lighting accentuated the lush curves of Betina's body. She moved sensuously to the groove, her motion sliding against the soft, sheer silk of her negligee. She was bare underneath except for a pink strand of cloth that gripped her waist and divided her round ass.

Her motions were grown up, not like the hard bounce, swing and strut of the first time Hutch had seen her, mesmerized by the way she clapped her ass like a pistol shot. No. This performance was for a more discerning crowd. One of maturity and exposure. She was a different woman. All hard edges gone, replaced by a supple invitation to an advanced look into the wiles of an intuitive woman. She induced a soft trance in her audience as she moved across the small stage as if gliding across ice.

Her beautiful body took on a different meaning. Where before she evoked notions of lust, she now commanded reference to art. To lines and curves. To height and dimension. To depth and perception. She'd transformed before their eyes. The two who appreciated her effort most were the ones smiling when the final drum tapped out. Kilroy and Arizona Ron were nodding their heads. They exchanged a knowing glance with one another. Each congratulating the other for years of survival and succeeding in the game. Betina was a rare treat deserving of an audience that understood perfectly the subtlety of the romance she'd introduced. Through a song and movement. Milo and

Hutch felt as if they'd been initiated into another level of manhood, seated in the same room with two generals of the game enjoying a show they couldn't describe if someone were to later ask them what they saw or felt.

Chapter Twenty Seven

"Come grandchild." G'Ma gestured to Dimp. He was watching her from the pool table in the game room as she cut a piece of cherry pie. G'Ma was in rare form as she moved around the brightly lit kitchen.

It was almost 10 a.m. and Milo was happy to see G'Ma up and around. She'd slept all day the day before, too tired to move. Jody was exhausted at the end of the night. She'd spent the day tending to G'Ma's every need, making sure that she took her medication and was comfortable in her motion bed. Jody was now reclining in a straw chair in the sunroom, occasionally laughing out at something she was reading in a novel.

Jasmine was only too happy to be of use helping out around the house. She was now beside G'Ma seasoning fish to put on the outside grill.

"Okay, G'Ma," Dimp responded. "Let me make this

last shot." He lined up the cue ball to slide a striped ball down the side of the rail into a corner pocket.

"Can you make that shot?" Milo asked Dimp with questioning eyes, prodding him. Milo stood to the side, resting against the wet bar on the far wall. "That's a tough shot nephew. I don't know..." Milo taunted.

Dimp was unmoved. He furrowed his brow in concentration, letting his tongue slide out the corner of his mouth in focused intensity. He snapped the pool stick against the cue ball and stayed frozen after the shot as the ball bumped against the striped ball. The cue ball struck the striped one with a soft knock, sending it rolling gently against the rail straight into the corner pocket. Dimp stood straight with victory and looked at Milo. "It's all in the stroke," he counseled before turning for the high stool at the kitchen counter where G'Ma was waiting with a smile.

Milo sauntered after him and sat on the next stool where G'Ma put a slice of cherry pie. "Luck," Milo said, cutting into his pie.

"There's no such thing as luck," Dimp replied, his mouth full of cherries.

"Child!" G'Ma said, looking at Dimp so that he would not talk with his mouth full.

The expression on her face was one satisfied with the spirit to chastise her grandson.

Milo was impressed with his nephew. Dimp was smart and competitive. Milo could already see that Dimp was going to be a factor in whatever filed of work he chose. But having a woman will never be a problem, maybe having too many. Throughout the morning he watched Dimp field calls from girls older than him on his cell phone. No sooner had he hung up with one, then another would call demanding his attention and made him smile. They were disappointed to find out that he was away from home all the way out in Chatsworth at his uncle's house.

Missy was out with Keashon. This provided a good opportunity for Dimp to spend time with G'Ma. Plus, Milo wanted to know what Dimp thought of his mother's new boyfriend.

"Why all them girls call you?" Milo asked, slicing into this pie. It was a juvenile question to test Dimp's awareness.

Dimp shrugged his shoulders, embarrassed that G'Ma heard Milo. She cut a quick eye at him waiting for his response no doubt. "They like me, I guess," he answered shyly, making sure to swallow the cherry pie in his mouth first.

Milo smiled, exchanging a wicked grin with G'Ma. "Why you think they like you?" Milo prodded, enjoying Dimp's shyness.

Dimp seemed to take a while to think about Milo's question. Milo was beginning to think the boy had suddenly loss his hearing. "I have no idea," Dimp answered humbly.

G'Ma smiled with her back turned, getting another cherry pie out of the oven.

Milo could see her cheeks spread from his angle. "Well, remember to treat all women right and fair. Find one girl that you like and that likes you more. Stick with her."

Dimp stopped short of digging his fork into his slice of pie. He looked up at Milo with a serious expression. "Why? When they all like me?"

Milo was amazed at how strong Dimp's face was. He had no flaw in his dark skin with thick, shiny black eyebrows and lashes. His large dark eyes were like bottomless wells under dark curly hair. "Because when you find the right girl, she's going to think she should be enough and won't like it if you have another girl too."

Dimp's face grew pensive, his fork still hanging over his pastry. "What if she do like it?"

Milo smiled again, this time catching quick eye contact with G'Ma as she opened the refrigerator. She was amused. "That's rare. If you find one like that, let me know," Milo said, spooning from the vanilla ice cream G'Ma set in front of him.

Jasmine came around the corner with the tray of seasoned fish in her hand. She stopped between Dimp and Milo on her way to the backyard. "When you find the right girl, you won't think of any one else. And if you find one that don't mind you being with other woman, run away from her as fast as you can. She's crazy and might try to cut your little thing off," Jasmine warned, snipping her fingers together like scissors.

"Jas!" Milo exclaimed, feeling the pain of her comment.

Jasmine gave a short laugh and rubbed her hand across Dimp's chin. "I'm just playing. No, for real though," she said quickly and turned into the sunroom laughing out loud.

Dimp looked at Milo for confirmation that Jasmine was being funny and assurance that his "little thing" would be okay. "Don't trip on Jas," Milo assured his young nephew.

"Ohhh ..." G'Ma exhaled with her morning effort. "I tink to sit out wit Jody in da sunroom," she said as she came around the counter and headed for the cool wicker chair confines of the place where Jody was enjoying her novel.

Dimp slathered his ice cream on what was left of his pie. "I'm too young to be thinking of that stuff anyway," Dimp said, speaking with his mouth full now that G'Ma was gone. He wanted to talk more about girls without her watchful eyes and ears.

"Yeah. You won't have to worry about that for a little while. Still, you not doing so bad right now. I didn't have that kind of action when I was your age."

Dimp looked up at him in surprise, as if Milo was ruining his image. "Serious?"

"Yeah, nephew. G'Pops had me go to an all boys school. No girls. And the ones on the block Missy chased away. She didn't want any girls around me." Milo reminisced.

"Mom didn't want you to have a girlfriend?" Dimp asked with a surprised lift in his thick eyebrows.

"Not even one. But you're lucky. You go to school with girls. And their parents have money so they should be alright. Don't they seem alright?"

"There's this one girl name Amber. Her mom is pretty too. She brings me candy to school. But this other girl named Brittany, she tries to bring me better stuff so I won't talk to Amber."

Milo chuckled. "Serious? Cool stuff?"

Dimp was enjoying himself now. "Yeah," he breathed out. "Friday she gave me a Will Smith CD. And Amber was mad too. I tried to tell her to be okay, but Amber wanted to talk to Brittany about it."

"See what I tell you? They don't like it when you have someone else on the side."

Dimp screwed up his face. "But we're not even old enough to have sex! And I only kissed Amber two times!"

Milo was laughing now. "Really? You kiss Brittany too?" he asked, trying to control the big smile on his face.

Dimp smiled with him. "Uncle," he said in a low voice. "Brittany showed me her chest. And she let me touch her."

Milo's brow furrowed. "Touch her where?"

"On her coochie," he whispered.

"Y'all do anything else?" Milo wanted to know.

"She let me grind her."

263

Milo nodded his head in thought. "So that's the one that brings you the CDs? Who's idea was that?"

"Hers. She just started bringing me stuff."

"Brittany..." Milo said aloud. "You know what her parents do? What kind of jobs they have?"

"No. I never asked her that. But her dad drives a Mercedes, the big one. And they own property. They rich," Dimp said as a matter of fact.

"Richer than me?" Milo grinned at him then.

Dimp gave this some thought. "I don't think so."

"Well, this Brittany girl sound kind of cool. You like grinding on her and touching her?"

"She likes it."

"Do you like it?" Milo asked again.

"It's alright. I like kissing better. Brittany always tastes like strawberry. Amber likes to kiss for a long time. Brittany doesn't," Dimp said.

"Which one do you like the best?"

"I like both of them for different reasons."

Milo started to tell him about keeping them both happy and what he quickly realized was a grown up way of dealing with his two girlfriends. He decided to let Dimp learn his lessons naturally so he would appreciate them. "G'Ma made some good pie nephew. Make sure you thank her before she goes to bed," Milo said, getting up to put his plate and bowl in the dishwasher. "You finished?" he asked from the other side of the counter.

"Yeah," Dimp said, stifling a yawn as he passed his

bowl and plate over to Milo.

"You not sleeping good?" Milo asked.

A shadow passed over Dimp's face with the question. "No. Not really."

"What you mean?" Milo pressed.

Dimp looked sadly to a spot over Milo's head. "I have bad dreams."

"What kind?" Milo was facing him now across the counter.

"Just bad," Dimp answered evasively.

Milo was silent for a few beats.

"How do you like your mom's new boyfriend?" he asked.

Dimp screwed his face up. "He alright," Dimp answered unconvincingly.

"He alright or is he not alright?" Milo asked pointedly.

"Sometimes..." Dimp faltered, then regained his purpose. "Sometimes he watches me and it make me feel funny."

"Watch you how? When you play or on the phone?" Milo's heart quickened.

Dimp looked up at him now. "When I use the bathroom. He watch me sometimes."

Milo could tell that this was making Dimp uncomfortable. "You tell your mom?"

"No."

"He's not supposed to watch you use the bathroom. When you sit or stand?" Milo asked.

"When I pee. He said he wanted to make sure that I was doing it right." He looked at Milo for some assurance that he was doing it right and for what else all this could mean.

"I'm sure you're doing it right. He shouldn't be watching you. Don't worry about it. You're doing everything right. Milo assured him as a slow fire burned inside of him at what Dimp just revealed. Milo came from around the counter and tapped him on the shoulder. "Come on. Let's play another game of pool. If you win, we'll go to the 3-arcade in Burbank."

"Cool," Dimp said excitedly. "Can G'Ma, Jody, and Jasmine come?" Dimp asked as he hopped off the stool.

"I don't think so. Jody and Jasmine might need to stay here and look after G'Ma. Hutch might come though."

"Uncle Hutch? Cool! Rack' em up, since I won the last game."

"We didn't even finish the last game." Milo protested.

"I still had more balls than you. Unless you want to finish this game. It's my shot." Dimp suggested hopefully.

Milo thought quickly. "I'll rack," he submitted, glad that Dimp's mind was off his revelation. Milo forced himself to concentrate on the game all the while sorting out in his mind the meaning of what Dimp told him.

Boring. That's what jail was. Boring. Meal time was like an indicator for what stage of the day it was. You never knew what time it was until either the noon medication issue time or the four p.m. count time to be soon followed by the five p.m. dinner. After that it was a dark span of time until you figured it was or had to be close to midnight. Most times your best calculations were wrong. When you think it must be near eleven at night because of the time you've spent alone, quiet in a cell, when actually only two hours have passed since the last medication issue at six p.m.

Billy Bob had his supply of magazines: XXL, Smooth, Black Men, and King. They all made him stress. He thought he would enjoy them, but the novelty soon wore off. He couldn't wear the clothes, drive the cars, buy the DVDs or get the new set of 24" rims for his Navigator. And the fine ass women showing their asses just made him sick. He wanted to hold Florence in his arms. Maybe get a cool blowjob. The way it looked they were trying to lock him up forever. The new music, watches, hot spots, and new methods to lovemaking meant nothing to him except as a reminder of his former life.

So Billy Bob lay on his bunk listening to the chatter around him. He'd know nothing more until either

Mr. Rubin came down for an attorney visit or he went to court. Until then life was just plain boring.

Billy Bob didn't know how long he'd been laying on his bunk. It had to be late by how clear the humming from the overhead florescent lights sounded against the quiet on the tier. A deputy was walking down the tier doing and early morning count. He flashed his light in on Billy Bob and seeing his eyes open he moved on.

"Barlow!" the deputy called into the next cell.

Billy Bob was waiting for Cecil to curse him out like he normally did when the deputy shined the light in his eyes. He didn't. This time there was an eerie silence. Billy Bob listened, his eyes looking at the ceiling.

"Barlow!" the deputy repeated, slamming his flashlight against the bars. The clanking rattled against the quiet like iron thunder.

The steel bars that made up the door slowly moved open. The deputy stepped into the cell and called Cecil again, poking him across the leg with his flashlight.

Billy Bob's heart was pounding in his chest as he listened for any sign of life. Then the alarm went off, soon followed by tapping booted feet. An announcement rang out over the static intercom, "Medical emergency Alpha row 4300." The intercom crackled dead. Billy Bob moved to the front of the cell and sat on the floor against the wall. He watched the crowd, mostly green uniformed legs moving around for position and white pant legs given priority to space. They all concentrated at the front of Cecil's cell. It looked serious.

Sheriff deputies with stripes on their shoulders and bars on their lapels milled about apart from the main group of regular deputies. They whispered among themselves. The medical staff were all inside Cecil's cell moving with lazy urgency. A stretcher was carried past his cell into Cecil's. Not long after, Cecil Barlow was brought out strapped into the stretcher. His body was limp under a white sheet that was pulled over his face. The procession of sheriff and medical staff filed past Billy Bob's cell, some taking the time to peer into the darkened cave. An old white Sheriff with a Lieutenant's bar on his lapel stopped in front of his cell and glanced casually in. Billy Bob was at his feet, seated on the floor watching him. It took a second glance for the Lieutenant to notice Billy Bob was there. He looked down at Billy Bob with an inspecting gaze. The locked eyes momentarily not saying a word. Sharing the death between them.

Long after the tier became empty and quiet, Billy Bob remained seated on the floor. He thought about nothing and everything. He filled up the loneliness with the reality of being alone in a cell, knowing that Cecil died alone in the cell next to him. Billy Bob was too numb to feel. Too numb to move. His head rested on his arms crossed over raised knees, eyes closed against the emptiness.

Chapter Twenty Eight

The sun was fading fast on the horizon after having done its duty for the day. Milo looked into the rearview mirror at Dimp who was on the phone sharing a private joke with a girl on the other end. Hutch was in the passenger seat chilling, bobbing his head to Ludacris' Red Light District. Milo coached the 2006 Lexus GS at a cool clip down the 405 freeway on his way to Missy's house to drop Dimp off after a full weekend of fun and games. Milo hadn't worked out how he would broach the subject of what Dimp had told him. *I'll just be straight up with her*, he thought to himself. He knew Missy would not want to believe it, but if Dimp said it, it had to be believed. Boyfriend or no boyfriend, love or no love. Dimp came first. Not to mention Milo's objection to her moving so fast with someone nobody knew.

When Milo pulled onto the posh LaDera Heights street he saw an unfamiliar rust colored Brougham on gold Dayton hundred spokes parked in the driveway. His anger was fresh in his chest when he saw Keashon and Missy coming out the front door laughing together, hugging arm in arm. Milo didn't bother pulling into the driveway and instead pulled to the curb, halfway blocking the driveway.

"Stay in the car, Dimp," Milo warned as he jumped out the driver's side into the street. He began taking long strides around the back of the car towards Keashon and Missy.

By the time Hutch got out the car Milo was already up the slight grade of driveway. He recognized the familiar menace in Milo's voice and hurried to catch up.

Milo took long strides up the inclined driveway looking straight into Keashon's eyes. Missy looked into her brother's face and saw there a determination that alerted a warning bell inside her. Before she could form the question or issue a command Milo was swinging heavy blows to Keashon's face. He caught him square in the nose, making blood squirt out like a squeezed citrus fruit.

"Milo! What?! What the fuck are you doing?" Missy screamed, standing away from the swinging arms. She looked at Hutch. "Stop him! Stop them!"

They were exchanging blows until Milo caught him again across the bridge of his nose, knocking him back into the rose bushes against the front of the house. He quickly advanced on Keashon and kicked him in the head as he tried to get up out of the rose bushes.

"Milo... stop!" Missy screamed, again looking to Hutch. "Hutch! My son is watching!"

Hutch looked back at a wide-eyed Dimp. He was staring out of the backseat window at the fight. Hutch ran over to pull Milo off of Keashon. Milo pulled free of his grip and advanced on Missy shouting, "This nigga watch Dimp take pisses and shit. He having bad dreams 'cuz this nigga a pervert!" Milo breathed hard.

Confusion raced across Missy's face as she looked back at her son. She looked over to Keashon who was just now rising from the dirt holding his bleeding nose. His clothes were dirty and disheveled. "Is this true?" Missy asked him.

"Hell no!" Keashon mumbled beneath the palm of his hand.

Milo tried to rush him again, but Hutch caught him around the shoulders. "Get outta here!" Hutch screamed to Keashon.

Keashon ran to his Cadillac and started the engine. Missy was banging against the windows. "Where the fuck are you going?! What is he talking about?!" Missy shouted.

Keashon pressed down on the accelerator, making Missy spin off the car and fall down to the ground. The Cadillac bounced down the driveway and slammed across the back of Milo's Lexus. Both cars rocked from the impact. The sound of crushing metal could be heard loudly in the dusk-night sky. Dimp was thrown away from the window and onto the floor. Keashon backed the Brougham up with a quick jerk and put it back in drive. He burned rubber around the crushed back end of the Lexus and made a quick left down the street.

Missy hurriedly limped down the driveway toward the Lexus. "Dimp! Dimp!" she screamed with tears rolling down her face. When she got to the car, Dimp was unconscious on the floor. She tried to open the door, but it was stuck. She jerked on it, her entire body pulling for the life of her son. She ran around to the other side of the car to try the other door. It came open with a quick jerk. She reached down to the floor and grabbed Dimp up in her arms and knelt down in the middle on the street. "Wake up, baby. Wake up," Missy whispered with her son cradled in her lap. She pulled him to her breast and rocked him against her body. "Please, Lord. Please," she cried over his head. She kissed his forehead and wiped the trickle of blood that ran down his temple. "Oh my baby," Missy cried, looking around her for help.

Milo knelt down beside her. "The ambulance is on the way, sis," he said, the sirens echoing closer to prove what he said was true.

Dimp stirred in her arms. "Dimp! Come on baby!" A smile show through the tears streaming down her face. She moved her hands over his hair and brushed at his cheeks. "Baby, come on. Wake up for Mommy," she whispered, still rocking him against her.

"Mom," Dimp said hoarsely. "Uncle Milo," he whispered.

"I'm right here, nephew. You alright? Don't move. Are you hurt?" Milo asked, kneeling on the asphalt facing Missy, Dimp between them.

Dimp opened his eyes and looked around him. First up into his mother's crying eyes and then over at Milo. "You were fighting." He smiled.

"Ohhh!" Missy exhaled and rocked him against her again, happy that he smiled.

"Yeah little man. Everything's alright. Just stay still," Milo advised as the ambulance turned the corner followed by a police car.

The Black female paramedic was the first to jump out the passenger side of the ambulance, followed by her male Hispanic counterpart. They converged on Missy and Dimp as they kneeled in the middle of the street. Missy was reluctant to let Dimp out of her grasp against prodding hands with reassurance from the paramedic.

The Black officers emerged from the squad car and moved over the scene, taking in the damaged Lexus with broken glass and fresh crushed metal at its rear. They motioned Milo to the rear of the Lexus to ask what the situation was. Missy was in no shape to offer anything as she was paying close attention to the care of Dimp.

One of the officers reminded Milo of Rolando. He was at 6'4 and 250lbs with Mississippi greasy black skin. He seemed to recognize who Milo was. He squinted his eyes as he held his small note pad in his hand to write down what Milo had to say. "You look familiar to me," Officer Brown said.

Milo was looking at the damage to his car and glancing over at Missy who was following Dimp to the back of the ambulance to sit inside for a check-up. "Yeah. My sister's friend crashed into my car," he said almost incoherently.

"Your name is Milo right?" Officer Brown asked.

"Yeah. Milo Sempier." He looked up at the questioner with a note of familiarity.

"I thought so. You own Haitian Jack's." Officer Brown said with a smile. "What happened here? Who did this to your ride and why is the boy in the middle of the street?" he wanted to know.

"My sister's boyfriend was parked in the driveway. We got into a fight and he got in his car and ran into mine. My nephew Dimp was in the backseat and got knocked around. He was unconscious for a minute." Milo rubbed his hands across his face in frustration.

Officer Brown was looking at Milo's torn shirt and dirty pants. "Why were you guys fighting?"

Milo looked over at Dimp. "Man... um... just a little argument that got out of hand." Milo went into boss mode recognizing that Officer Brown really wanted to help. "Yeah, it was just something that got a little heated. I'll take care of it myself. I'm not pressing charges or nothing. Cool?" He looked at the officer for the OK.

Officer Brown appraised Milo's reasoning. "You got it, Milo. We'll put a patrol around this house just in case he comes back. Does you sister want a protection order?"

"Does she have to be involved to do that?"

"Not officially, but I will need a description if I want to personally be on the lookout for him."

Milo gave Officer Brown a description of Keashon and an unspoken invitation to the V.I.P Lounge at Haitian Jack's.

Missy was told that Dimp was okay, but to keep on the lookout for any dizziness, sleeplessness, or fainting. He appeared to be fine and all tests were normal. When Missy finally got Dimp into the house and the neighbors dispersed she made Dimp a cup of cocoa and laid him down to rest. He fell asleep immediately. She went into his room periodically to check on him. She'd lower her head to his face to see if he was breathing.

Milo had his shirt off as he talked on the phone in the kitchen. He was leaned against the sink when Missy walked in with red-rimmed eyes from all the crying. She'd changed into a pair of shorts. Her leg was bandaged around the knee from her fall away from Keashon's car as he sped away. Missy walked up to Milo and hugged him around the waist, her head resting on his shoulder. "Missy's cool... naw... Gwen is on her way, she'll drop me off. Okay baby... see you in a minute," Milo said into the phone before hanging up.

Missy looked up into his face with an expression of disbelief and apology. "I'm sorry," She whispered. "I never imagined that he could do something like that."

Milo was silent. He held his sister in his arms, trying to absorb her pain.

"Thank you for being a big brother. For loving me enough to hurt my feelings. Loving me harder than anyone in my life. Thanks for remaining mentally strong to survive because my greatest strength is seeing yours," Missy confessed.

Milo continued to hold her as she silently wept against his chest. She was stronger than pride, he thought to himself.

"What's wrong baby? You're not yourself this evening. Tell Momma what's wrong," Joanne coaxed, as she snuggled against Big Red.

It was true. Big Red was not himself. He usually came to see Joanne baring gifts and a grandiose persona most likely due to having recently duped a drug dealer or setting someone up for an arrest, getting jacked, or murdered. But he was different this night.

His skin was sallow and his spirits low. He was visibly worried, something Joanne had never seen before in him. This was a turn off. She had to admit she'd been turned off a long time ago, but due to the fact that Big Red paid for her home and was responsible for her flower shop, she put up with him until she could find a way to get from under his large thumb.

They lay under the covers after having made love. It wasn't as passionate as it used to be. Big Red tried to blame this on the long hours he was working, but Joanne knew better. She prodded him for an explanation. "So you're going to keep it all to yourself? Let it grow inside you like a cancer?" She knew it was no use. She'd been trying for years to get him to admit that he was a crooked cop. She knew this but could not get any specifics. Maybe Big Red knew that she would betray him if she had the opportunity.

"It's just the hazards of law enforcement. It might be time for me to retire," Big Red admitted. The federal investigation was heavy on his mind. He hoped that he could make it to retirement or that he would be offered retirement in lieu of any criminal prosecution. Everything was in jeopardy. He was lucky not to be in jail. If the Feds found out all the allegations were true, Big Red knew that his whole life would be washed down the drain. He was surprised that his dick even got hard with the amount of stress he was under.

"You always tell me that," Joanne pressed. "I feel I deserve better than that. You treat me like I'm some whore," Joanne complained, looking for him to reassure her since that is exactly how she felt.

Big Red was silent next to her.

"You make me sick! I don't know why I put up with your shit!" Joanne fussed, getting out of the bed and moving to the foot of it. She stood naked with her legs apart staring down at him. "Can you answer me that? Why do I put up with you?"

Big Red gazed at her dark skin. The thickness of her legs. The pubic hair hanging from her pussy filling in the gap. Her titties stood firm, the nipples surrounded by large black circles. He waved his hand out to his sides, indicating the house.

"Motherfucker! You think this shit is charity? You think I got something for nothing?!" Joanne continued to argue with her hands on her hips. She didn't bother to cover up. She wanted Big Red to see exactly what it was he was in love with. Why he did the things he did for her.

Big Red still hadn't answered. He watched the blaze in her brown eyes. She stood tall at the foot of the bed. He'd been here before. Her arguing in vain for something she knew the answers to already. He didn't feel like stroking her ego or her pride. He needed stroking this night. He was the one in pain. Now here she was putting on one of her acts again. He just hated that he would have to get up to leave. He wasn't ready to leave, but he knew after this tantrum, the one he wasn't about to give in to this time, he would have to leave. He wished she would just get back in the bed and suck his dick.

"So you just gonna lay there and look at me like I'm stupid huh?" she hissed, looking down at him. *White cracker motherfucker*, she thought to herself. *If my husband wouldn't have died you would have never tasted this black pussy. You bastard.* She stared at him, cursing him in her mind. "You make me sick!" she said, and turned towards the bathroom. She sat on the toilet and starting peeing. The stream of urine shot into the toilet. She didn't close the door, forcing Big Red to listen to her piss.

Dumb ass black bitch, Big Red said to himself as he listened to her piss hit the toilet water. *How the fuck I get involved with this black bitch?* he asked himself. *I'm going through hell and all this bitch can do is think about herself.* Big Red was upset with himself for loving her.

Joanne flushed the toilet and stomped back into the room and took up position at the foot of the bed. She didn't even wash her hands. "You still here? Go back home. Or can't you stand to be around the bitch you got at home. Her titties don't stand like this huh?" Joanne asked, holding up her titties. "Her pussy ain't juicy like this huh?" She swayed her hips. "Her skin ain't tight like mine huh?" She rubbed her face. "Why don't you just divorce that dried up prune? Didn't you know that she would wrinkle like raisins? See, Black don't crack," she teased, jutting her chin out at him.

They had a love/hate relationship. Each hating each other for needing one another. And loving each other for the fulfillment of that need. Every now and then this wound had to be opened for all its ugliness. They hated themselves for the need and the slicing of the wound to reveal the putrid puss inside.

Big Red threw the covers off of him. He had to leave. He couldn't take anymore. So much was on his mind at a time when Joanne decided to spaz out. He didn't know where he would go. Maybe to the bar, but then he'd have to go home drunk. And that in itself would be murder because his wife would nag him so tough that he'd end up leaving again. He couldn't divorce her because she'd leave him destitute; homeless and without a pension. But he had to leave.

"You leaving? Good! Get your ass out of my house! Yeah, you bought it. So what! Get the fuck out if you leaving!" Joanne screamed, privately upset that he was leaving. She was being denied her act. She wasn't finished yet and he was cutting her performance short. "Don't leave. I'm sorry," she pleaded.

It was too late. Big Red looked back at her sadly as he opened the front door. She'd killed his spirit with her black venom. Cut his balls off with her revenge. He let out a deep sigh and closed the door behind him.

"Leave then nigga! Fuck you!" Joanne screamed, yanking the door back open. "Go back to that dried up prune motherfucker! Tired ass cracker!" she yelled.

Big Red opened the car door and got in. He tried

not to move too fast letting her know he was running from her tirade. He took deliberate steps and eased into the driver's seat shutting the door on her continued insults. The car was parked in the driveway. It was dark outside. Through the front window he could see her mouth moving, shouting obscenities. He turned the ignition. Something strange happened. The starter didn't catch immediately. Big Red heard a beeping sound. It all took less than a second. Big Red knew what it was before the thought formed in his mind. The explosion filled the night sky, knocking Joanne back into the house. In her driveway, Big Red's car was ablaze, the smell of burning rubber and gasoline filled the air. Joanne lay naked, unconscious on the floor of her living room as flames licked at t

Chapter Twenty Nine

When Milo woke up, Jody was sitting in an overstuffed chair in the corner of the master bedroom. She was bathed in morning light from the window behind her. A small book was in her hand as she read from it. The words formed on her lips, but now words escaped. She was deep in concentration. Milo watched her from hooded eyes for a while. He was content to lay in the peace of their bedroom watching his wife read from the purple book with cursive writing on its cover, her small hands holding it from its base.

Milo took a deep breath and thanked God that he was able to wake up once again and take part in the bounty of God. He silently prayed that the Lord would use him for a good purpose and forgive him his sins. He silently thanked the Lord for the mercy shown him in his life and for the blessings seen and unseen that have been bestowed upon him. He asked that the Lord shield him from the wicked and merciless plots devised by Satan.

"How did you sleep?" Jody asked from across the room, sensing that Milo was awake.

Milo opened his eyes slowly, a smile spread across his lips. "Good. How long have you been up?"

"Long enough to know that my love for you is true. How are you feeling?" she asked crooking her finger into the page she was reading and lowering the book to her lap.

Milo thought about the horrible events of the day before. He was thankful that Dimp and Missy were all right. It seemed like an important chapter was closed that was causing him some irritation. "Cool," he responded, stretching under the covers. "What are you reading?" he asked, stretching his hands to his side as if reaching for Jody.

Jody smiled and flipped open the book to the page she had marked with her finger. She read, "Sometimes we find satisfaction in self-pity. The reason is that it is our nature to find satisfaction in love; and when we are confined to ourselves we begin to love ourselves, and then self-pity arises because we fill our limitation." Jody looked over the book at Milo. Her large hazel eyes were smiling at him. "Want me to finish?"

Milo nodded.

"But the love of self always brings dissatisfaction, for the self is not made to be loved; the self is made to love." Jody marked her place again and placed the book in her lap. She looked up at Milo. "I love you," she whispered across the room.

"I love you, too, sunshine. How's my son doing?" He nodded towards her stomach. "All this drama isn't affecting him is it?" He could have been asking this for Jody.

Jody smiled at his thoughtfulness. "Your son's okay," she answered cryptically.

"Good. I'd hate for him to come out with all this stuff unresolved in his head like he had to take somebody's fade."

"He's a lover not a fighter, just like his daddy. But I'm sure he won't be a punk. Just like his daddy," Jody joked. "Shall I continue?" she raised the book.

Milo nodded.

Jody cleared her throat. "The first condition of love is to forget oneself. One cannot love another and oneself at the same time, and if one says, 'If you give me something I will give you something in return,' that is another kind of love, it is more like business." Jody closed the book and placed it in her lap. She looked over at Milo, watching him contemplate the words she'd just read.

"Well... at least now I know you aren't over there reading pornography," he joked.

Jody was out of her chair like a cat, jumping onto the bed. She straddled Milo and began kissing him all over his face. Between his smiling lips. On his raised cheeks. Across his thick eyebrows. Squarely on his broad nose. She wrestled the covers off him and fought her way to his underwear. "Oh! Look what we have here," she said in surprise, looking at his erection. "So it's you who are having pornographic thoughts." She laughed.

"Still I rise." Milo smiled.

"Indeed you do," she responded, pulling his erection through the opening in his boxers and placing her full lips over his swollen head.

The phone rang.

Jody continued to suck as Milo picked up the phone. "Hello," he managed through clenched teeth. "OK." He hung up just as quickly as it had rung.

Jody raised her head up. "Who was that?"

"Kilroy," he answered looking down the length of his body at her.

She smiled and bent her head back over the swollen meat in her petite hands and continued wishing Milo a good morning.

Sometimes a little gangsterism is needed Milo thought. All the pieces were falling together. Now, all he had to do was call Rubin and let him know that Big Red was dead, if he didn't know already. The day was starting out good. He needed to hear that it was enough to get Billy Bob out of jail. Between the feeling of success and Jody massaging him so well, Milo came with a burst inside her mouth. She continued to smile, squeeze, and suck the morning nectar of him while groaning in pleasure and ecstasy.

By the time Milo made it downstairs after show-ering and satisfying Jody under the spray of water, Jas-mine was in the kitchen making peach danishes from scratch. Milo was happy to see G'Ma lounging in the sunroom sipping on herbal tea instead of still laying in her bed too tired to get up.

"Hey, honey," Jasmine greeted him warmly when he came into the kitchen.

"That smells good, like peaches. What you got in the oven?" Milo asked as he was on his way to wish G'Ma a good morning.

"Pastries," Jasmine said quickly as she moved around the kitchen. "Hutch is on his way and Missy said to call her."

Milo nodded his head at the messages that he must have missed while he was in the shower with his wife making love. He turned toward the sunroom and leaned over G'Ma's wooly head to give her a kiss on the cheek.

G'Ma reached her dark hand up to Milo's cheek as he kissed her. "Top of the morning grandchild. How sweet of you. Have a seat awhile," she said, tapping the seat next to her.

Milo was glad to have a seat. The sun glanced ac-ross G'Ma's wooly oiled hair. Milo was casually dressed in a pair of sweats and a t-shirt. He relaxed in the wick-er love seat next to G'Ma, taking in her fresh cinnamon scent. She set her teacup onto the glass table in front of them and relaxed back into the seat with a satisfied exhalation. "'Tis a beautiful morning don cha tink?" G'Ma asked, looking out into the back yard and over the pool.

"Yeah, it's shaping up nice, G'Ma." Milo answered, knowing something else was on G'Ma's mind. He patiently waited for her to ask him the direct question. He didn't have to wait long.

"So dat boy Missy was seein'... he gon' away for good?" She was looking Milo in his eyes now.

G'Ma could have asked him about a number of things and he wouldn't have been surprised. Her question made him think of something he should have given some thought to. Never leave an enemy to fight again. Destroy him completely. "I can't really say, G'Ma," Milo admitted.

"Watch out for him," G'Ma warned with sage advice. She continued to look into Milo's face. "Ronnie still here?" she asked seriously. G'Ma had been calling Arizona Ron "Ronnie" ever since her son Jack had introduced him to her. That was so long ago. Ron considered G'Ma as dear to him as his own mother.

"I haven't heard from him today, but I believe he's still here. You know he can't leave without saying goodbye to you." Milo smiled with this.

"Better not. Maybe Sherrie wants him to stay?" G'Ma had an amused expression on her face.

So she feels that too huh? Milo asked himself, looking into G'Ma's deep brown eyes. "Maybe G'ma. It might be good for her."

Jody appeared at the edge of the sunroom looking delicious in a pair of white linen pants and black wife-beater. "Hutch here and you have a phone call," she said to Milo as she moved into the room smiling at G'Ma. As Milo vacated the seat next to G'Ma, Jody sat down, kissing her on the cheek. "Good morning."

When Milo walked into the kitchen, Hutch was already fussing with Jasmine about the peach danish she was putting on a plate. "Look boy, I'm not Gwen. You better go sit down somewhere," Jasmine suggested as she scooped pastries off the pan and onto plates.

Milo caught Hutch's attention. He turned away from Jasmine, forgetting the witty reply he had planned. "Bru." He extended his hand for dap. "Jasmine tripping." Hutch nodded his head towards Jasmine hoping Milo would offer a word or two on his behalf.

Milo shrugged his shoulders as he reached for the phone.

Jasmine stuck her tongue out at Hutch.

"Hello," Milo said into the phone. "You gone? G'Ma wants to see you. She say you better not leave without saying goodbye... Sherrie won't like it either I bet. Yeah, that was nice work. The construction crew is going to have a hard time putting that one together... Okay... I'll let her know... Later, Bru," Milo finished, hanging up the phone.

"Was that Ron?" Jasmine asked, closing the refrigerator with a jug of milk in her hand.

"Yeah. He say he got to roll. He'll be back though," Milo responded.

"I think he'd be good for Sherrie," Jasmine offered with a sly grin.

"You not the only one." Milo nodded towards the sunroom.

"G'Ma?" Jasmine was pleasantly surprised.

Milo nodded in the affirmative.

"Then it's all set," Jasmine pronounced.

Hutch had been sulking until Jasmine put a danish in front of him. "Don't Ron got some say so in this?" he asked.

"We do the choosing. Y'all ain't got a say in nothing," Jasmine teased.

Milo nodded his head in agreement. Hutch had to be reminded that this was true.

"Don't he have a bunch of property in Arizona? Like a ranch on a million acres or something like that?" Jasmine asked.

"Yep," Milo answered.

'You think Sherrie would move to Arizona?" Hutch asked Jasmine since she seemed to know so much about women.

Jasmine shrugged her shoulders.

Milo for the first time thought about what it would mean for him if Arizona Ron wanted Sherrie to move away. He hoped that if they did hook up, Ron would move and Sherrie could stay. Milo took a bite of the danish Jasmine gave him as these thoughts ran through his mind. He wasn't surprised that Arizona Ron had to roll like Michelin. It was only right after the deed had been done. He didn't know when he'd be back, but whenever it was, it would be right on time.

Chapter Thirty

The cute district attorney looked disappointed. She was the first person Billy Bob saw when he was escorted into the courtroom in platinum ankle and handcuffs. The deputy led him to a chair beside Mr. Rubin. Before he sat down he turned to wink at Florence and his mother who sat side by side. Milo, Hutch, and Dubb were behind them in the second row. Billy Bob's eyes gleamed, reflecting the dapper attire and gold diamonds his family casually wore. They looked beautiful to him. A reminder of reality against the hell he'd been in where everything was one of two colors—neither bright nor vibrant.

 The Judge entered through a door behind the raised desk he moved towards. He sat in the fat leather chair and looked out over the courtroom. "Do the people want to be heard before I rule on this motion?"

the Judge asked, looking over at the district attorney.

The day before, Mr. Rubin had gone down to the jail to see Billy Bob. He explained that the cop who arrested him had been blown up in a car accident. Billy Bob smiled then, exchanging a knowing glance with Mr. Rubin, who'd been involved with defending the family of Milo for over a decade. Mr. Rubin explained that they would be having a dismissal hearing due to the fact that the cop was the arresting officer and he was under federal investigation. Any testimony he could have provided or any notes he gathered investigating any crimes alleged against Billy Bob were tainted and inadmissible in court. *Up out this motherfucker,* Billy Bob had thought to himself as Mr. Rubin explained the situation.

The chubby district attorney stood up. She was very pretty and Billy Bob once again paid attention to her every move. She looked over briefly at him and turned towards the judge. "Your Honor, the people are in no position to move forward at the present time," she said briefly and stood for the judge's reply.

The judge seemed agitated as he shuffled some paperwork on his desk. He looked up suddenly with a sigh and peered over his round gold-rimmed glasses at Billy Bob. "Mr. Mason," he took on a fatherly tone, "to take a life is no small matter. And if you did a fraction of what is in these files here." He patted the folder in front of him. "Then you are a dangerous road that will lead back to me."

He glanced at the people in the audience then turned his eyes back on Billy Bob. "From the looks of it you have a very supportive family. Most young men who sit where you sit, have no one here for them. I suggest you take stock of your life before you end up dead or in jail for the rest of your life. You don't get many chances to roll again," the judge said, done with his fatherly duty. He cleared his throat and squared his shoulders. "Mr. William Mason is free to go home. All charges are dismissed without prejudice." He looked over at the district attorney. "Do the people plan to re-file this case for prosecution?"

She seemed uncertain. "Well, I'm sure law enforcement will continue to investigate any outstanding crimes. The people reserve the right to prosecute should the need arise."

The judge looked over at Billy Bob. "Mr. Mason, keep your nose clean. Go to school or something. You're free to go," he said, folding up the papers on his desk.

As Billy Bob was being led back through the door in which he'd come he looked out at his family. His mom and Florence were hugging each other. Milo winked at him. Dubb was excited and had to be escorted from the courtroom because he made so much noise shouting "HoodRich" over and over again. Billy Bob couldn't wait to get out. He knew processing would take all day. He wouldn't actually be free until at least six or seven at night.

When Billy Bob got back to his cell after the customary waiting in dirty holding cages for hours, he was finally called to be escorted up to his row. He started to call Cecil's name. Then he remembered that he was no longer next door.

His cell was stocked with pastries, candy, cup-o-noodles, trail mix, and cosmetics. None of this stuff would have any meaning on the streets. He didn't know anyone else on the row so he decided to leave everything in the cell for the next guy who happened to come through. He lay down on his bunk, looking out onto the tier where the overhead light danced across the back of a giant cockroach that inched its way along the wall. He watched the bug until it was out of sight, all the while thinking of what he would do first.

Nothing seemed real to him. Not until he was actually on the bricks would he feel free. Now that he knew it was time to go, the orange jumpsuit seemed that much more brighter and uncomfortable. He couldn't wait to put on his own clothes and drape his platinum chain around his neck. He could feel the wood grin on the steering wheel of his Navigator. He didn't realize that he was smiling until he thought of Drak and a frown formed on his face. *I gotta go see Drak's grave*, he thought to himself. The realization that Drak wouldn't be waiting for him when he got out made him sad. He couldn't think anymore. Really couldn't be happy. He lay somber on his rack until a deputy appeared at his door with orders for him to get his stuff together. He was leaving. Billy Bob left everything in the cell. There was nothing in it that he wanted except his personal letters.

"Milo, I can't thank you enough for what you did for my son," Elaine said, giving Milo a tight hug when he stepped through the front door. She let him go and turned to Hutch. "Hey, Mr. Man. You wanna hug too?" she asked seductively.

Hutch was tempted to feel her under the sheer print sundress. Her ass and hips forced the fabric to tighten at the curves. She was looking delicious as usual. "Wish I could," he said, holding up the platinum wedding ring on his finger.

"You were supposed to marry me years ago. If you would have stopped back by that time we might be married right now," she teased, referring to the time he and Milo stopped by after Billy Bob shot that guy who gunned Milo down in the street. Milo had come by to check on Billy Bob fresh from the hospital and give her some cash and gift certificates.

Hutch smiled. "No doubt about that," he said.

Milo moved into the living room. "Where you boy at?"

Billy Bob appeared at the end of the hallway, his

body still wet from the shower. His platinum chain hung to the rim of the towel wrapped around his waist. "What's up, Bru?" he asked with a giant smile on his face.

Milo met him in the middle of the living room to give him a hug. "How you feel?" Milo asked, stepping back from him, not minding that his cashmere blazer was damp.

"Better now."

"Stop by Haitian Jack's later on. I got someone who wants to meet you," Milo said.

"Who that?" Billy Bob asked eagerly.

"Don't trip." Milo turned to Elaine. "You come to."

Elaine smiled, jangling her diamond bracelets around her wrists. "Oh, don't worry. I'll be there."

"We out. Got business to handle," Milo said as Hutch led the way out the front door.

"Damn! Milo, when you cop this? What happen to the Lex?" Billy Bob asked, moving off the porch towards the driveway still wrapped in the towel.

"Just picked it up," Milo answered. The setting sun shown the deep purple gloss of his new BMW 760. It was squatted on 22" chrome rims with magenta spokes. The windows were tinted lavender. "The Lex is a long story," Milo said with a wave.

"I need to ride with you!" Billy Bob exclaimed as he moved around the big body BMW. "This joint is fat! It's a monster! Where you on your way to?" He looked up hopefully from the other side of the car.

Milo looked at Elaine for an unspoken instruction. "I got business, Bru. Ride with Moms. I'll be at the club when you get there."

When Milo and Hutch pulled off, Billy Bob was standing on the porch with Elaine. They hugged each other around the waist. It was amazing to Milo how much Billy Bob had grown. He put his hand over his heart as he pulled off down the street, happy that Billy Bob came through without a scrape.

Haitian Jack's was boiling with the excitement and energy of an extra inning game. It was filled to capacity with the beautiful and the bold. Players shooting pool and dime pieces at the bar sipping bright colored drinks. Milo was coming out the back office when Billy Bob came through door. His mom, Elaine, was next to him.

The guest DJ announced his arrival, "And the man y'all be hearing about and waiting for is here. Billy Bob back from the belly of the beast." There were applause and cheers from those who'd either heard of or knew Billy Bob personally. Milo met him in the foyer.

"Thought you wouldn't make it," Milo said, aware that all eyes were on them.

Billy Bob brushed at his suit jacket. "Had to represent, Bru," Billy Bob responded with a smile, flipping the lapel of his Hugo Boss suit jacket. A white skull cap peeked from under his Bossalino hat. He was looking gangster.

"My type of get up," Hutch said as he walked up and gave Billy Bob dap. "And you looking right," he said to Elaine. She rewarded him with a smile.

"Come on. I got somebody who wants to meet you," Milo said, gesturing for him to follow him to the V.I.P. room.

Billy Bob looked up at the dance floor. He spotted Missy immediately. Her long black hair being thrown by her energy on the dance floor. He followed Milo up the stairs leading to the V.I.P. room.

Billy Bob was amazed at the sight of Betina on the stage. She was making her ass bounce to a Lil Jon growl as he commanded her to shake her ass. Then Billy Bob couldn't believe his eyes when he noticed The Game lounging on a leather love seat.

You know Game right?" Milo said.

Game got up from his seat. "Call me Charles," he said with a crooked smile. "I heard a lot about you. Dre let me listen to your demo and I wanna put you on my album."

Billy Bob tried to be cool, but his insides were jumping like pop rocks. "That's cool. You still with G-Unit?" he asked, trying to confirm the rumors.

Game smirked. "Naw. That was then. It's Black Wall Street now."

"I feel you," Billy Bob said, giving Game dap and then moving to the couch with Game to enjoy the show and chat some more.

"I'm out. Holla if you need anything," Milo said as he dipped out to head to the main floor.

Sherrie was at the bar when Milo pulled up beside her with Elaine in tow.

"I'm going to dance," Elaine said, peeling off, leaving Milo at the bar with Sherrie.

"You're straight?" Milo asked, noticing her dour expression.

She looked up at him. "Where's Ron at?" she asked.

Milo smiled. "He had to shake for a minute. He'll be back though."

"When?"

"I've never known you to be open like that," Milo teased.

Sherrie didn't respond.

"G'Ma say he might be the only one right for you."

"She did?" Sherrie asked in surprise, recognizing the green light.

Milo nodded his head.

Sherrie's expression brightened. "I'm glad everything worked out for Billy Bob."

"Yeah, me too." Milo sighed, taking a seat next to her.

They sat silently looking out over the success and activity of the night. Everything had worked out, Milo thought appreciatively.

It was almost Midnight when Missy found Milo by the pool tables talking to Kwame Brown, who had just been traded to the Lakers from the Wizards. "I'm going home, brodda," she said, then looked up at Kwame, offering an inviting smile. "Hi. You're tall. You play basketball or something?"

Kwame extended his hand. "I'm Kwame. Yeah, I play for the Lakers."

"That figures," Missy said, dismissing him. She turned to Milo and gave him a sweaty embrace. "I'll call you when I get home. I have to stop by the babysitter to pick up Dimp."

"Cool. Be careful." Milo advised, before Missy could walk away. He watched her stop for a minute and talk in animated gestures to Jody and Sherrie by the bar. They laughed together and touched on the arm or shoulder to emphasize a point or respond to one well received.

Milo was having a conversation with a local businessman who was trying to interest him in some cross promotional opportunities with his surf shop when Milo saw Missy finally leave out the front door.

Missy was exhausted. Dimp was ready to go to bed.

He'd been woken up at the babysitter's house for the ride home. He immediately trudged to his room when they got into the quiet house. Missy reminded him to take off his clothes before he got into bed. She knew how tired he was and would simply lay across the covers. Missy undressed as she made her way to her bedroom in preparation to take a quick shower.

She was in her bra and panties when she checked her messages, seated on the edge of the bed. Several calls ended with no one saying a word. Then she heard Keashon's voice on the sixth call. "You know I didn't do it. Why haven't you returned my calls? We need to talk." He sounded at first casual then his voice turned angry. Missy hadn't returned any of his calls since Milo beat him up. On her way to the shower she heard the front door close. Missy reached under the bed and grabbed her chrome .380. Her fingers tightened around the grip. It couldn't have been Milo because she just left him at the club. G'Ma was in Chatsworth and she wouldn't be coming into the front door at two in the morning. Missy tiptoed out the bedroom and into the hallway.

A shadowy figure dashed across her line of sight. She quickly moved to the edge of the hallway and ducked inside the bathroom halfway down. She moved behind the door, listening for the inevitable footsteps. The gun was raised over her shoulders. Then she heard it. The hard wood floorboard creaked under the weight of the intruder. She waited, sweat greasing her palm against the warm metal of the gun. When Missy burst from the bathroom, the intruder was right in front of her, startled with his mouth open and eyes wide. The gun was pointed right at his face. Missy let off three quick bursts, sending bullets through the dark ski mask. The heavy body crumpled to the floor at her feet. Missy was shaking. She knelt down to peel the ski mask back. Keashon?

Missy heard something behind her. She looked back. Dimp was at the door of his bedroom with an aluminum bat in his hand.

"Go back in your room, Dimp!" Missy shouted.

Dimp didn't move. He stood there with the bat in his hand looking at the dead man in his house.

"Shit!" Missy hissed, rising to grab the phone in the living room. She dialed 911 and then called Milo.

Haitian Jack's was quiet except for the employees and a few friends who sat around the bar exchanging jokes and stories. Milo's cell phone rang. It was an odd ring. Jody, who was seated next to him, looked at Milo strangely. Milo put the phone to his ear. "Hello," he said into the tiny device. The blood drained from his face. "What!?" The air was knocked out of him. "In the house... Dead! I'll be right there," Milo said, hanging up the phone. He looked around him for a split second as his friends looked at him for an explanation. "That was Missy... and..." He was at a loss for words. He shot up out his seat and dashed for the door. Hutch was right behind him.

When Milo pulled onto Missy's street, the block was ablaze with the colors of paramedics and police officers. It looked like what it was in front of Missy's house: a murder scene. Sleepy neighbors braved the early morning frost to be nosy. Hutch and Jody managed to catch up and ride with him. They were followed by Jasmine and Sherrie. Milo pulled up to the curb careful to leave a way for the official vehicles to leave.

Missy was huddled with Dimp on the back of a fire rescue truck parked in the middle of the street. Milo marveled at the response in her rich neighborhood. He thought back to when his father died on the block, the only cars were one squad and an ambulance. He didn't remember the immediacy of the situation that he witnessed here. He jumped out the BMW and ran towards the cordoned off section of block, behind which Missy and Dimp sat. Missy saw him at the edge of the commotion followed by Hutch, Sherrie, Jody, and Jasmine. A detective stopped them at the yellow tape.

"That's my sister." Milo said.

"We're all her family," Sherrie joined in, letting the officer know they would not be turned back.

He lifted the yellow tape for them.

Milo was the first to reach Missy and Dimp. They hugged, quieting the confusion around them.

Forensics experts and detectives moved in and out of Missy's house with briefcases and notepads. The young white detective that let them under the tape came over.

"Maybe you guys want to get out of here. We've gotten enough out of your sister for the night," he said compassionately. "Just fill out this paper work so we can know where to contact her." He handed Milo an official form attached to a wooden clip board.

Keashon was still dead in the house. One thing all murder scenes had in common were that it took a long time to get the body away.

"I can't go back in there," Missy said from the back seat of Milo's car. She hugged Dimp close to her, sharing the blanket she was wrapped in with him.

"Don't worry about it. We'll get your stuff out of there. It's about time you shook the spot anyway." Milo comforted his sister, thinking that it would be impossible even for him if Missy still lived there. Even after finding BoDeen dead in the driveway. She stayed. But to kill someone in your own house, he knew, took something out of you.

What a day, Milo thought to himself as he turned onto the 405 freeway Chatsworth. G'Ma will like having Dimp there, Milo knew. The sun was hinting at an early sunrise by the time Milo approached Chatsworth's off-ramp. He looked in the rear view mirror at his sister. She was strong, he thought to himself. *We'll get through this together*, he promised. He caught her eye contact in the mirror. She smiled, proof that she heard him though he didn't say a word. There was no room for 'I told you so' or 'you shoulda did this or that'. The only room they had was for support and love for one another.

This book is in memory of

My Grandfather

Cecil Barlow

He died in prison in 2004.

And my uncle:

Andrew Barlow

1969-1997

A tragedy born of the ghetto.

I love y'all.

Rest in peace.

SOUR:

HoodSweet Pt. 2

Written by:

Isiko Cooks

At Pleasant Valley State Prison

On June 23, 2005

On C Yard- Bldg.2 – Cell 234

rawest ever. truest ever. realest ever.

desire. motivation. Dedication.

Peace. Power. Position.

MANIFEST SUCCESS !!!

Sour

your game is...

A KING PRODUCTION

All I See Is The Money...

Female Hustler

A Novel

JOY DEJA KING

Prologue

Nico Carter

"I don't know what you want me to say. I do care about you—"

"But you're still in love with Precious," Lisa said, cutting me off. "I can't deal with this anymore. You're still holding a torch for a woman that has moved on with her life."

"Of course I have love for Precious. We have history and we share a daughter together, but I want to try and make things work with you."

"Oh really, is it because you know Precious has no intentions of leaving her husband or is it because of the baby?"

"Why are you doing this?" I shrugged.

"Doing what... having a real conversation with you? I don't want to be your second choice, or for you to settle for me because of a baby. Nobody even knows about me. I'm a secret. You keep our relationship hidden like you're ashamed of me or something."

"I'm not ashamed of you. With the business I'm in and the lifestyle I'm in, I try to keep my personal life private. I don't want to make you a target."

"Whatever. I used to believe your excuses, but my eyes have been opened. I'm a lot wiser now. I've played my position for so long, believing that my loyalty would prove I was worthy of your love, but I'm done."

"Lisa stop. Why are you crying," I said, reaching for her hand, but she pulled away. "I was always upfront with you. I never sold you a dream."

"You're right. I sold myself a dream. More like a fairytale. But when I heard you on the phone with Precious that fairytale died and reality kicked in."

"What phone conversation?" I asked, hoping Lisa was bluffing.

"The one where you told Precious she and Aaliyah were the loves of your life and nothing would change that, not even the baby you were having with me. It was obvious that was the first time you had ever even mentioned my name to her."

"Lisa, it wasn't like that," I said, stroking my hand over my face. "You didn't hear or understand the context of the entire conversation." I shook my head; hating Lisa ever heard any of that. "That conversation was over a week ago, why are you just now saying something?"

"Because there was nothing to say. I needed to hear you say those words. I knew what I had to do and I did it."

"So what, you're deciding you don't want to deal with me anymore? It's too late for that. We're having a baby together. You gonna have to deal with me whether you want to or not."

"That's not true."

"Listen, Lisa. I'm sorry you heard what I said to Precious. I know that had to hurt, but again I think you read too much into that. I do care about you."

"Just save it, Nico. You care about me like a puppy," Lisa said sarcastically.

"I get it. Your feelings are hurt and you don't want to have an intimate relationship with me any longer, I have to respect that. But that doesn't change the fact you're carrying my child and I will be playing an active role in their life so I don't want us to be on bad terms. I want to be here for you and our baby."

"You don't have to worry about that anymore. You're free to pursue Precious and not feel obligated to me."

"It's not an obligation. We made the baby together and we'll take care of our child together."

"Don't you get it, there is no baby."

"Excuse me? Are you saying you lied about being pregnant?"

"No, I was pregnant, but..."

"But what, you had a miscarriage?"

"No I had an abortion."

"You killed my child?"

"No, I aborted mine!"

"That was my child, too."

"Fuck you! Fuck you, Nico! You want to stand there and act like you gave a damn about our baby and me. You're such a hypocrite and a liar."

"You had no right to make a decision like that without discussing it with me."

"I had every right. I heard you on the phone confessing your love to another woman and the child you all share together. Making it seem like our baby and me was some unwanted burden. Well now you no longer have that burden. Any child I bring into this world deserves better than that."

"You killed my child because of a phone conversation you overheard. You make me sick. I think I actually hate you."

"Now you know how I feel because I hate you too," Lisa spit back with venom in her voice.

"You need to go before you meet the same demise as the baby you murdered."

"No worries, I have no intentions of staying. As a matter of fact, I came to say goodbye. I have no reason to stay in New York."

"You're leaving town?"

"Yes, for good. Like I said, there is nothing here for me. I don't want to be in the same city as you. It would be a constant reminder of all the time I wasted waiting for you," Lisa said, as a single tear trickled down her cheek. "Goodbye, Nico."

I watched with contempt and pain as Lisa walked out the door. I couldn't lie to myself. I almost understood why she chose not to keep our baby. I wasn't in love with Lisa and couldn't see me spending the rest of my life with her. The fucked up part was it had nothing to do with her. Lisa was a good girl, but she was right, my heart still belonged to Precious. But I still hated her for aborting our baby. I guess that made me a selfish man. I wanted Lisa to bless me with another child that I could be a father to, but have her accept that she would never have my heart.

At this moment, it was all insignificant. That chapter was now closed. Lisa was out of my life. In the process, she took our child with her and for that I would never forgive her.

Seven Months Later...

"Look at her, mommy, she is so beautiful," Lisa said, holding her newborn daughter in the hospital.

"She is beautiful," her mother said, nodding her head. "What are you going to name her?"

"Angel. She's my little Angel." Lisa smiled.

"That's a beautiful name and she is an angel," Lisa's mother said, admiring her granddaughter. "Lisa, are you okay?" she asked, noticing her daughter becoming pale with a pain stricken expression on her face.

"I'm getting a headache, but I'll be fine," Lisa said, trying to shake off the discomfort. "Can you hold Angel for a minute. I need to sit up and catch my breath," Lisa said, handing her baby to her mother.

"I would love to." Her mother smiled, gently rocking Angel.

"I feel a little nauseated," Lisa said, feeling hot.

"Do you want me to get the nurse?"

"No, just get me some water," Lisa said. Before Lisa's mother even had a chance to reach for a bottle of water, her daughter began to vomit. In a matter of seconds Lisa's arms and legs began jerking. Her entire body seemed to be having convulsions."

"Lisa... Lisa... what's the matter baby!" Lisa's mother said, her voice shaking, filled with fear. "Somebody get a doctor!" she screamed out, running to the door and holding her grandbaby close to her chest. "My daughter needs a doctor. She's sick! Somebody help her please!" she pleaded, yelling out as she held the door wide open.

"Ma'am, please step outside," a nurse said, rushing into Lisa's room with a couple of other nurses behind her and the doctor close behind.

Lisa's mother paced back and forth in front of her daughter's room for what seemed like an eternity. "It's gonna be okay, Angel. Your mother will be fine," she kept saying over and over again to her grandbaby. "You know they say babies are healing, and you healing your grandmother's soul right now," she said softly in Angel's ear.

"Ma'am."

"Yes... is my daughter okay?" she asked rushing towards the doctor.

"Ma'am, your daughter was unconscious then her heart stopped."

"What are you saying?" she questioned as her bottom lip began trembling.

"We did everything we could do, but your daughter didn't make it. I'm sorry."

"No! No! She's so young. She's just a baby

herself. How did this happen?"

"I'm not sure, but we're going to do an autopsy. It will take a couple of weeks for the results to get back. It could be a placental abruption and amniotic fluid embolism, or a brain aneurysm, we don't know. Again, I'm sorry. Do you want us to contact the father of your granddaughter?" the doctor asked.

Lisa's mother gazed down at Angel, whose eyes were closed as she slept peacefully in her arms. "I don't know who Angel's father is. That information died with my daughter."

"I understand. Again, I'm sorry about your daughter. Let us know if there is anything we can do for you," the doctor said before walking off.

"I just want to see my daughter and tell her goodbye," she said walking into Lisa's room. "My sweet baby girl. You look so peaceful." Lisa's mother rubbed her hand across the side of her face. "Don't you worry. I promise I will take care of Angel. I will give her all the love I know you would have. Rest in peace baby girl."

Read The Entire Bitch Series in This Order

P.O. Box 912
Collierville, TN 38027

A KING PRODUCTION

www.joydejaking.com
www.twitter.com/joydejaking

ORDER FORM

Name:

Address:

City/State:

Zip:

QUANTITY	TITLES	PRICE	TOTAL
	Bitch	$15.00	
	Bitch Reloaded	$15.00	
	The Bitch Is Back	$15.00	
	Queen Bitch	$15.00	
	Last Bitch Standing	$15.00	
	Superstar	$15.00	
	Ride Wit' Me	$12.00	
	Ride Wit' Me Part 2	$15.00	
	Stackin' Paper	$15.00	
	Trife Life To Lavish	$15.00	
	Trife Life To Lavish II	$15.00	
	Stackin' Paper II	$15.00	
	Rich or Famous	$15.00	
	Rich or Famous Part 2	$15.00	
	Rich or Famous Part 3	$15.00	
	Bitch A New Beginning	$15.00	
	Mafia Princess Part 1	$15.00	
	Mafia Princess Part 2	$15.00	
	Mafia Princess Part 3	$15.00	
	Mafia Princess Part 4	$15.00	
	Mafia Princess Part 5	$15.00	
	Boss Bitch	$15.00	
	Baller Bitches Vol. 1	$15.00	
	Baller Bitches Vol. 2	$15.00	
	Baller Bitches Vol. 3	$15.00	
	Bad Bitch	$15.00	
	Still The Baddest Bitch	$15.00	
	Power	$15.00	
	Power Part 2	$15.00	
	Drake	$15.00	
	Drake Part 2	$15.00	
	Female Hustler	$15.00	
	Female Hustler Part 2	$15.00	
	Female Hustler Part 3	$15.00	
	Female Hustler Part 4	$15.00	
	Female Hustler Part 5	$15.00	
	Female Hustler Part 6	$15.00	
	Princess Fever "Birthday Bash"	$6.00	
	Nico Carter The Men Of The Bitch Series	$15.00	
	Bitch The Beginning Of The End	$15.00	
	Supreme...Men Of The Bitch Series	$15.00	
	Bitch The Final Chapter	$15.00	
	Stackin' Paper III	$15.00	
	Men Of The Bitch Series And The Women Who Love Them	$15.00	
	Coke Like The 80s	$15.00	
	Baller Bitches The Reunion Vol. 4	$15.00	
	Stackin' Paper IV	$15.00	
	The Legacy	$15.00	
	Lovin' Thy Enemy	$15.00	
	Stackin' Paper V	$15.00	
	The Legacy Part 2	$15.00	
	Assassins - Episode 1	$11.00	
	Assassins - Episode 2	$11.00	
	Assassins - Episode 2	$11.00	
	Bitch Chronicles	$40.00	
	So Hood So Rich	$15.00	

Shipping/Handling (Via Priority Mail) $7.50 1-2 Books, $15.00 3-4 Books add $1.95 for ea. Additional book.
Total: $_____FORMS OF ACCEPTED PAYMENTS: Certified or government issued checks and money Orders, all mail in orders take 5-7 Business days to be delivered